SHOWDOWN

The man Spur chased wore a blue shirt and dark pants. There were few buildings this close to the water. At the end of the pier, Spur saw the man running between two small buildings where fish were displayed to be sold.

Spur surged between the buildings with his Colt fisted and ready for action. The man hid at the corner of one of the buildings twenty feet away and snapped off a shot as Spur blasted around the structure. The round missed. Spur returned the fire with one round and thought he hit the man in the leg, but he vanished around the corner.

Spur ran to the corner of the frame store and stopped, searching the area. There were lobster pots, nets, an old fishing boat, a rack of oars and dozens of wooden boxes to hold just-caught fish. He scanned each area where a man could be hiding, then went back over them again.

Something had moved.

The third wooden fish box on the left. Spur watched it. It moved again and this time a hand came out beside it with a .44 in it. Spur angled his weapon toward the spot and the moment a face appeared around the side of the box, Spur fired twice.

Once had been enough....

SPUR

SAN DIEGO SLATTERN
Dirk Fletcher

LEISURE BOOKS   **NEW YORK CITY**

A LEISURE BOOK®

August 1996

Published by

Dorchester Publishing Co., Inc.
276 Fifth Avenue
New York, NY 10001

Printed in the United States of America.

SPUR

SAN DIEGO SLATTERN

Chapter One

Archer Grundy slouched on his sorrel on a slight rise and looked down a quarter of a mile at the smoke trailing up from a log shanty that the homesteaders had put up since his last visit.

Bile boiled up in his throat and he wanted to scream at them, "This is my land, damn it, and you're trespassing. Get the hell off my range and take your scrawny cattle with you."

Grundy didn't scream. Three times he had said those same words to the riffraff who had squatted on his range. Three times was his limit for anyone.

Archer Grundy was a large man, raw-boned, hewn from the same material as the granite boulders that spotted his 18,000 acres of rangeland. His face was windburned and leathery after more than fifty years in the saddle tending to ornery beef cattle. Pale blue eyes glared at the world from under heavy dark brows, asking no quarter and giving none. He had come to this outback country east and south of the tiny village of San Diego in California when there was little there but the old Spanish Presidio and a limping trade in cattle hides that went by sea to New England.

He staked out his claim thirty-five years ago in the valley south almost to the Mexican border and started his herd. There were no rules and laws about land back then. It was there for the taking, and he took it. Every year he published a notice in the small newspaper in San Diego, specifying his land boundaries. As was the custom of the times, most other cattlemen abided by the boundaries. More than a dozen times over the years he'd had to evict squatters off his land. But since the homestead act of 1862 things had gotten worse.

For years he had sold hides, and later the beef as well. With the coming of the train he could sell live cattle to points north and sell more cattle to the slaughterhouse right there in San Diego. Things were starting to go his way. Now this new squatter.

For thirty-five years he'd been building this cattle ranch, and just because some idiot said he had the right to homestead on unclaimed land didn't make no damn difference.

When the time came in '62, Grundy had homesteaded all the land he could. He'd laid out his 160 acres one hundred yards wide in stretches along the stream and the small lake. He had three cowhands homestead too, and then later bought out their rights for fifty dollars each. He had tied up over ten miles of the valley center and the little stream and the lake. The man who controlled the water in an area controlled the land. His land was ten miles long and up to three miles wide in spots. A place to build a ranch for his grandsons. If he had any.

Grundy grunted at the memories, looked over at his

son, who rode with him, and pointed.

"There the bastards are. Just like I told you. We call them out and shoot them. No talk, no questions. Just blast them bastards into hell where they damn well belong."

"The woman, too?" Grundy's son asked. His glance wouldn't hold his father's stare. He looked away, and Grundy spat a stream of brown juice into the dry California dirt.

"When in hell you gonna grow up a little, Lester? Now, damn it, we go down there and do what we have to do, and I want to see that six-gun of yours smoking just the way I trained you."

Lester Grundy was not a chip off the granite block his father was chiseled from. Lester was slight, clean-shaven, had his mother's dark eyes, brown hair and delicate hands. He was a late life child but at twenty-eight still had none of the talents or skills of a rancher. He could ride, but a rope was useless in his hands. His father kept trying.

Grundy scowled. "Damn right we shoot the woman. You want to leave a witness? We hit them both, then burn down their shack and let the horses loose. Somebody might think it's Indians or some damn rawhiders."

They nudged their mounts into motion and rode down the slope with six-guns out. One saddled horse stood tied near the back door of the small shack. Grundy nodded.

"Figured that bastard would be here about noon for some grub. We'll get this over with quick and get back to that north valley. We got to do some more cutting out of calves to get them branded."

They were fifty yards from the house when a rifle shot screamed over their heads, and both ducked.

9

"Hold your shooter down so he can't see it," Grundy growled.

They rode forward at the same walk, and another shot slammed into the ground beside them.

"Hold it right there or I'll shoot your damn horses and chase you home on foot," a voice bellowed from the shack.

They could see the rifle sticking out of a crack where the door had been opened.

"Johnson, we need to talk to you about them critters of yours we rounded up," Grundy lied. "Figure we got about thirty of them and want to know where we drive them to."

"Strays? You found thirty of my strays?"

"What I said, Johnson. If'n you cain't hear, ain't my problem. Guess we'll go back home."

Grundy started to turn his horse. They were within thirty feet of the shack now, and a man stepped out with the rifle aimed at them.

"You said you got thirty head of my brand?" Johnson asked. He wore range clothes but no hat. He looked to be about thirty years old, slender with full beard.

Grundy and his son rode forward again. Grundy nodded. "Damn right. The man can hear after all. Where you want my men to drive them scrawny Box J brand critters?"

The man frowned. "Why you have a change of heart, Grundy? Usual you ain't this pleasant." Johnson lowered the rifle and looked back into the house. "It's all right, Martha. We just talking about some strays."

As soon as Johnson looked away, Grundy brought up his six-gun and fired three times. Two of the rounds hit Johnson in the chest, one killing him instantly. Grundy slid to the ground, groaning from his rheumatism as he hobbled toward the fallen man and the shack.

A shotgun muzzle showed out the door, and Grundy dove to the ground just before it roared. The double-aught slugs rocketed just over his body, caught his horse in the side and head and knocked it to the ground, where it thrashed, kicking its way to death.

Grundy rolled, lifted his six-gun and fired the last three rounds. He always carried six loads on a mission like this. All three rounds jolted through the open door over the barrel of the shotgun, and he heard a scream.

Lester turned his horse and galloped for the ridge-line. Archer Grundy rose out of the dirt, ran to the side of the shack, pushed the spent shells out of his weapon and thumbed in six new ones.

He went around the shack carefully, listening for any sound, any movement. He could hear nothing. He rushed through the black hole of the open door and tripped over a body. Grundy sprawled on top of the woman and rolled away, panting heavily.

He groaned as he got to his knees. Now he saw the woman lying on her back, one hand to her chest where a large red stain showed. She turned her head toward him, and the words came clear but softly.

"Help me. Please help me."

Grundy scrambled back in shock. His six-gun came up again and he fired at the woman twice. Both slugs hit her in the chest and she gave one short cry; then her hand fell and she was dead.

Grundy staggered out of the shack, searched until he found a can of coal oil. He wet down the outside of the shack, then sloshed the rest into the open door. He lit a match and the vaporized coal oil whooshed into flames.

The man was away from it and wouldn't burn. No matter, Grundy decided. He limped to the Box J brand horse tied at a short rail near the cabin and untied her. After three tries, he got into the saddle and rode to the small corral, where four horses stood. He had the gate open and pulled wide in a moment, and rode in, chasing the mounts out of the enclosure. When they did the calf branding, he'd have to remember to blank out the Box J brand on the horse and put on his own Bar G brand.

Grundy looked over the scene and nodded. The shack had almost burned down, the horses were gone. Could have been a robbery aimed at stealing the horses. He nodded again and rode up the slope the way he had come. He wasn't concerned about tracks from the horses. By the time anyone found the body at this out-of-the-way place, the wind would have scoured away any trace of hoofprints.

As Grundy came over the rise of the slope, he found his son on his knees on the ground retching. Grundy rode up within a few feet of the young man and sat there waiting.

When Lester Grundy looked up at his father, the older man's voice came with thunder and derision.

"You through making a fool of yourself, son? You ready to try to get up on that mount and go back to work with me in the north valley? We got work to do, boy. Let's get your ass in your saddle and go do it."

Lester shook his head in total surprise. "You murder a man and then his wife and now you're going back to work as if nothing happened? Those people's deaths don't mean no more to you than swatting a fly or shooting a coyote, do they?"

"If you weren't my flesh and blood, boy, I'd beat you into the ground like a fencepost. Right now we got work to do, and you got some spine to be firming up. Now get up on that horse and let's go to work. Convince me that I should pretend for a while longer that you're my real son and not some foundling we took in from a passing gang of rawhiders."

Lester stepped into the saddle and glared at his father. "Some day, old man, some day."

Grundy swung his horse around. "Some day, kid? Some day? Why not right now? You want to use your fists or maybe your six-gun or that rifle in your boot? Hell, you can't use any of them halfway decent. Maybe it's like the men say in town. Lester Grundy should have had tits instead of balls. Is that the way you really are?"

Grundy sat there watching his son for a minute more. The young man didn't move, didn't look at his father.

"Hell, boy, we'll settle this some other time. Right now, let's get to work."

Chapter Two

Spur McCoy lay back on the warm sand and watched another perfect Pacific Ocean wave rise, form and break and the crashing foam rush toward the clean brown beach sand in an unending roll. He took a deep breath of the tangy ocean air and relaxed as the San Diego sun warmed him after his swim only a few minutes ago in the blue waters.

The United States Secret Service agent had just finished a demanding assignment in Los Angeles one hundred miles to the north, and swore that he would take a week off. No telegrams, no letters, no word even to his boss, General Wilton D. Halleck in Washington, D.C., to let him know where he had settled in for a rest. Spur was tired in body and mind and needed a break.

Spur McCoy was in his prime, thirty-two years old, a veteran of the Secret Service, six feet two inches tall and a trim, hard-muscled 200 pounds. He wore his

14

black hair a little longer than most men of the day, was clean-shaven and had green eyes under heavy brows. He was an expert with all weapons, from handguns, rifles and sabers to explosives, fighting knives and axe handles. He was a Harvard University graduate, and his father owned several large retail stores in New York City, but he had chosen the Secret Service for his career.

Now he handled most of the federal law-enforcement problems west of the Mississippi with the help of some U.S. deputy marshals.

The Santa Fe Railroad had just been extended to San Diego from Los Angeles in this year of 1884, and four days ago he had taken the first train south out of Los Angeles he could find. He stared at the breakers that kept rolling in one after another.

"They don't even turn them off at night," his companion for the rest and relaxation said beside him. She was Ginny Lambeau, one of the ladies involved in his recent Los Angeles fracas, and she promised to show him San Diego if he put off checking in with his head office for a few days. Now she sat up, her skin a golden tan, her blond hair a shade lighter than it had been a week ago, courtesy of a lot of time in the sun.

She was one of the prettiest women Spur had seen in a long time and had helped him in the Los Angeles case with some vital information. She also made a delightful companion.

"How long can you hold your breath?" Ginny asked.

Spur shrugged. "A minute, maybe a minute and a half. Why?"

"Your next introduction to San Diego is spear fishing. See those pads just off shore? Those are bull kelp. Their long stems go to the bottom and lock onto rocks and sand, then they grow from the sun and the nutrients from the ocean water. They also provide food and hiding spots, so they are home to hundreds of kinds of fish and other sea critters."

"We swim out, dive down and spear the fish?" Spur asked.

"Some of us do. But for guests we always launch a small boat through the waves and row out, anchor our boat and then dive from that. Think you can get down twenty feet?"

"Easy," Spur said, hoping that he could.

Ginny rose up on her knees and stared at him. Her stylish black swimsuit covered her from shoulders and elbows to well below her knees. The wet fabric clung delightfully, revealing the curves of her breasts.

"Spur McCoy, you don't look like you want to go spear fishing at all. What's the matter with you? You just worked hard up in Los Angeles with those nasty old bank robbers, and it's your turn to take a short vacation."

"You're right. My turn."

Ginny pouted and reached over and smoothed out the frown on Spur's face. "Just because you're fooling your boss back in Washington, you're feeling bad, like you're cheating him or something. You've earned a few days off. Now relax."

"Not true, Ginny, about feeling bad. I know I need a vacation. I've had three glorious days and nights. Figured I should tell you, I sent a telegram this morning before you got up. I'll probably have a new assignment as soon as we get back to the hotel. We lost two agents last month and we're stretched a little thin."

Ginny stood and tugged at his hand. "Then come on, we won't go back there. We'll go spear fishing and then take a long hike down the beach and have supper out and go to that concert at the opera house tonight. We won't even look in your box behind the room clerk when we go in well after midnight."

16

Spur McCoy sat up and pulled her down beside him. "Like to do that, sweet Ginny. I really would. But I wouldn't be good company. Three days off is the most I can manage." He stood and lifted her up beside him. "Time to check out the Horton House Hotel and see what kind of mail I have."

"No, McCoy. I won't let you. I'll drown myself. I'll run out in the surf and go under and you'll have to come rescue me."

Spur laughed and leaned down and kissed her cheek. "Not a chance. You swim like a harbor seal. You'd end up saving me. Let's take a quick look at the hotel. Even if there is a telegram from the general, we won't open it until tomorrow. Agreed?"

She half shut her blue eyes and stared at him, her mouth a thin, hard line. "Well, if you really mean it. Not until tomorrow morning. With you, I bet tomorrow could be midnight plus one minute. So you have to promise me that tomorrow means tomorrow morning after breakfast, right?"

"Yes, yes. Now come on. One more quick dive into a breaker to wash the sand off us and then back to the buggy and get into some clothes. That is, if that horse and buggy are where we left them."

A half hour later, they scurried into San Diego's showplace, the Horton House Hotel, and up to their second-floor room.

"I'm going to have a bath in that glorious tub with the hot and cold running water," Ginny said. "Gee, hot water right out of a faucet. What won't they think of next? I've lived in San Diego for four years and I've never even been inside this grand hotel before, let alone stayed here for four nights. I'm really enjoying it." Ginny vanished into the separate bathroom, humming a song.

Spur kicked out of his beach clothes and slipped

17

into dress pants and shirt and some low shoes. He combed his hair and hurried down to the lobby. The room clerk saw him coming and held out three telegrams. All were in envelopes, so there was no way to know which one had been sent first or who they were from.

He pushed the envelopes into his shirt pocket and went back to the room. He'd read them later.

Late that afternoon they had an early dinner in the hotel dining room. Fresh Pacific lobster were in season, so they were served one whole lobster each, with the huge claws already cracked and the delicate meat of the claws and tail ready to scoop out and dip in melted butter.

After the meal they walked around the heart of San Diego in "newtown" where the city had expanded from its origins in Old Town near the old Spanish Presidio.

There was a traveling troupe of actors in town doing Shakespeare's *Hamlet*. Ginny had never seen it, so they went in and enjoyed a performance.

After the play, the restaurants and cafes were closed, and even the Horton House Hotel's dining room had shut down before they got there. They went up to their room, and Spur showed Ginny the three telegrams.

"Three? I've never known anyone who got even one telegram, let alone three in one day. I'm dazzled."

She snatched the telegrams from his hand and held them. "I'll keep them until after breakfast. Remember, you said you wouldn't read them until after we eat in the morning."

Spur lifted his brows and took a long breath. "Seems like a great waste of time. What in the world are we going to do between now and breakfast?"

Ginny smiled and walked toward him, her hips swinging, her breasts pushed out in front. "I bet we

18

can figure out something." She kissed him and pressed her breasts against his chest.

Spur growled through the kiss and picked her up and carried her to the bed.

She waved at him. "This time let's try it different. Let's be soft and gentle and slow. I know—we can pretend it's the first time for both of us and we're a little shy and don't know exactly what to do. How about it?"

Spur set her down on her feet at the side of the bed and grinned. "I think we can arrange something like that. Just so you don't get excited and try to seduce me."

Ginny laughed. "I'll try to hold myself in control."

Three times that night they both kept in check and made love softly and gently.

At breakfast the next morning, Spur took his time with his bacon, eggs, pancakes and sausages, and only when he finished his coffee did he look over at the three telegrams still in their envelopes lying on the table in the hotel's dining room.

"Aren't you the least bit curious about those three wires?" Ginny asked. Her smile came a little forced. "Goodness, I could never sit there and have breakfast not knowing what they said."

"You made me promise," Spur said.

"I know, but breakfast is over. Can I open one of them?"

He waved his hand at them, and she picked up the one from the bottom and carefully opened the sticky flap of the envelope. She handed the yellow paper message to Spur. They were printed out on a machine at the telegraph office automatically these days.

He took the sheet of paper and scanned it, then handed it to Ginny. She read it.

TO SPUR MCCOY. HORTON HOUSE HOTEL SAN DIEGO CALIFORNIA. CONGRATULA-

Dirk Fletcher

TIONS ON LOS ANGELES ARREST. U.S. MAR-
SHAL THERE PLEASED. NEW ASSIGNMENT
COMING SOON. STAY WHERE YOU ARE FOR
NOW. SIGNED GENERAL WILTON D. HAL-
LECK, WASHINGTON D.C.

Ginny looked up. "So one of the other wires has
your new assignment?"
"Probably. Pick out one."
She handed another envelope to him. He opened it
quickly. It held two pages of paper, and he began to
read:

TO SPUR MCCOY HORTON HOUSE HOTEL,
SAN DIEGO CALIFORNIA. MORE DETAILS ON
YOUR NEW ASSIGNMENT.

He dropped the wire and opened the third one.
"This one needs to come first," McCoy said. He rushed
past the heading to the message.

NEW ASSIGNMENT IS THERE IN SAN DIEGO.
FOR SIX MONTHS COUNTERFEIT $20 BILLS
HAVE BEEN SHOWING UP IN BIG CITIES
ACROSS THE COUNTRY. CHICAGO, ST.
LOUIS, NEW YORK, PHILADELPHIA AND
OTHER PLACES. NO REPORT OF ANY BILLS
PASSED IN SAN DIEGO. THE BILLS ARE EVI-
DENTLY SENT BY MAIL TO BUYERS, WHO
ALSO PAY FOR THEM BY MAIL.
   QUALITY OF BILLS IS EXCELLENT, HARD
TO DISTINGUISH FROM ACTUAL CURRENCY.
ONLY WAY TO SPOT THEM IS BY THE SERIAL
NUMBER, WHICH IS THE SAME FOR ALL
BILLS PRINTED. SAMPLE OF THE COUNTER-

20

FEIT BILLS TO BE SENT BY REGISTERED MAIL FOR QUICKEST DELIVERY TO YOU.

ONLY LEAD IS A SAN DIEGO HAND-STAMPED POSTMARK ON A SCRAP OF ENVELOPE THAT HAD BEEN USED TO MAIL ONE BATCH OF BILLS. WE DIDN'T RECOVER THE BILLS OR THE PERSON PASSING THEM.

SUSPECT A STOLEN PLATE FROM THE BUREAU OF ENGRAVING BY AN UNHAPPY EMPLOYEE. PAPER AND INK ARE NOT ALWAYS THE BEST QUALITY. BILLS ARE "WEATHERED" TO MAKE THEM LOOK USED.

U.S. MARSHAL FOR LOS ANGELES ALSO COVERS THE SAN DIEGO AREA. CONTACT HIM FOR ANY AID NEEDED. THE PRINTER IS IN SAN DIEGO. FIND HIM, DEFACE THE PLATES, THEN SHIP THEM TO ME. DESTROY ANY BILLS FOUND IN ANY STAGE OF PRINTING. GOOD LUCK.

Spur handed the wire to Ginny to read and went back to the last telegram.

MORE DETAILS ON YOUR NEW ASSIGNMENT. WE HAVE ONE NAME, ANGELO. A CHECK OF BUREAU EMPLOYEES OVER LAST FIVE YEARS SHOWS NO ANGELO LISTED. PROBABLY AN ALIAS.

ONLY $20 BILLS PRINTED. PRINTING EQUIPMENT IS HIGH QUALITY. MAY BE MADE AT SOME LEGITIMATE PRINTING FIRM.

MORE TO FOLLOW AS THE CASE DEVELOPS. THIS CASE MARKED URGENT BY SECRETARY OF THE TREASURY WALTER GRESHAM. PRESIDENT CHESTER A. AR-

THUR HAS EXPRESSED "SERIOUS CON-
CERN" ABOUT THIS PROBLEM STATING
THAT IT COULD UPSET THE WHOLE PAPER
CURRENCY BALANCE IN THE UNITED
STATES.

ONE DEPUTY U.S. MARSHAL HAS BEEN
KILLED SOMEWHERE BETWEEN SAN DI-
EGO AND LOS ANGELES WORKING ON THIS
COUNTERFEITING CASE. THAT'S WHY THEY
REQUESTED YOU COME IN ON IT.

ALL SPEED WILL BE WELCOMED IN SOLV-
ING THIS PROBLEM.

SENDING: GENERAL HALLECK.

Ginny looked up from reading the telegram, a big
smile on her face.

"Good! Now you'll be staying right here in San Diego."

"Maybe not so good. Maybe the counterfeiter already knows that I'm in town, so he'll pull his defenses
in close and lay low. Maybe he'll decide to kill me instead of worrying about me."

"They wouldn't dare even try that," Ginny said.
"They'd have to deal with me."

Spur thanked her with a nod, then began evaluating
the problem. The fact that there had been no distribution of the bills in San Diego made the job a dozen
times harder. The printer was smart, choosing not to
foul his own nest with the bogus bills.

By now San Diego had 12,000 people, maybe more.
Spur couldn't open up every warehouse and business
building in town and search it for printing equipment.

The general's idea of a legitimate printer letting his
press be used for such a purpose was not reasonable.
However, the counterfeiter might have a breakdown
in his press and need some quick spare parts or advice.

22

Spur would check with the best printers in town on that aspect.

The bankers would be no help, since no bad money, at least from this counterfeiter, had surfaced here.

The post office might help. It seemed to Spur that any such operation would use registered mail to cover any loss. The post office had such records. But searching for one man or a small firm that shipped twelve items over a six-month period might result in fifty or a hundred names. Still, it was a starting place.

Ink, paper. Where did a man get the kind of paper the Bureau of Engraving used for the bills? It was a highly specialized type of paper and might even be regulated by the government.

Spur scowled and stared out the window at the San Diego street bathed in warm sunshine. He had a big job ahead of him so he better get started on it.

Chapter Three

Dr. Philip Brown stared at the San Diego County Sheriff and shook his head. "I can't guarantee anything, Will. That bullet is too close to the heart. It's got to come out, but I'd say there's a fifty-fifty chance the patient won't survive."

Sheriff Will Raferty rubbed his hand over his face and scowled at the medical man, who had blood on his hands. His white apron too was streaked with the outlaw's blood. They stood in the operating room at the doctor's clinic in San Diego and stared at the man on the table.

Sheriff Raferty stood five-ten, had a pot belly, a six-gun slung low, forty-two years of living experience and twelve years as a lawman. He looked more like an accountant than a lawman. He was fast with his six-gun, color-blind, wore town clothes contrasted with cowboy boots and a low-crowned Stetson. He'd never taken a bribe in his life.

Juan Sebastion was alive and conscious. He had just killed three men in a bank robbery attempt and taken two bullets himself, one breaking his leg. Two men got away, and Sheriff Raferty wanted to find out who they were.

"I'll talk to him now," Sheriff Raferty said. "You stop me if he's getting too weak. I want to hang this man for everyone in town to see and send a warning to other outlaws that we're a tough town on killers. Three good men he gunned down today. I want to hang him real bad."

The sheriff moved up to the bloody table where the man lay strapped down and stared down at the pale face. The bank robber had lost a lot of blood.

"Sebastion, can you hear me?"

A short nod of the bearded face.

"I want to know who was with you today at the bank. You're dying, Sebastion. You might as well go out with a clear conscience. Who were the other two bank robbers?"

Sebastion shook his head.

"You tell me their names and I'll bring in a priest for you, Sebastion."

The dark eyes flickered, and Sebastion's face worked a moment; then he sighed and shook his head as if saying a priest would make no difference to his soul.

Three times more, Sheriff Raferty asked the bank robber but got no answer. At last he shook his head in disgust, jammed his well-worn Stetson on his head and marched out of the room.

"He's all yours, Doc," Sheriff Raferty said as he left.

Dr. Brown smiled as he moved toward the patient. "Sounds like you weren't cooperative with the sheriff, Mr. Sebastion. He should have let me help." Dr.

Brown took a probe and pushed it into the bullet hole in the man's chest.

A scream of agony crashed around the all-white operating room. Two large electric lamps lit the room. Dr. Brown had set them in place only that month with a new electric generator to power them.

"Well now, Mr. Sebastion. I believe we need the names of your two robber friends." Dr. Brown held the probe poised over the wound.

"Bastard," Sebastion whispered.

"True, but I'm the bastard with the probe and you're the bastard on the operating table. The names, Sebastion, or I'll go on poking around in that bullet wound like I'm digging a new posthole."

"Bastard!"

The doctor probed again and this time felt his tool scrape the lead bullet. The patient screamed for five seconds before he passed out.

Dr. Brown smiled. He was a tall, slender man with elbows and knees that sometimes flew in all directions. He loved surgery and would have stayed in St. Louis's finest hospital if it hadn't been for a small problem he'd had with the supervising physician. He had piercing gray eyes, thinning brown hair and a nose that kids could use for a sled run. Right now he stared hard at the patient.

The doctor applied a cold cloth to Sebastion's forehead and the back of his neck, and the patient revived.

"Now, Mr. Sebastion, we were talking about names." Dr. Brown held the bloody probe in front of the patient's eyes.

"Russell Smith and Hernando Martinez. The two men I was with at the bank. Now make me well."

"I've been thinking about that, Sebastion. We don't need you anymore. Sure as hell, if I saved you, the court or a smart lawyer would get you off somehow so you wouldn't have to pay the price for shooting those three men. The committee has voted that it will be better if you expire quietly right here on my operating table. The sheriff knows of the risk. Good-bye, Mr. Sebastion."

Dr. Brown lowered a cone covered with sul-ether over Sebastion's nose and mouth. Sebastion breathed in a moment as he struggled against the tie-downs, then passed out.

Dr. Brown probed again for the bullet, pulled it out and dropped it in a tray. Then he inserted a scalpel in the wound and moved it carefully until he felt the blunt side of the scalpel touch the rubbery artery leading into the heart. He reversed the instrument and sliced deliberately down and inward. Blood welled up from the wound. Dr. Brown withdrew the scalpel and pushed a gauze pad over the wound to contain some of the blood.

Four minutes later, Juan Sebastion bled to death.

Dr. Brown put his instruments in the metal pan he used to sterilize them and sat down and stared at the body.

"I do not condemn thee, Juan Sebastion. Go, and sin no more. The Gospel According to John, chapter eight, verse eleven. Now, may the almighty God have mercy on your soul."

Dr. Brown sat watching the dead man a minute more, then rose and went into another room, took off his bloody apron and put it in the laundry basket. Then he washed the blood off his hands. He would report the names of the other two robbers to the sheriff on his way home and tell him of the patient's death. It had been a good day. A murderer had met his maker and by now was deep in the pits of hell stoking the everlasting fires.

Dr. Brown smiled. Yes, it had been a good day.

Chapter Four

The next morning, Spur McCoy talked to the three biggest printers in town. One at the newspaper said that her equipment wasn't half good enough to print counterfeit currency.

Next he went to the R & B Printers on Broadway and found a neat young man in the front office working on the books. He glanced up and grinned, put down his pencil and came forward to the counter across the front section of the store.

"Yes, sir, how may I help you?"

"Are you Mr. R or Mr. B?" Spur asked.

The young man grinned. "Actually I'm the son of the R if that makes any sense. I'm Randy Rawlins. How may I help you?"

"Looking for a printer here in town who can provide me with some ultra-high-class, first-rate quality printing on some new stock certificates I want to issue. I don't want the stock variety, but something worked up from scratch."

"Looks like you know a thing or two about fine printing. We simply don't have the equipment to do that quality of work. You'll want a Balboa 200. We had an old one that outprinted our newer equipment until we wore the thing to pieces. We have a few parts now for salvage if we ever get another one."

"What about your competition, Bradley Printers over on C Street? Could they do it?"

"Not a chance. Their presses are older than ours. We have the best quality in town, but not what you'd need for stock certificates that couldn't be counterfeited. San Francisco is probably the closest place you'll find the Balboa 200 in working condition."

Spur thanked him and left. He passed the Horton House Hotel on the way and stopped to check his box. Another telegram from the general. Briefly, he said that the first appearances of the bills were about six months ago, and they moved across the country from the Pacific Coast eastward. He also said he had sent wires to the county sheriff and the postmaster to urge them to give Spur complete cooperation in his investigation. He also gave the name of the deputy U.S. marshal killed while investigating the case: Jeffrey Lang.

The wire made a connection for Spur. The railroad to San Diego went in about six months ago. The bills began showing up about six months ago. Could the counterfeiter have shipped a press from San Francisco to San Diego to start up his new business?

Spur walked quickly toward the train depot beyond Front Street. The station master looked over Spur's credentials and nodded. He was short, fat and

German, talking with an accent that couldn't be mistaken.

"Unt what might I do for you?"

"You were here that first month of operation?"

"You betcha."

"Do you remember any heavy shipments, a big bulky item such as a printing press? It would be extremely heavy, and probably come in a wooden crate of some kind."

The station master frowned for what seemed like a half hour, then shook his head. "Not me remember, but Snodgrass maybe. He runs the freight office."

Five minutes later, Spur had described what he wanted to Melvin Snodgrass, the freight superintendent.

"No, sir, I don't remember one, but we've had hundreds of shipments through here. I can look it up for you. About how much do you think such a press would weigh all crated?"

"Fifteen hundred pounds, maybe a ton. These bruisers are big and heavy."

"Come into the office. Six months ago ain't too far back. I worked out of San Francisco for a while. Record books up there are huge and heavy things."

At the end of the station they went into a large room that held freight at one end where people came to pick up small items, and an office at the other end where two clerks worked. Snodgrass talked to one redheaded man, who nodded and found a book and began looking through it.

Snodgrass took another book and began leafing through it from the back. "You said the first month or so we were in business here, right?"

Spur assured him that was right. Snodgrass had his book almost checked through when the red-headed man came up with a grin over his whole face.

"Got it," he said. "You mentioned maybe a printing press. Got one, a Balboa 200 printing press out of San Francisco. She came in, and a guy loaded it off the freight car right onto a heavy wagon and took her away."

"Who was it shipped to?" Spur asked. Was it going to be this easy?

Snodgrass took the book and ran his finger down the page. "Shipped to the Pacific Printing Company. Signed for by one J. J. Pacific."

Spur frowned. "You ever heard of this Pacific Printing Company before?"

Snodgrass shook his head. "Nope, but it gives an address. 842 H Street. Might ask them there."

Spur asked to look at the record and made sure of the address. Then he thanked the two men and walked quickly toward H Street. There were a few business buildings on the 600 block, only one store on the 700 block and no business buildings at all on the 800 block. It was a phony address.

The wagon? A wagon suitable to haul a heavy press could have been rented or borrowed from two dozen different places. No one would remember it after six months.

Spur then walked to the post office. The odds were a thousand to one that they would be able to help. His only chance was the registered mail records.

Postmaster Tom Fogiletta listened to Spur lay out his problem.

"Now, Mr. Fogiletta, is there any way you can help me find this individual who is sending these packages?"

"You said the packages would be valuable. Then the person would send them by registered mail."

"Register a package containing five thousand dollars in twenty-dollar bills?"

Fogiletta shrugged. "Could. How heavy are these packages?"

Spur groaned. "Didn't think you would need to know that. I'll find out. About how many packages do you register each day?"

Postmaster Fogiletta laughed. "Every day? Hell, some days none at all. Some days up to twenty, twenty-five."

Spur nodded. "I'll find out the weight and approximate size of the bundles we're hunting. My guess is that one has been going out each month for the past six months. I'll be back."

Spur marched up to the San Diego First Bank and went to see the manager. He explained who he was and that he needed some information.

"How big a package would five thousand dollars worth of twenty-dollar bills make?" Spur asked.

"That's a strange question." The manager, Mr. Gray, stared at Spur. "You sure you're with the government?"

"I'm sure. We don't have to use twenties, make it ones or five's, they'll be the same size and weigh the same."

Mr. Gray took Spur into the vault and showed him stacks of twenty-dollar bills still in their wrappers from the Bureau of Engraving in Washington, D.C.

"There's a hundred bills to a stack, that's two thousand dollars worth of twenties. You want five thousand dollars worth, make it a hundred and twenty-five to a stack and put them side by side and you have it."

Spur saw a wooden ruler on the table in the vault and measured the stacks of bills the banker had laid out side by side. Each bill was 7⅜ inches long and 3⅛ inches wide.

"So the package would be about eight inches long and seven inches wide. The whole thing wrapped with cardboard on both sides would slip into a large envelope."

"Yes, and it could be mailed. But you know the mail gets robbed sometimes, and lost sometimes. We don't recommend sending money through the U.S. Postal Service."

"What if it's registered? Sounds pretty safe to me. Thanks. I won't need these bills as samples. Thanks for your help, Mr. Gray. Oh, I'd appreciate your not saying a word about our conversation to anyone. I must insist."

The banker looked properly concerned, and Spur walked out of the bank and back to the post office. He found a smiling Tom Fogiletta, the postmaster.

"We may be in luck here, Mr. McCoy. Lots of people register letters, but not many register packages. We can tell how big the item is by the amount of postage to mail it. The registration fee is the same but the amount of postage differs. We checked quickly on this month so far, and only ten packages of any size were registered. There were two dozen letters registered. We know because they had charges for postage of only three cents, plus the registration fee."

"That's good news. I figure the package I'm looking for would go in a large envelope, nine by twelve, something like that with some cardboard protection. Say it would weigh eight to ten ounces."

"Now we can do you some good. I'll put one man on checking the records since the train came in here six months ago. That's what you want, right?"

"Right. I'm looking for a pattern, like a ten-ounce envelope sent by registered mail once a month by the same individual. The name of the sender is on the receipt record, isn't it?"

"You bet, and the name it's sent to as well. Yes, I think we can help you."

"How long will it take?"

"Most of today, I'd guess."

"I'll be back to check on it."

Spur left the post office and walked to the county courthouse. It seemed to be a temporary location. He found the sheriff's office and went in. A deputy wearing spectacles looked up and frowned.

"Like to see the sheriff if he's in," Spur said.

"Could I have your name and your business with the sheriff?" the deputy asked.

"I'm Spur McCoy and I have some government business to discuss with the sheriff."

"McCoy, come on in here. I just been reading this damned wire from Washington by God D.C. Door on your left there."

Spur went through the open door into the room the booming voice had come from. He found a man sitting behind a cluttered desk smoking a cigar.

"Yeah, Spur McCoy, an honest-to-God federal agent. Never seen one of you boys before. Guess we're in the same kind of business. Shut the door and let's see if I can help you any. Understand this is to be kept on the quiet side."

Spur liked this lawman who wore his cowboy hat with his town clothes and now reached out a hand for a weak shake.

"Sit down and fill me in on this situation."

"Not sure what the general told you in his wire. Briefly, we've got a major counterfeiter here in San Diego pumping out five thousand dollars' worth a month, and he might be doubling that by now for all we know. My job is to find and stop him."

"Big job, McCoy. We have near thirteen thousand folks here in town and nearby. Can't talk to all of them."

"I hoped you might give me some help. Along the

line sometime this counterfeiter might just try to spend some of his phony money right here in town simply to massage his ego. Just to see if he can pass the bogus bills. He makes only twenties, so that makes it a little easier. So far I understand no such bills have surfaced here, but we want to warn you and the bank so if the bills do show up, we'll have another way to track him down."

"You got samples?"

Spur reached in his wallet and brought out two twenty-dollar bills, United States Notes, perfectly crafted.

"The best way to spot these is to look for the serial number. It's the same on both of these bills. If he spends any here in town, they will all have the same serial number."

"You'll contact the banks?"

"How many?"

"We have four here in town."

"I'll see them today, but it's a long shot he'll spend any of the bogus bills here."

"How can I help you?"

"I don't know yet. Just wanted to check in, show the colors and say hello. Right now I'm working the railroad and the post office. You have a store in town that sells paper and ink?"

"Nothing commercial. One of the printers can get special paper from his catalog out of San Francisco."

"Might have another talk with them. Good idea." Spur stood and held out his hand. "You hear about any fake twenty-dollar bills, you give me a holler. I'm at the Horton House.

"Now about my other problem. What can you tell me about a man killed up north a ways by the name of Jeffrey Lang? He was a deputy U.S. marshal out of San Francisco judicial district."

"Lang. Yeah, I remember. Came into town, talked with me one day, and the next day they found him dead about a mile out of town. Shot. His six-gun was still in leather. Surprised him, I guess. No witnesses, no clues. I reported it to his U.S. Marshal."

"No local tie-in at all on his death?"

"Wasn't here long enough. Don't even know what hotel he stayed at. Here today, dead tomorrow."

"That's another dead end. Literally. Well, thanks for what you told me. I'll stay in touch."

They shook hands and Spur went out to the street. He walked down to the last printer he had talked to, Randy Rawlins at R & B.

"Paper? We don't have anything good enough that anybody could use to print money. I heard that it ain't even for sale. Government has it made special somewhere in France."

"What about paper almost that good? Could it be ordered from San Francisco?"

Rawlins pulled out a catalog filled with various sizes and shapes of different paper stock. He thumbed through it and picked out one.

"Could use something like this. High rag content, holds ink extremely well, but it tends to bleed through to the back side. That wouldn't do. I'll keep looking. Nothing special about the ink. All you need is one that will hold up for two or three months, just time enough to pass off all of the counterfeits, right? I'll look at the ink catalog, too. But it ain't promising."

"Thanks, and I'd appreciate it if you didn't say anything about our conversation."

"What's to say? One thing's certain. We don't have a Balboa 200 and we don't print twenty-dollar bills. Sounds like a fast way to make money, though."

They both grinned, and Spur walked back out to the sunny street of San Diego. It was warm but not hot. A cooling breeze came from offshore and kept the June temperature in the mid seventies.

He thought of taking Ginny to lunch, but one thing would lead to another and he wouldn't get anything else done all afternoon. He had a quick bowl of soup at a cafe and went back to the post office.

The postmaster saw Spur come in and motioned him over to a Dutch door. The top half was open.

"We have something for you to look at, Mr. McCoy."

Fogiletta led Spur into the rear of the post office to a table where a young man worked on some record books.

"Registered mail is one thing we keep remarkably good records on. It's signed off from one person to another the whole distance to its destination. Ed here has been going through our registration records. Tell us what you've found, Ed."

Ed was about twenty with blond hair cropped short, a long neck and spectacles perched on the end of his nose.

"In January only ten packages in the ten-to-twelve-ounce class were registered. In the next months there were sixteen, ten, five, fourteen and so far in June ten."

"You have a list of the dates and the persons sending the packages?" Spur asked.

"Right. I wrote them out for you."

Spur took the sheets of paper and began reading the names. One name kept popping up, twice in each of the first three months and once in each of the next three. Each mailing was for twelve ounces. The name of the sender: R. C. House.

Spur wrote the name in a notebook he carried in his pocket. "You have an address on this R. C. House?"

The postmaster beamed. Ed nodded. "Yes, sir. He's listed on each of the receipts at 1401 Fifth Avenue. That would be up the hill a ways from downtown."

Spur grinned and slapped Ed on the back. "My friend, you may just have solved a dastardly crime." He shook his hand, then that of the postmaster and hurried out of the post office and up the street. He'd seen Fifth Avenue. Now all he had to do was walk up fourteen blocks and find 1401. He checked his six-gun. Yes, it was in its leather home and loaded and ready to go. He had no idea what or who he might find at 1401. He hoped it was a Balboa 200 grinding away in a back room of the house or some shed, and the printer and counterfeiter.

He tested the six-gun in his holster and marched up the dirt street toward the 1400 block.

Chapter Five

Bernard Dennis sat in his basement workroom and stared in wonder at the Balboa 200 printing press he had just been working on. It was the best press in the world and it was his. Much better than the ones he had struggled with at the Bureau of Printing and Engraving in Washington, D.C.

But those days were now only cloudy and unhappy memories. He rose and went to the freshly printed stack of twenty-dollar bills and smiled. He was working on another 5,000 dollars' worth of bills. Fantastic. The bills were printed one at a time, instead of twelve as he used to do in Washington. These bills were absolutely perfect. Not even the best Treasury agent could pick out one of his bills as counterfeit.

All it took was advance planning. He had been working at the Bureau of Printing and Engraving for twelve years as a master printer when the new superintendent came in and took over. At once Bernard knew he was in trouble.

The tall man with white hair and brown eyes simply couldn't stand to look at Bernard. Yes, Bernard knew he wasn't a handsome man and that he had a few disfigurements, but his work had been outstanding and his relations with his fellow employees exemplary before Godfrey took over. There should have been no conflict. It was entirely Superintendent Godfrey's doing.

Bernard Dennis was a small man, barely five feet two inches and slight of body. His hands were works of art with sensitive fingers that had a delicate touch in the fine printing trade. He only had one eye, the other lost in an accident and replaced with a glass eye that stared unblinkingly ahead day in and day out regardless of what his good right eye did.

He knew that his bad eye took some getting used to. What irritated his supervisor more was the deep purple birthmark that covered most of the right side of his face. He knew that took some getting used to as well.

He had achieved the top of his profession at the bureau not through good looks but through his remarkable skills and almost fanatical work habits. Then in six months his new superintendent had had him demoted and at last fired on charges of insubordination.

Godfrey had paid for his crimes. Bernard Dennis was a smart man and had predicted the eventual result of his almost daily conflicts with Godfrey. The man was a red badge, had the power and authority to make Dennis look bad. Soon after Godfrey took over, Dennis began his planning.

First he stole the paper that he would need, that special paper that the bureau had made for itself and itself alone so it could not be copied. He didn't take the large sheets. He figured what he would need and instead found selvage and slightly irregular sheets that were assigned to be cut up and destroyed.

He cut them into four-by-eight-inch pieces and sneaked them out of the building in his leather work case twenty or thirty at a time. After three months he had enough of the official paper to print up 100,000 dollars' worth of twenty-dollar bills. He had over 5,000 four-by-eight-inch sheets, which he stacked carefully in a box and sealed shut.

The ink was simpler. He took home in his leather work case the almost empty bottles of the specially made green, black and red ink. Each bottle had to be checked in and out, and that was part of his responsibility. In this way he soon obtained more than enough ink to do the job. When he got the bottles home he poured what was left of each color into a second bottle until it was filled.

Next came the harder part, getting a pair of engravings of the front and back of the twenty-dollar bill. It took him three months to get them, but when the chance arose, he took it gleefully and no one suspected.

Ten plates were due to be replaced by new ones carefully hand engraved by their master engravers. The old plates were not worn out and had several million impressions left on them, but the superintendent had been ordered to insert a new series date and a new signature, so the old plates were taken out of use and ordered to be destroyed.

On that particular day, Bernard Dennis wore his jacket with the big side pockets and brought to work two coppered steel plates the same size as those he was instructed to destroy.

When the opportunity arose, he substituted a pair of front and back plates of the twenty-dollar bill with a pair of metal sheets from his pocket and ceremoniously dropped them into the caldron with the other eight real plates, where they would be melted down and the metal reused. It went off without a flicker of suspicion by any of the watchers, and later he walked out of the building with the perfect twenty-dollar engraved plates in his jacket pockets.

Two weeks later he created a wild incident of insubordination with Godfrey and was suspended immediately. He was discharged without pay or pension the following Friday afternoon. He screamed and raged at his hearing, and the Secretary of the Treasury, Walter Q. Gresham, listened, then in the best bureaucratic style approved his dismissal.

That same afternoon Bernard Dennis arranged to sell his home in Washington. He was widowed and had one child who now lived in New York. Dennis's wife had died four years earlier.

Next he bought a small two-shot derringer at a pawnshop and ammunition for it. That was Godfrey's night to play poker with some Washington cronies. He always walked the two blocks to a friend's house where the game was held. Dennis met him halfway there, stepped from behind a large tree near the sidewalk, and shot Godfrey twice in the belly.

"Not even our best surgeons can save you from a belly shot, Godfrey. I should leave you in pain for an hour before you die, but by some miracle you might live and identify me."

Dennis reloaded and placed the muzzle of the .32 against Godfrey's forehead, saw raging terror in the superintendent's eyes, and then pulled the trigger.

Dennis escaped in the darkness before anyone in the rich neighborhood thought to investigate what could have been shots.

The next morning, Dennis was on the train for San

Francisco with the money from the sale of his house tucked in a money belt. In the city by the bay, he went in search of a Balboa 200 press that had an eighteen-by-twenty print capacity and the quality of printing he required. He bought a new one from a supply house and told them to hold it for him.

Then he traveled on to San Diego, figuring that this was the farthest he could get from Washington, D.C., and investigated the possibilities. After a week, he bought a run-down building at the edge of the business district that had a half basement with access from the rear slope of the property. He moved his press from San Francisco to San Diego by rail and went to work.

He smiled again remembering, then felt he'd given the ink long enough to dry. He went to the receiving tray and jogged the sheets with the fronts of the U.S. twenty-dollar greenbacks on them and stacked them on a rough table. He would print the rest of this group of 250 bills before he stopped.

The 250 bills would make 5,000 dollars in almost perfect U.S. currency when he was done. The only flaw in the bills were the serial numbers. The eight numbers and the one letter on the front of each bill were identical. He didn't have the expensive equipment to give each bill a different number. It didn't matter. The way he spread them around the country, he would have his fortune, be out of the business and living in a beach-front cabin down in Mexico with a pair of young and beautiful senoritas to keep his bed warm.

He would complete the first run today. The toughest part came next. He had to run the sheets through the press twice more and get the color registration exactly right. That was the joy of this press. Dennis would position the piece of paper exactly for the first color run, then place the bill in the same spot for the second and third color, and the press would print it in precisely the same position as the first color.

It was a matter of authenticity, but with Dennis it was also a matter of pride.

A knock sounded on the door at the top of the wooden stairs he had repaired when he moved in. He wiped his hands and went up the steps and unlocked the door.

When he swung it open he saw Consuelo standing there with a cup of coffee and a sweet roll for him. Consuelo had left the buttons open on her blouse, and when she moved her arms her fine, rose-tipped breasts showed from her blouse.

She handed him the coffee and he grinned and sipped it, then put his arm around her so his hand covered one of her breasts and moved her along the hallway toward living quarters he had built in the back of the run-down building.

"Make love," Consuelo said and laughed softly. They were the first English words he had taught her after he found her on the street looking for work. Now she cooked and cleaned and shopped for groceries for him, did whatever he asked her to, and never went into the basement of the old store.

Consuelo smiled and fed him the last of the sweet roll in the bedroom, then gently undressed him. The first day she had told him that the purple mark on his face did not bother her. She was almost as tall as he was and she liked that. Sometimes Dennis figured that Consuelo might have been a whore walking the San Diego streets, but he didn't worry about it. He had always had trouble with women, but not this one. He gave her more money than she had ever seen in her seventeen years of life. As the oldest of fourteen children, she had been pushed out the door when she

San Diego Slattern

reached sixteen. The closest town was San Diego, and she came here and stayed.

She stripped off her clothes and knelt over the naked printer and teased him a moment, then eased down on his quivering tool and heard him moan. He would be fast and try for a second time as always and not be able to.

Consuelo smiled. She remembered when a boy from her village had taught her about making love. He had climaxed twelve times that afternoon. As she remembered, they both had been fifteen years old. Now she settled for one lovemaking and kept her man happy. For her it was the best arrangement she had ever made, and she wanted it to last until she was old and withered up and had no desire for a man.

Bernard Dennis rolled away from the slender Mexican girl and sighed. He couldn't remember the last time he had been able to climax twice in one day. At forty-three he was getting old. He laughed and she looked at him.

"It's fine, Consuelo, you're the best woman I've had in years. Just keep your little pussy hot and ready and we'll get along fine. Maybe in another two or three months we can go down to Mexico and find that little *casa.*"

Her eyes lit up and she lifted away from him. *"Casa en Mexico?"*

He grinned at her, nodded and got dressed and went back down the steps to do the rest of his day's production.

Chapter Six

Spur walked up the slope on Fifth Avenue. There were plenty of houses along here. Not like on his other hunt for the counterfeiter. He needed 1401 Fifth. Three more blocks ahead.

The houses here were bigger and better, some of the nicest in town, and showed lots of tender care.

He came to the end of the 1300 numbers and looked across the dirt track of a side street and saw a stately house on a big corner lot.

That had to be it. He crossed the street and went through a wrought-iron gate and up a concrete sidewalk to the front steps. As he went up the painted wooden steps, he saw the name plate on the door. It read: "1401 Fifth Avenue. Jonas M. Meikoff, M.D. Internist, General Practitioner. Hours 8 to 5 Monday through Saturday. By appointment only."

Spur stared at the name in his notebook beside the address. R. C. House was the name of the person who

46

sent the packages of counterfeit bills and gave this as his return address.

Spur had a sinking feeling that he'd been out-smarted again.

A mistake? Not five times in a row.

Spur opened the door and stepped into an ornate waiting room. This was not a doctor for the poor and unwashed of San Diego. Soft music played from a rec-ord machine somewhere out of sight. The room was tastefully furnished and showed touches of elegance. A woman in a clean white uniform came through a beaded curtain and smiled.

"And how may I help you today, sir?"

"I'm looking for a Mr. R. C. House at this address. Do I have something mixed up?"

"You just may, sir. This is 1401 Fifth Avenue, the office of Dr. Jonas M. Meikoff. I've been with Dr. Mei-koff for over five years now, and I know nothing of anyone named R. C. House."

Another phony name and address. This counter-feiter was not only smart and talented, he was clever. He had used the same name and return address five times. Maybe he'd be bold enough to do it again. If the post office clerks could be alerted to watch for the name at the time of mailing, they might have a chance. Spur thanked the lady in white, assured her it was his mistake, and retraced his steps out the front door and back to the post office.

Ten minutes later the postmaster was sympathetic. "Yes, I see what you mean. This man is ingenious. Un-fortunately, we require no proof of identity when one is sending a registered item. We do require strict iden-tity when one is picking up such an item."

Spur told the postmaster his suggestion.

"You want me to post this name and address on the cover of every pad of registered item forms we have, and urge our clerks to memorize them and to call the sheriff at once if anyone tries to mail a package with this name and using that address?"

"That is my best bet so far to find this counterfeiter. He's the cleverest one I've ever had to hunt. Usually they make one big mistake and that's enough for us to catch them. This man seems to be extremely smart, and so far he's been unusually lucky."

The postmaster agreed to the plan to identify the name and address on the registered letter and package pad of blanks and on the registry books.

"Don't know if it will work, but we'll try it. When was the last package mailed?"

They looked at Spur's list. It had been twenty-four days ago.

"Maybe within a week he'll have another package to mail," Spur said. "I just hope to hell we can catch him mailing it, and then it can become damaged in transit and have to be opened and repackaged. Then we'll find the fake bills and nail this damned counterfeiter."

The postmaster smiled. "You've worked with some post office people before and some postal inspectors. I'd say we can do that and not get into too much trouble."

Spur shook the postmaster's hand and went out into the warm San Diego sunshine.

A man across the street waved at him, and Spur waited as the gun-toting gent hurried across the street, dodged a team of oxen and then a farmer's heavy wagon, and came up to the boardwalk in front of the post office. Spur recognized the man as one of the deputy sheriffs he had seen in the county office.

"Mr. McCoy?"

"Right."

"Sheriff would like to see you. He says he wants to

do some horse trading, but I don't know what he meant by that."

"Would now be a good time to talk to him?" Spur asked.

"Indeed it would. You know where he is?"

Spur said he did and walked down to the courthouse and to the sheriff's department. Sheriff Raferty stood in the door to his office holding a cup of coffee.

"Cup?" he asked, and Spur nodded. A deputy brought him a cup of dank black coffee. They sat down in the office and the sheriff closed the door.

"McCoy, I'm obliged to do all I can to help you when needed on this counterfeiting charge. You find the scallywag, and me and the boys will help you nail him to the wall.

"Figured you might want to do me a little help in exchange. This morning somebody reported finding a shack burned to the ground and a dead man laying outside. Looked like he'd been dead a day or maybe two. He brought the body into town. Turns out to be a homesteader, one John Johnson. He's on file with the land office. Picked himself out a plot of land out east in the area where the county's biggest rancher thinks he owns the whole damn valley for twenty miles."

"I've met his type before. Self-made man, small homestead, but he controls a huge chunk of rangeland."

"About the size of it. His name is Archer Grundy. He's a bit over sixty, has one son. His wife died five years ago. He tries to make the kid into a rancher, but he ain't. He's more of a poet.

"Grundy has a history of rough tactics with what he calls squatters on the land he claims as his."

"The land this Johnson was on was unclaimed federal land and he homesteaded it?"

"True. Can't say for sure that Grundy killed this homesteader Johnson. But that's my guess. He had a wife, but she wasn't found. Wondered if you'd mind riding out there and looking over the site? I'm ready to ride if you are."

"Guess I owe you, Sheriff. But this damn counterfeiting is my first call. When I get a lead on that, I'll drop your case like a hot branding iron in a glove full of holes."

"Done."

Spur changed pants, used a county mount and rode with the sheriff and a deputy east from San Diego. They followed a dry watercourse for a mile or two, wound through a low pass and then down to a larger valley where water had pooled in some deep holes along what appeared would be a fair-sized stream in the rainy season.

Three miles up this valley the sheriff stopped them. He pointed east and south.

"Down there a few miles is the Grundy spread, the Bar G. He's got more damned cattle than he knows what to do with. Furnishes the slaughterhouse in town with all the beef they want. Now he's shipping steers on the hoof to Los Angeles." The sheriff pointed up a small valley to the left.

"Up here three or four miles is the Johnson place. I checked the land office map before I came. It's a legitimate homestead, damn near proved up. Heard Johnson had about twenty head of breeding stock and was looking forward to his first drops. Now hard telling where his cattle or his horses are."

They rode into the small ranch yard an hour later, and the smell of burning flesh was still in the air. Spur caught the scent when the wind changed. He probed the ashes of the burned-out shack with a long stick and soon found the remains of a human body.

"Wife, looks like," Sheriff Raferty said. "Now we have two killings instead of one."

They worked for a half hour gently removing the remains of the woman, wrapping her in canvas and putting her three feet down into the hard California soil.

Spur had checked for tracks when they first rode in, but a fresh wind evidently had blown out any sign of them. He had seen a seep fifty yards from the house where some chaparral and a solitary cottonwood tree grew, and walked up there, the sheriff trailing along behind. The seep had a spring at its head that had been dug out and a small trough inserted to run out a pencil-sized stream of water. It fell into a three-foot-wide pool a foot deep.

Spur sampled the water, then drank a double handful. He walked down fifty yards before the thirsty soil soaked up all of the water and the ground turned hard and dry again.

Almost at the end of it, he came to a place that was twenty feet wide where the water had seeped into a flat area and caused some straggly grass, a host of weeds and a few wildflowers to grow. Across the moist area he found two sets of hoofprints deep and well defined.

The mounts had both been walking. One was a heavier horse, slightly larger than the other one and packing a bigger load.

Spur stood and looked at the sheriff. "This Grundy, is he a big man, two hundred to two-ten?"

"Yeah. How did you know? He's over six-one and I've seen him at two-twenty to two-thirty. Some Mex woman is cooking for him now and he ain't eating as well."

"A heavy man and a lighter rider went across here within the past three days. The sides of the mud prints

51

haven't dried up much yet. Pushed up that way, they'll dry out in five days or so depending on the sunshine. These mounts are heading away from the Johnson homestead, evidently in the direction of the Grundy spread."

"Interesting, but nothing I can take to the judge. If Grundy did it, I need some hard evidence."

"Six-gun don't leave no brass like a rifle would," Spur said. "They have ways now to prove which rifle fired which lead bullet, if they can get a good enough bullet out of a victim. Some Jasper back in Virginia says he can do the same thing with a six-gun that has rifling in the barrel. Uses a microscope or some such device. Afraid I don't know how to do it."

Sheriff Raferty grunted. "Damn it to hell. I been expecting old Grundy to do something like this. Last time somebody homesteaded on what he calls 'his' range, he raped the woman, beat up the man, burned their wagon and drove off their brood cows. Couldn't prove it was him, but the man raised a stink about it and the district attorney went out and had a long talk with Grundy. Maybe he figured not to leave no witnesses next time."

They walked back to the ranch yard, mounted and checked the small corral. The gate was open and no animals were inside. The outbuilding had two saddles and some tools, little else. Not much to show for a man's life.

They could see no cattle or horses from where they sat and decided not to search for them.

"Some running irons and those 'stray' cattle and horses could wind up with the Bar G brand easy as not," the sheriff said.

They made better time riding for town. As they went down H Street, the sheriff eyed Spur a moment.

"How would you like to settle down on a homestead

out here in Grundy-claimed land?"

"Not about to settle," Spur snorted. "Using me for bait so I can get my head blown off by some insane old rancher toting a double-barreled Greener?" He laughed. "Not a chance, Sheriff. Pick on somebody else."

"Can't. Grundy knows most of the folks around here who would try homesteading out there. He'd smell a setup quicker than scat. I need somebody who would threaten him, talk nasty to him, spread some hot lead around his boots next time he comes to town."

"Sheriff, all I need to do in this town is to find myself a counterfeiter, ruin the plates and send the man and the engravings up to San Francisco to the U.S. marshal."

"Then at least help me get one of the bullets out of Grundy's six-gun. How would we do that?"

"Fire his gun into a bale of cotton or a bunch of blankets, something that wouldn't distort the shape of the grooves and lands on the slug. First you'd need something to compare it with, say a slug from the dead homesteader's body."

"Oh, we have that. Two of them, in fact, that old Doc Brown dug out of the dead man. I've heard about them rifling marks, too."

"So, no problem. Grab Grundy, take his gun away from him, fire a round into the blankets and hope it matches."

"Microscope, you said?"

"Sure. Your doctor friend should have one in his office. Let him do the matching job for you."

"Might work," the sheriff said. "Only how the hell do I get that six-gun away from Grundy long enough to fire a test round?"

Spur shrugged. "Your problem, Sheriff. I got worries of my own. This counterfeiter could run off a half million dollars' worth of phony money. My job is to stop him."

When they rode up to the sheriff's office just before dark, Spur was starved. He turned the horse over to a deputy and headed for the closest cafe that looked like it wouldn't give him food poisoning. A disturbance up the street caught his attention. Then a brass band struck up, and Spur walked the half block to see what was going on.

He was there before he realized it was a political rally. A small man in a black suit and a black derby hat stood on the back of a farm wagon, and when the band stopped he began shouting at the fifty people who crowded around. They cheered everything he said.

"When we get more students, then we'll build a new schoolhouse. Right now we got three of them. Enough for any town our size. We need them older boys out working, earning a living, not studying things like literature and poetry and fancy books.

"Elect me next Thursday and I'll cut the school budget back to where it was two years ago, and make our teachers earn their pay by teaching more hours. We can't go soft on them teachers or they'll just want more schools and fewer students in each class.

"We got more kids with book learning now than we need. Let them learn how to earn a living with their hands."

The cheers broke out again, and one man who protested was quickly hustled off to the side.

A man standing near Spur didn't let that stop him.

"What about training more doctors and scientists? You saying we don't need scientists?"

The small man looked sharply at the questioner and held up his hand when his muscle men headed toward him.

San Diego Slattern

"Well now, Dr. Brown. I expected you here tonight. Yes, we need doctors. Two in a town our size. We've got three and another one is trying to get started. You want more competition? Be reasonable. You weren't taught here in San Diego. Neither were the other three doctors in town. Let us educate our own kids the way we want to."

The crowd cheered again. Spur looked at the doctor. He was a tall man, slender, with elbows and knees that seemed to stick out with nowhere to go. He had thinning brown hair and a large nose that Spur wouldn't soon forget.

The doctor mumbled something and walked away from the rally. Spur soon left, too, and had his supper in the Elite Cafe. A small Mexican man loaded Spur's plate with four kinds of Mexican food Spur didn't know the names of. Three were rolled-up pancake-looking things stuffed with meat and cheese. The last one was a folded-over shell filled with shredded chicken, lettuce, cheese and chopped-up tomato and onion. The meal was delightful and filled him. He had a second cup of coffee and headed for the post office. It was closed.

He retreated to the Horton House Hotel and went up to his room. Ginny Lambeau lay on the bed reading a lurid magazine about sex crimes. She pointed to a picture and giggled.

"I don't see how in the world she could ever do that." Then she tossed it aside. She wore one of his shirts, which didn't quite cover her crotch where she sat on the bed. She smiled at him.

"Hope you had supper? I got starved and went down to the dining room," she said.

"Good. What can you tell me about the big rancher out to the east, Archer Grundy?"

"Grundy? Ugh! He's big and rich and mean. Thinks

55

he can have anything he wants. I've heard he's a terror when he goes to the Sartorial Parlour House. That's the best whorehouse in town. One day he stopped me on the street and asked me if I'd want a job cooking at his ranch. Only twelve men and some Mexicans to cook for and I'd have a helper.

"I told him no. He followed me. Said the job paid twenty dollars a week and I'd get Sunday off and that there might be some extra benefits if I wanted to work late one or two nights a week. I screamed at him and rushed down the street. He stood there humping his hips at me and laughing."

"He sounds like a real choir boy."

"That for sure he ain't."

"He come into town often?"

"Used to come in every Saturday night, get into a game of poker, then get roaring drunk and wind up in a whorehouse. He's been a little quieter lately. I'd guess he's over sixty years old."

"Hitting his prime years."

"Why so interested in him? He ain't no counterfeiter."

"True. Sheriff asked me for a favor."

Ginny smiled and unbuttoned his brown shirt and took it off, revealing her young, naked, firm, female body. "Hey, I'm the one looking for a favor tonight. I just hope to fuck that you're not too tired." She smiled and leaned over and kissed him.

Spur grinned. "Too tired? You've never seen me too tired at least for two or three times. Maybe not all night, though, this time."

She pulled his hands up to her breasts. "My titties have missed you. See if you can get acquainted again."

As he caressed her breasts, she unbuttoned his vest and shirt and peeled them off him, then toyed with the black hair on his chest.

Ginny sighed and nodded. "Oh, yes, Mr. McCoy, I think we're going to be able to get acquainted again. Look at my nipples. They're rising and hardening. I love it."

He stripped out of his boots, pants and shorts and pushed her down on the bed on her back. Her knees lifted and spread and he went between her silky white thighs and probed only a moment before he thrust forward hard and jolted all the way into her.

"Oh, God!" Ginny brayed. "So wonderful. Just wonderful. Fuck me hard and fast. I need it right now, right this second."

Spur obliged. He pounded at her hard, set up a rhythm that she matched, her slender hips humping up at him in exact synchronization, surging his desire. He broke into a sweat.

He bent and sucked on her orbs, and she screeched in wonder as she climaxed before he knew it, then she came again and again. Six times she exploded as her body writhed and twisted, shook and vibrated. Her voice began low, but with each satisfaction, she surged higher and higher until she screeched one last time and went limp.

Then her eyes opened and she saw him still pumping and she began again to match his thrusts.

A moment later he exploded. He was sure the room had disintegrated around them, that the stars were blown out of their spot in the heavens, that the universe had collapsed back into a void of nothingness and he was the supreme being of the whole wild mishmash of matter and light and energy.

Then slowly the universe came back together, the stars came out again, planets resumed their proper orbits, and the moon gleamed down at him and the woman on this small spot on a third planet orbiting a fifth-class star in a tiny galaxy way out on the wrong side of the tracks in the massive universe.

"Oh, God!" Ginny said.

Spur couldn't talk for a moment. When he could find his voice and get back some of his strength, he nodded at the girl below him.

"Oh, God, you're right. That was a fine one."

They lay there for ten minutes listening to each other breathe. Then he rolled off her and she cuddled against him and they slept.

When he awoke an hour later, it was dark outside. He went to the window and looked down. Two saloons showed bright and sounded loud. There was a torch-light political rally just out of sight. He could see the glow of the torches and hear the politicians talking through megaphones.

He turned back to the bed. Ginny sat hugging her knees to her chest.

"When you lived down here where did you stay?" Spur asked.

"With my parents. Then I ran away to Los Angeles."

"Maybe we should stay in another hotel. I'm feeling a little like I'm on display here. I'd be easy to find if someone came looking for me."

"Somebody looking to shoot you down, Spur?"

"Could be. Never can tell. I've put a lot of men into prison. Lots get out and come hunting me."

"They don't know where you are."

He shrugged. "You're right. So far I haven't made any killing enemies here in town. Now all I have to do is find out who's printing up all those counterfeit twenty-dollar bills."

"He don't spend none of them here in town?"

"Not a one. That's going to make it harder to find him."

"Maybe he'll change his mind and spend some."

"I hope so. Got some ideas I want to try tomorrow.

Maybe we better get some sleep."

"Just one more time?"

Spur shook his head. "Not tonight. I know we couldn't beat the one we just had, so why push our luck? Rest up for tomorrow."

"Promise?"

"I promise."

He didn't get to sleep right away. He lit the lamp and went over the material he had on the counterfeiter. Ginny slept through it like the healthy young woman she was. What a sexy young thing. He shook his head and went back to his notepad. If he were the counterfeiter, how would he work the mailing? He was still making circles and squares on the pad an hour later. He couldn't give up yet, he had to get an idea. It would come. It had to come.

Chapter Seven

Dr. Philip Brown tousled the hair of an eight-year-old boy and handed his mother a bottle of medicine.

"Mrs. Horst, this should clear up that cough in a day or two. Give it to him four times a day and whenever he wakes up at night coughing. Nothing to worry about. If it doesn't go away in two days, come back and see me. Okay, Seward?"

The boy nodded, coughed in one final demonstration and went out the door to the hallway and into the waiting room.

A woman came out of a room and frowned at the medic. She perched one fist on her full hip and shook her head. "You really have to see him. He's been waiting for twenty minutes and he's getting impatient."

Dr. Brown nodded at Hilda, his receptionist, nurse, housekeeper and wife. She had weathered over the years like everyone did, but on her the age had seemed to make her sweeter, more tender and caring for him as well as his patients.

"I know. What does he say ails him?"

"Poor man can hardly talk. All that shouting and yelling at the rally last night. You two tangle again?"

Dr. Brown nodded, gave an exasperated sigh and went into the next small treatment room. A man on a chair stood up quickly.

Lothair Clinton had one hand on his throat, the other held out in supplication. "Help me, Doc. Hurts like hell." The words came out slowly, croaking like a giant bullfrog down on Glendenning's pond.

Dr. Brown nodded, felt the man's throat a minute and then peered down it trying to get the light from the coal-oil lamp in the room at the right angle. He felt a chill settle over him and lifted his brows. One more. There had to be one more. It was for the good of the town, the children.

"Well, Lothair, looks like you brayed and bellowed too much last night. Your vocal cords must be raw and inflamed from all the speechmaking.

"I'll give you something to help. Most important thing is to let your voice rest for at least three days. Don't say a word unless you have to to stay out of jail. I'll have to do a mix on some medicines I have. Take it by mouth a spoonful every four hours. Got that?"

Dr. Brown held up his hand. "Don't answer me with words, just nod." Lothair Clinton nodded, his thanks showing on his face. "All right. You just sit there a minute and I'll get your medicine. Won't take me but a minute."

Like most other doctors in the smaller towns of the West, Dr. Brown kept a good supply of medications for his patients. Few small towns had stores that carried or specialized in medicines.

Dr. Brown went into the small room he called his laboratory, where he kept most of his medications. He felt the chill again and nodded, accepting it this time. Yes, the conditions were right, the principle was undeniable, the need for action was absolute, and the means were at hand. It would be quite simple, really.

He took down a drug that would help heal the vocal cords. It was a sop of a sort. Lothair's condition would heal itself in a week if he refrained from talking. Most people wouldn't do that. He added to the medicine an ounce of laudanum. The tincture of opium would help keep Lothair calm. Then he hesitated. One of three drugs would do the job. He considered them carefully. At last he chose the more potent of the three. It should be effective in forty-eight hours with four doses a day.

Dr. Brown carefully mixed the three medicines and poured them into a small bottle that had dosage marks on the side. When he was satisfied that the contents were completely mixed, he pasted a small label on it, using only the name of the throat medicine, but didn't sign it. He put on the date.

No one this side of San Francisco could analyze the exact contents of the bottle. There was almost no risk. He took the bottle out to Lothair Clinton and handed it to him.

"Remember now, no talking. Take the medicine one tablespoonful four times a day. Check back with me in a week."

Lothair began to say something but Dr. Brown held up his hand again. "About last night. No hard feelings. I realize you were talking on the stump as a politician. No reason why we still can't be friends. Now get home and shut up for a few days."

Lothair grinned and nodded and walked out of the examining room, through the waiting room to the street.

San Diego Slattern

Dr. Brown watched him go. Lothair had been a friend years ago. But that all ended when he began to shortchange the children and their schooling in the San Diego School District. That was where the city's future lay. In educated, hardworking, forward-looking young people. That meant their education would cost more money, a lot more money. More and not less should be spent on the children's schooling.

He lifted his brows and watched his wife come out of the waiting room with a baby in her arms. She never could resist the lure of a baby. It was too late for them now. He took a deep breath and went back to his medical practice.

Consuelo stared at the papers on the floor of the living quarters Bernard had fashioned from the old run-down store, not believing what she saw. There next to the wall were several of the sheets of paper that had been printed with the twenty-dollar plates. Bernard must have dropped them. How could he be so careless?

She scooped them up and heard him coming up the steps from the basement. She quickly pushed the printed bills under a newspaper on the small table in the section of the old store that had been turned into a living room. The bills had been finished, but not trimmed off on the sides. She had no idea how many there were. She should take them to Bernard at once.

Consuelo hesitated, then smiled slyly. He might throw her out and she'd be back on the street at any time. She had no hold on him. Yes, she knew about the money he printed, but he realized that she would never tell the *policía*. Everywhere the police were scoundrels and cheaters who took what they wanted. No, she would never go to the police about the bad money.

Bernard came into the room, waved at her and went to the kitchen area. He made a sandwich for himself and uncapped a bottle of warm beer. He always took a snack in the afternoon.

"Hey, woman. We're out of bread. Go to the store and get two loaves and find some pickles and some of that canned sauerkraut. Yeah, love that stuff. Here. Here's two dollars, should be plenty. Bring me back the change. I'll be busy until late."

He took the food and went back down the steps. The door slammed behind him.

Consuelo hurried to the door but could hear nothing from below. She returned to the table and looked under the newspaper. The bills lay there, clean and bright. She'd seen Bernard trim the bills and crumple them and fold them so they looked used. Should she? She stared at them. There must be six or eight. She counted them. Ten! That was more money than she had ever dreamed of having. It could all be hers! Two hundred U.S. dollars.

She walked around the room three times, then found some scissors and trimmed one bill the way she had seen Bernard do. Then she folded it, crumpled it and straightened it out. Yes, it did look older now. She wadded it up, then smoothed it out and put it with the two one-dollar greenbacks and walked to the grocery store three blocks over.

She found what Bernard wanted, paid for it with the two dollars and had sixty cents left. Folded carefully in her other hand was the twenty-dollar bill. She had never had one before. She had seen them, but only briefly.

She thought of the gambling tables at El Razza saloon on the south end of town where the Mexicans all lived. She had been a player there when she worked the streets and had money. Sometimes she'd take her gentleman friend down there and watch him gamble. They knew her there.

She turned and ran south. The package in her arms became heavy and unimportant, but she clung to it. She stopped outside the door to the saloon, wiped the perspiration from her face and combed her fingers through her long black hair.

She walked in and saw that the roulette wheel was still there and that two men played on it. She stood by and watched a minute, then El Chico looked up and saw her. He was running the wheel today.

He said something to her in Spanish and grinned. She scalded him with a look and waved the twenty-dollar bill at him.

"Chips, you whore's whelp. I have more money than you do. Give me chips."

She put the sack of food on the floor by the table and watched the wheel two more turns. They hadn't started to cheat with it yet. She had a chance. Twice she bet on the red and twice she won. She was four dollars ahead. The next three bets she lost; then she put ten dollar chips on red 24 and held her breath.

The ball rolled around and around and bumped over the slot and at last came to rest—in red 24. Consuelo shrilled in delight.

"I'm on a roll, I'll break this little wheel." Then she remembered how they could rig it when they wanted to. El Chico warned her with his eyes, but she didn't want to believe him. She played against the others on the table. If most went black, she played red. She won steadily until she had more than forty dollars' worth of chips.

The others players dropped out and it was her against the house.

In five minutes she was broke. El Chico lifted his

65

brows. "I warned you," he whispered as he raked in her last five-dollar bet.

She took the sack of food, hurried back to the run-down store and went in the side entrance. Nothing had changed. She could hear the muffled sound of the printing press below. So he hadn't done all of his printing yet.

Consuelo put away the food, then cut herself a thick slab of bread, spooned honey on it and ate it quickly. She burned the scraps of paper she had cut from the twenty-dollar bill in the small kitchen cookstove, and made coffee.

She sat there thinking about the other bills. She shrugged, retrieved them from between some books in a small bookshelf and stared at them. With the scissors she had used before, she trimmed the last nine bills, and burned the strips of paper in the stove. She "weathered" the bills until they no longer looked new, then found a hiding place.

She put the bills behind a mantel clock that struck the time. Bernard had bought it at a secondhand store just after he arrived. The money would be safe there.

She went to the door and called down about supper. Bernard couldn't hear her. She went down the steps and asked him what he wanted to eat. He said he'd eat later, he wanted to finish up this batch before he quit.

"Take me a least two hours more. We'll decide then."

She went back up the steps, ran to the clock, took out two more twenty-dollar bills and walked out the door and down the street toward H Street and the shops and stores. She bought an ice cream at the Anderson cafe, and the clerk made no comment about the twenty-dollar bill. That was as much money as a workingman made in two weeks of toil and sweat.

She spent more of the money in a women's wear store, getting some of the silky bloomers and short underwear that were being worn by women in the East now. It looked scandalous. Maybe Bernard would notice.

Twice she read the big clock outside a jewelry store, and the second time she rushed back to the old store and slipped in the side door. She put the other new twenty-dollar bill and the change behind the clock. Before, she had left the sixty-cents change from the grocery shopping on the kitchen table beside Bernard's plate.

She planned a supper and had it well in hand before the short man with the purple mark on his face came up the steps. He sniffed, then saw the stew cooking and nodded. She had saved some of the roast from the day before in their icebox, and put in onions, carrots, potatoes, turnips and parsnips. The roast beef would add just the right amount of flavor.

That evening, Bernard was cheerful and happy. He had finished another group of bills that would be mailed the next day. He always was happy when he had another shipment ready. Consuelo knew, too, that tonight would be a fine time in bed. His need was especially high when he finished a printing. She kept hoping for three times, but so far two was the best the little man could do even with her expert assistance.

She thought of all the money behind the clock and she shivered. It was delicious having some money of her own. Just like the old days. Only now she got to keep it all, not just ten cents on the American dollar.

Spur McCoy spent most of the day talking with the managers and tellers at the three biggest banks in town. He showed them a sample bill and asked them if it was genuine. Every teller and bank manager declared it to be genuine. Then Spur brought out a second bill and asked them the same question.

Only when Spur pointed out that the serial numbers on both bills were identical did he convince them that the twenty-dollar bills were counterfeit.

One banker still protested. "The paper in this bill is absolutely genuine. The ink is exactly correct. If I didn't know better, I'd say it came from the same ink pot that printed the rest of my paper money."

"There's a good chance it did," Spur said. He explained how some disgruntled employee could have stolen ink and paper in small quantities over months or years, and then somehow got plates and went into business for himself.

At the end of his meeting at the third bank, Spur gave up for the day. He found a handy saloon, had a fair steak dinner and then spent three hours drinking six beers and losing eighteen dollars at a dime-limit poker table.

When he got back to the Horton House and his second-floor room, he found Ginny Lambeau stretched out across the bed, naked and sleeping soundly. He repositioned her without waking her, then covered her with a sheet and slid in beside her. He could use a good night's sleep.

The next morning, Spur debated about going to the fourth bank. It was the smallest of the four, and evidently served the lower end of the money chain in town. He had a slow breakfast, then got to the bank about eleven o'clock.

He worked his counterfeiting game with the manager. The man was delighted and did the same game with his tellers. Both missed the serial-number problem.

"So, that must make you a federal government agent of some kind," the manager said. He was Felix Nelson, manager and part owner of the California Merchant's Bank.

San Diego Slattern

"Right. We think someone is printing this fake money right here in San Diego. What we need to do is find him. This man doesn't foul his own nest. So far none of the fake bills have surfaced here in San Diego. We're hoping they do somehow. If you could have your tellers watch for this particular serial number, I'd appreciate it."

"Mmm. I guess we can do that. We don't deal in many large bills. We might get thirty or forty twenties in a good day. I'll write down that serial number and post it with both of my tellers. They're good lads."

As they spoke, one of the tellers came into the manager's office with a puzzled expression.

"Beg your pardon. I was trying to remember that serial number. What was it again?"

Spur knew it by heart. "It starts with a capital A, then two, eight, one, one, two, three, six and a star."

The teller took out a bill and looked at it a moment. "Yeah, that's what I figured you said it was." He handed Spur a twenty-dollar bill. Spur scanned the number. It was the same.

"Matches," Spur shouted. "Where did you get it? Who deposited it? Was it today or yesterday?"

The bank manager looked at the bill and nodded. "By God, you're right, Seymour. Same number."

Seymour frowned. "I know it came in today. This morning. I had only two deposits of any size. One from a small store and one from a saloon. Can't remember which was which."

"Think on it," Spur said. He took out his billfold and removed two legal twenties and handed them to the teller. "In the meantime, I have to confiscate that fake twenty. Here's a twenty to replace it, and a twenty-dollar reward for you for finding the bad one. Now, think who gave you that particular bill."

After a half hour the teller couldn't be sure. He said

he'd take notice of any twenties from then on and make sure he knew who gave him another fake twenty-dollar bill. He gave Spur the names of the two stores who usually had twenties in their deposits. It could be one of them. One was the El Razza saloon down in Mex town, the other the Tiny Thimble Ladies' Apparel shop.

Spur knew it was too early to check with the small store and the saloon. If one bill showed up, there would likely be more. Maybe the counterfeiter was showing his bravado. Maybe he'd changed his operation. Maybe he was getting ready to leave town, so he'd flood the place with fake bills.

Spur spent the next two hours talking with the bankers he had seen yesterday, informing them that one bogus bill had been found, so there could be others. They each checked their unbanded twenties but found no more fakes. Spur reminded them there was a twenty-dollar reward for each counterfeit bill the tellers found.

Spur had lunch at the closest eatery at noon, and Sheriff Raferty found him there. The lawman took off his Stetson, then noticed that Spur still wore his and put it back on.

"Figured you never missed a meal, McCoy. Worked out any way to get hold of Archer Grundy's six-gun yet?"

"Nope, figured that was your job."

"How about homesteading? I can get you fixed up with a place right in Grundy's front yard if'n you want me to."

"Figure that's a good way to tempt getting gunned down late at night from ambush."

"McCoy, you don't sound too keen on helping me much here."

"About the way it is. Got me some problems with getting shot."

"So you won't do it?"

Spur took another bite of the ham and cheese sandwich and chewed it thoroughly. "Sheriff, I didn't say I won't. Just haven't said that I would. Big difference."

"You want to close out your own case first."

"Be a big help. One of the counterfeit bills turned up here in town today. Getting a line on the gent, I hope."

"Thought you said he was smarter than that."

"Maybe he isn't. I want to stick close to town next few days, hoping we can nail whoever's spending the fake bills."

"Yeah, your job. Course it sure don't help me a hell of a lot."

"You have a gun law in this town? No six-guns in the city limits to be worn in holsters in public?"

"Seems to me some wild-assed county politician rammed through a law like that a few years back. Nobody paid no attention to it."

"Check and see if it's still on the books. If it is, you can grab Grundy's piece as soon as he rides into town. Take it to your place, shoot two or three times into a foot-thick pad of folded-up blankets. Then dig out the undamaged slug and try for a match with the rifling on that bullet the undertaker pulled out of that homesteader."

"By damn, it just might work. You don't even have to buy me lunch. I'm going to talk to the district attorney. Don't want to get some evidence and then not be able to use it."

The lawman waved and hurried out the eatery door. Spur settled back and enjoyed the rest of his sandwich and a second cup of coffee.

He wondered who had spent the counterfeit twenty-dollar bill and if that person would do it again. Now they had one more chance to catch the crook.

Spur pushed back from the table and headed for the post office. Time to check in with the postmaster again. Maybe the counterfeiter would get his month's production done early and mail his package before the thirty days were up. Maybe, but Spur wasn't counting on it.

When he found the postmaster, the mailman lifted his hands in frustration and shook his head.

"We've had no one mail a registered package with the 1401 Fifth Avenue return address. We're watching. You posting any reward?"

"Fifty dollars if they spot the person and we get there before that person gets away, or we run him to ground later and capture him."

"Sounds fair to me. These clerks will keep their eyes open wide if there's a chance to make an easy fifty dollars."

"Good, let's make it sixty. Spread the word and let's hope this lowlife is ready to mail another package of fake money."

"I'll do that. Hell, I'll watch, myself." They waved, and Spur went out the front door.

At least he was making some progress. He wished he knew who'd turned in that counterfeit twenty-dollar bill. That would be a big leg up on the case. When he stopped by the small bank again, it was closed and they were gone for the day. He'd have to wait until tomorrow and hope.

He walked past the El Razza saloon, where the bogus bill might have been passed. It looked like a drinking establishment catering to the large Mexican trade in town. Back up the street a block he found the Tiny Thimble shop. Not many women in town would be spending a twenty-dollar bill on clothes. This woman might just have the key to his problem.

As he started to cross the street, a gaggle of riders galloped into town, racing straight down H Street, scattering pedestrians and single riders. The seven cowboys angled for the biggest saloon and gambling establishment in town, the Crowing Rooster.

Spur jumped back off the street to the boardwalk as the horses charged past. He shook his head and looked at another man who had escaped.

"Who the hell is that?" Spur asked.

"You must be new in town. That's old man Grundy and his six bodyguards. He don't come to town no more without them. Don't know how fast they are, but all of them pack iron, and I've seen them shoot."

Spur watched the riders drop off their mounts, tie them and swagger into the saloon. He started toward them and saw Sheriff Raferty and one deputy coming the other way.

"Stay out here," the sheriff told Spur. "Or at least stay out of the confrontation."

The lawmen went into the Crowing Rooster, and Spur went in a minute later. When he came inside, he saw the sheriff talking to Grundy.

"That's about the size of it, Mr. Grundy. You remember when the county board passed the law. Any firearm carried into any incorporated town may be picked up by the county sheriff and held until the owner leaves the jurisdiction, when the weapon will be returned."

"Hell, I been in town fifty times since they passed that damn law. Nobody said a word. Just riding in we saw men all over town with sidearms. You ain't taken their weapons away from them. Why me?

"Because the law stipulates that anyone brandishing or causing public concern about safety may be required to turn over his weapon on demand."

"That's what you're doing?"

"Right, Mr. Grundy. As a responsible land owner in this area, we expect you to set an example for the others. I'd be obliged if you'd hand over your six-gun and tell your men to do the same. They'll all be safe in my office when you get ready to ride out of town."

A man slid up beside his boss, his hand dangling over the butt of his six-gun.

"Want me to take him, Mr. Grundy? I kin do it." The speaker was young, holding a bottle of beer in his left hand and grinning at the sheriff.

Grundy frowned, shook his head. "Nope, Ned. I need you. Best if we do what the lawman here says. We're law-abiding citizens. Next time maybe if I only bring two of you boys we won't look like a threat. Yeah, Sheriff. We'll give you our guns. I'll be staying overnight. The rest of the boys will be out of here by midnight. Be sure you have somebody at your office so they don't got to wait around."

"I'll be sure. Appreciate your cooperation. You're helping to make San Diego a civilized town." Sheriff Raferty took the pearl-handled six-gun Grundy handed over, then the weapon from the man siding him.

Grundy bellowed and five more men came up, nodded to their boss and handed over their weapons. The sheriff had an armload of hoglegs. He grunted at the men, waved at his deputy to put away his handgun and headed for the door.

Spur waited two minutes, then went out the door as well. He wanted to be at the sheriff's office to fire the rounds from the Grundy gun for comparison. Who knows, that microscope in the doctor's office might find them a killer after all.

Chapter Eight

Archer Grundy groaned when he eased his leg out of bed the next morning. Too much damn rotgut whiskey. He had enjoyed the poker. Won almost thirty dollars. He pushed to sit up on the side of the bed and let out another groan of pain.

It was getting harder to get up every morning. Lying in bed all night got his rheumatiz kicking up. It seemed like every morning when he stood up he found a new place to hurt. Damn this getting old.

He eased his feet down to the floor and stood up, battering down the stabs of pain in his hips and shoulders. He knew that his fingers wouldn't work right until they got warmed up. Rope burns and scar tissue and some strange little knobs of bone on three of his fingers made them hurt most of the time now. By noon they would be halfway back to normal.

He looked at the alarm clock ticking away on the box beside the bed. Six-thirty. He was glad he'd changed his mind last night and had come home rather than stay in town. He had most of what he needed right here, except for the drinking with the men and the gambling. He especially liked the card playing.

By the time he got dressed and downstairs to the kitchen, Lester had cut off and fried a slab of bacon and had some hot-cake batter waiting to go on the cast-iron griddle over the wood-stove fire.

"Morning, Pa."

"Yeah, morning."

Lester poured a cup of scalding coffee, and Arthur took it black and gulped down a throat-burning mouthful. The heat soaked into his hands and he welcomed it. He eyed his only heir working at the stove. He might not be much of a cowhand, but he did know how to get breakfast.

Sometimes he made the morning meal for the two of them and let Josefina handle breakfast for the crew. His mother had taught him to cook when she knew she would have no daughters. She taught him too much the ways of women. Damn, but the boy was weak. How in hell did he ever hope to take over running a ranch this size?

Two thick flapjacks dropped on Archer's plate beside a patty of fresh-churned butter and a small pitcher of hot syrup. Archer forgot his problems for the moment and ate his breakfast. Four of the big hot cakes, four strips of thick-cut bacon and two cups of coffee and he was satisfied.

Lester finished eating before his father and busied himself clearing the table.

"Hell, boy, let Josefina do that. What we pay her for. We've got some cutting and branding to clean up in the north valley. Want you to come along and help. You missed most of the other branding. Every rancher's got to know how to brand and castrate his own steers."

Josefina came into the kitchen with a worried look, but Lester said something soft to her in Spanish and she brightened.

"*Buenos tardes*," she said.

"Yeah, good morning. All the crew should be back in time for chow at noon. We'll be tired and hungry. Make it good."

Josefina nodded. "Yes."

"Lester, you go out and get the horses ready. I'll be along directly. Need to talk to Josefina about the new order for food from town."

Lester nodded, grabbed his wide-brimmed hat and left the kitchen.

"Pantry," Archer said and walked ahead of the Mexican girl. She was seventeen, and he had hired her in town one day when his other cook had quit. She usually lived across the border in Mexico, but was in San Diego to visit her sister.

She had been thrilled to earn three dollars a week and had been working for him for over six months now.

In the pantry he closed the door halfway and stared a moment at her. Not much in the tits department, but she had a tight little twat.

"Do me a fast one, Josefina, little cunt." He caught her shoulders, eased her back against the wall and fondled her breasts. She frowned for a minute, then as his hand warmed her breasts through the thin white blouse, her nipples hardened and rose and she began to pant. Her hands went down to his crotch and found the swelling there and trilled in delight.

Quickly she knelt and opened the buttons on his fly and pulled out his thick penis. Her mouth went over it at once, and he began to stroke into it with his hips moving slowly. Then as he began to pant he drove harder and harder until she brought her hands up to hold his lance and limit his penetration.

"Oh, God, that's sweet. You've got a great mouth and a sweet little cunt. Oh, yes, this is good." He gasped and pounded hard six times into her mouth and bellowed in satisfaction. He paused a minute, then came out of her mouth and put his penis back in his pants. He patted her on her breasts and chuckled.

"You might not be the best cook in the world, but you do service a man mighty fine. Any hole, you don't care." He laughed softly, stroked his hand up through her crotch and pulled open the pantry door.

She heard the screen door slam and slumped to the floor. She lifted her skirt, pulled down her bloomers, and her hand found her crotch and the tiny node there. She strummed it a dozen times while her hips bucked and she trembled all over. She cried out softly and pumped her hips again and again until the climax had torn through her and swept away.

Josefina arranged her clothes, went back into the kitchen and watched the men ride out toward the north pasture.

Archer Grundy rode in front of the six other men as they headed north. He sat tall in his saddle at six-one and 220 pounds. Hell, he could keep up with these young kids any day. He put in just as hard a day's work as any of them. That's what Lester had to learn if he wanted to run this ranch some day. He damn well better learn how to deal with homesteaders.

Lester rode up beside his dad.

"Pa, I saw a big old cougar up there in the brush. Probably the one that's been feeding on our calves. I'm gonna go up and see if I can track him. Got my rifle in the boot just in case."

Archer waved him away, and Lester spurred up the

slight slope into a patch of brush and small trees. Archer snorted. When the kid wanted to, he could ride as well as any of the hands on the place.

A short time later they heard three rifle shots.

Lester joined the others just as they came to the north valley to start working the cattle. His father looked at him.

"Nope, missed the cat. He's a big one. Should put out some baited traps."

"You don't mind killing that animal?" Archer asked.

"If the animal is killing our stock, then I don't mind hunting him down."

The other riders had moved off to start cutting out and grouping the calves for branding. Archer turned to his son.

"So what's the difference between that big cat killing our cattle and the homesteaders moving in and chewing up the land where our cattle have to graze and killing them off that way?"

"A big difference, Pa. If you can't see the difference, you just ain't the man you should be."

Archer Grundy jolted back in his saddle as if he'd been shot with a rifle bullet. His mouth fell open, then snapped shut, and his eyes blazed.

"You take that back, son, or we're gonna have a lot of trouble. No cause to get mean and nasty."

"Not mean and nasty, Pa. It's what I think and it's right. You got no cause to kill them homesteaders. You wasn't even sorry about it. Them was two human beings out there doing what the law of the land said they could do. You should never have killed them."

"Here I still thought you were man enough to run the Bar G. Now I guess I got to admit that you ain't, and that you never will be. You're a yellow-bellied coward. I just ain't had to 'fess up to it before. What the hell am I gonna do with you?"

79

"Nothing, Pa. I'll be going back to the ranch right now and pack a bag and be on the train out of San Diego in the morning."

"Damn it, Lester. No son of mine is running out on me. You'll stay here and do what you're told. You don't have to go. I'll ease up a little. Maybe you just ain't cut out to manage the ranch. No reason for you to run off. Hell, you can hire a manager when I'm gone. Pay him to run it.

"You realize what this ranch and the cattle are worth, son? I've had an offer for three hundred and fifty thousand dollars. Think about it. We've got near a thousand head of brood cows. They're worth two hundred each on the market. That's two hundred thousand. There's over three thousand head of steers and calves that will eventually bring fifty dollars each, depending on the market. That's another one hundred and fifty thousand.

"Hell, son, this ranch is worth more than all the stores, shops and houses in San Diego combined.

"There's a dozen ways a man can get himself killed out here on the range. I could get gored by a range bull, my horse step in a gopher hole and throw me and break my fool neck, get hit by lightning or bit by a rattler half a dozen times. If that happens, then all this is yours, free and clear.

"You don't mean it about running out on me, do you, son? Then I've got nothing to work for. I'm building up this ranch so you'll have something. Sure, I started from nothing, but no reason you got to."

Lester shook his head. "Pa, you just don't understand. I'm twenty-two years old. I'm a grown man. I don't want to be a rancher. I want to be a musician like Ma was. I want to study the fiddle, go to some big city and be in a symphony orchestra. That's what I want to do."

"A fiddler? A starving musician? Play for barn dances and weddings? Hell, boy, that's what fiddlers do."

"Only I'll do more. There's a man in San Diego who teaches the violin. I've signed up to take lessons twice a week. That means I'll have to practice four hours a day. I'm starting late, so I have to rush."

"Four hours a day . . ."

"You want me to stay here, Pa, that's what I'm going to do."

Archer threw up his hands in frustration. "What the hell, a fiddler. In another five years this place will be worth a half million dollars. You want to be a fiddler."

"Maybe it won't be worth that much, Pa. We own the land along the river. All the rest of this is not our land. You know that. This ain't the sixties anymore when you could bluff the settlers off the land you controlled but didn't own. This is eighteen and eighty-four, and homesteaders are gonna keep coming. You can't kill them all."

"Usually I don't have to. I just scare them off and run them out. Damn, but you are pigheaded. Let's get some steers cut here and branded. We'll talk about this later."

"I'm going into town tomorrow for my first violin lesson, Pa. And another thing. I wish to God you'd stop screwing Josefina. She's only seventeen. She could make big trouble for you if she wanted to."

"Trouble? She's a Mex, not even a citizen. She enjoys the fucking more than I do. Don't worry about her."

"What if she gets pregnant?"

"Then I ship her back to her parents in Mexico."

"The way you've done before?"

"Yeah, if it's any of your business. Now let's ride. Enough of this damn talk."

"Pa, today I work the range for you. Tomorrow I start my music lessons. I'll be practicing most of every day. If you want to disown me and throw me out, so be it."

Lester Grundy whipped his horse around and spurred out to the area where the other cowboys cut out the calves that had been missed on the roundup and herded them into a bunch getting ready for the branding.

Archer Grundy watched his son ride away. At least the boy had some gumption about something. Grundy took a long breath, closed his eyes and let it out. Then he rode in and got the branding started.

Spur McCoy felt prickles of excitement tingling along his spine as he sat in Dr. Philip Brown's office. The sheriff sat beside him and held the two envelopes, one marked "Death slugs taken from Homesteader Johnson," the other "Slugs from weapon #1."

Dr. Brown came out of a room drying his hands on a clean white towel and nodded. The two men stood and went into his laboratory.

"Dr. Brown, this is Spur McCoy, who's helping me out on a case. What we're wondering is if you can match up these slugs and prove that they came from the same revolver."

"How would I do that?" Brown asked.

"Back East they're starting to do it by magnifying the marks made on the lead slugs by the lands and grooves as the bullet's slammed through the barrel when fired."

"The rifling in the bore," Dr. Brown said. "Yes, that I know about. Just how to match them to show that they come from the same bore, I don't know about."

"I hear they use a microscope to do it," Spur said.

"Microscope? These are much too large. Maybe a

big magnifying glass. But the grooves are small. I don't understand how they establish a pattern on one slug that can be compared with the pattern on another slug."

Spur shook his head. "It was a chance that looks like it didn't work out. We'll leave the slugs with you. Maybe you'll get an idea how to match them."

Spur and Sheriff Raferty walked out of the doctor's office and back toward the center of town.

"Maybe he'll come up with a way to match them. The district attorney said if the doctor can swear the slugs came from the same gun, he'll be able to use it as evidence in court."

"You better not count on it. Dr. Brown looked totally confused."

"So what's next? You going to volunteer to stake out a claim for me?"

"Probably not. First I have my own problems."

"The counterfeiter."

"Right. My turn to check the banks. Maybe some more of the bills have shown up. Oh, you might check the land office and find out how many homesteads have been filed on and then abandoned in the area that Grundy claims as his grazing rights. Might produce some witnesses for you."

Sheriff Raferty grinned. "By damn, I think you've hit on a fine idea. I'll go right over there now. Might turn up something interesting."

Spur checked at the closest bank. They had found none of the spurious bills. The second bank had found none. The third bank had better luck.

"Our teller noticed the bill as soon as it came in. He has the name of the store and the person who deposited it."

Spur took out two twenties and handed them to the

bank manager. He pocketed the fake twenty. "The name?"

Five minutes later he stopped by at the Anderson Cafe and had a cup of coffee. A middle-aged woman waited on him, and he figured she must be the owner or the wife of the owner. A Mrs. Anderson had made the deposit in the bank as she did early every morning.

"Mrs. Anderson?" he asked.

She looked up and nodded.

"Yep. That's me. Yes, I run the place. Have ever since my late husband died. What can I do for you?"

When he explained about the bogus twenty-dollar bill she scowled.

"Damn, I should have known. That little Mexican chippie gave me a twenty-dollar bill and I wondered at the time where she got it, but a sale's a sale, even if it was just an ice cream. Where would a girl like that get a twenty-dollar bill? But it was busy right then and I'd just burned some broccoli. You know how bad burned broccoli smells in the kitchen? Anyway . . ."

Mrs. Anderson looked up and frowned. "So what's the matter? You asked me to tell you about the twenty-dollar-bill girl."

Spur grinned. "True. Do you know what her name is, where I can find her?"

"Name? We aren't in the same social circles. Don't think I've ever seen her before. But I know the type. She's either a whore or works in a saloon somewhere or is some rich man's little lady on the side. Where to find her? Not the hint of an idea."

"This is tremendously important. I need to know everything you can remember about her. How tall is she? How long was her hair? Did she have dance-hall paint on? How was she dressed? All you can remember."

Mrs. Anderson lifted her brows, hurried away to the

kitchen, then came back. "Almost burned the cauliflower. Okay, now the slattern. She was maybe five feet one or two. Mex black hair down around her waist, straight. Bangs cut high across her forehead. Brown eyes, of course. Cute in a trampy sort of way. Not busty at all, kind of flat on top. Slender hips. She wore a tight black pullover shirt of some kind and a Mexican print full skirt. That's about all."

"That's a good description."

"So, I see them all. Only one problem with that description. It fits about two hundred young Mex girls on the street out there looking for work, looking for a man to keep them, or just looking for a man for a half hour and a quick fifty cents. I might watch for a year and never see this particular one again."

"I'll check back from time to time to see if you've seen her. If you do, try to get a name and address or have someone follow her home. You do that and find out where she lives and I'll give you a reward of fifty dollars."

"Well now, I'll pay special attention."

Spur thanked her and walked to the post office. Tom Fogiletta, the postmaster, groaned when he saw Spur.

"Afraid you were going to come in."

"Why afraid?"

"Someone mailed another package, registered with the same return address, and we missed it. We had one man out sick last three or four days and he didn't hear about the registered-package situation. The clerk who replaced him on the window found it. He's been trying ever since to remember who brought in the package."

A few minutes later, Spur talked with the clerk. After the apologies and assurances, they got down to cases.

"How many registered packages did you take in this morning?" Spur asked.

"Three. That's the trouble. I can't remember two of them at all, just a blur. I guess it was the medicine Dr. Brown gave me. Said it might make me a little sleepy. Boy, did it."

"Man or woman?"

"Just can't say."

"Tall or short?"

"Don't know."

"Was one of the two a young Mexican girl?"

"I have no idea. Really."

Spur shook his head. "You are in a dense fog, aren't you? Do you think any of it will come back?"

"Can't tell."

"If you remember anything about the other two people who mailed registered packages, you tell your boss and have him get in touch with me. Sorry we missed it. Thanks anyway."

Spur went back and talked with the postmaster.

"Sorry we missed him. Maybe next time, only I don't want to wait another month for another mailing."

"Best we can do on this end. We have the address where it's going to on the other end. You can wire your people in that town to watch for that particular package being sent to that address and have it stopped at the post office. We can do that with contraband."

"Yeah, then we'll know who it's going to and we can arrest them at that end of the rope. But it doesn't help us a damn bit on this end. I'll get a wire off this afternoon. What was that address where the package is being sent?"

The postmaster wrote it down, and Spur thanked him and went to the railroad station to send the wire to his boss, who would handle the other end.

On the way out of the train depot, Spur saw a Mexican girl who looked about fifteen or sixteen. She could have been the one who spent the counterfeit twenty-dollar bill in that cafe. But he couldn't stop and question every Mexican girl in town.

He thought about it. A Mexican girl, young and pretty. She wasn't the counterfeiter. She might be working for him or sleeping with him. She could have stolen a bill and spent it, not knowing the consequences. Could be. She was his best lead, only who was she and where did she get the bogus bills?

Spur headed back to make a survey of the banks again. He'd worry them so much they would check every twenty-dollar bill they saw. They would know that number by heart and dream about it. All he needed was one more good report on the girl. Someone who knew her or where she stayed.

Spur opened the door of the first bank he came to and walked to the teller cages.

Chapter Nine

Dr. Brown set down his black case on a straight chair beside the bed and stared at Lothair Clinton.

"Well, Lothair, your wife tells me you're not feeling well. How's the voice?"

"Little better. Hurts. Feel rotten. Stomach upset. Joints hurt like hell. Have trouble breathing sometimes."

Dr. Brown nodded. "Voice should come along in a day or so. Double that medicine I gave you. Two tablespoons three times a day. That will take care of your voice. Joints hurt and trouble breathing?"

"Yes, Doc. Hurts like hell."

"Been some of that going around. A pleurisy kind of thing that some folks get. I've got some new pills that should relieve those problems. Take one with each meal."

Dr. Brown stood and took a small bottle of pills

from his bag and gave it to Mrs. Clinton, who hovered nearby.

"Dr. Brown, he's really hurting. He never gets sick. You're sure this will take care of him?"

"Mrs. Clinton, these two medicines should fix him up all right and proper. If there's any change, send someone over to get me and I'll come at once."

Mrs. Clinton nodded. She put her hand on her husband's head and frowned. "I do hope this will make him well."

"Nothing to worry about, Mrs. Clinton. Keep him lying down and give him lots of fluids. If I don't hear from you, I'll stop by tomorrow afternoon."

Dr. Brown nodded at both of them, closed his bag and walked out of the house. It was only a two-block walk back to his office and clinic. He smiled grimly. Yes, Lothair, that double shot of medicine should do the job sometime in the small hours of the night. By then it would be far too late and the threat to the children's education in San Diego would be quietly laid to rest in the cemetery. The pills were sugar pills, placebos that wouldn't hurt him, but would do him no good at all.

Dr. Brown set his jaw firmly and marched back to his office. Sometimes a man had to take a stand. He had the ability to change the way things were done in San Diego. He intended to use his power to continue to better the community. He tipped his hat to Mrs. Logan, the banker's wife, and strode through his front door to find three people waiting in his outer office. Good, now he'd get back to healing.

Mrs. Anderson brought Spur McCoy a second cup of coffee and a piece of cherry pie and pushed them in front of him. He sat at the Anderson Cafe three

stores down from the bank and looked up when two
women came in the door. Neither was Mexican, and
both were too old.

Mrs. Anderson nodded. "Yep. Gonna be damn hard
to catch sight of that girl again who gave me that
twenty. I didn't remember seeing her around here before. Maybe she was just passing through."

"Nope. She lives here or just across the border. The
man I'm hunting must live here too, close by, but I
don't know what he looks like. The girl is my best lead
so far."

"Like I said, we must have fifty of them girls out on
the streets some nights. The local whores are getting
mad as hell about them cutting prices and taking all
the business."

"Life is tough all over," Spur said.

Mrs. Anderson grinned. "That's what I tell them
when they come in here bitching. I can't stand a
whiner."

Mrs. Anderson would not be mistaken for a lady of
the evening. She was forty-something, five-five and
about 160 pounds. Not quite as wide as tall, but solidly
built. She had a mole on her right cheek and a more
than faint crop of hair on her upper lip. She was not
what you'd describe as a beauty. But how she could
cook.

Spur had eaten lunch and now supper in the cafe,
always watching for the elusive Mexican girl. He figured he had to put in two days here watching, then he
wasn't sure what he would do.

If no more bills were cashed, he was in real trouble.
He hadn't failed on an assignment yet and he didn't
want this to be the first. He tried to figure what the
counterfeiter would do. As long as the man felt no
danger here, he'd stay. If he knew he was being chased
and the Secret Service was so close, he would proba-

bly disband his operation here, leave the press and take his paper and ink and his ill-gotten gains and head for some new town, maybe San Francisco or Seattle.

A new thought came to Spur. Say the counterfeiter was selling his bills for thirty cents on the dollar, which had been the going rate for a while. For a $5,000 package of fake bills, he'd get back $1,500. What would he do with the real money? Would he put it in a local bank, or would he simply drop it in a suitcase and keep it and use what he needed? He'd have to check the banks tomorrow for a $500 to $1,500 deposit six or seven times about a month apart to the same account. That might take some looking, but if he found a name, he could break this case wide open.

Spur sipped the coffee between bites of cherry pie and had another thought. What would a young Mexican girl do if she suddenly had four or five of the bogus bills? She might even know they were not real, but that they could be spent. She had spent one or two. What would she buy?

Spur had an expert on the subject in his hotel room. He would head for the Horton House as soon as he finished his pie.

Mrs. Anderson came out and said, "I'll watch for her tomorrow. If she comes, I'll send somebody to trail her and find out where she's staying. It won't be in no fancy hotel. If I see her."

He thanked her and hurried back to the hotel.

Ginny Lambeau was in the middle of trying on clothes when he came in the door. They were scattered over half the bed.

"You think the red blouse and the black skirt, or should I wear a red blouse and the gray skirt? I kinda like the red and black. It sets off my eyes better, don't you think?"

91

"Yes, red and black." Spur sat in the room's only chair and watched her strip the blouse off. She wore nothing under it. He grinned.

"Yes, yes, I know you like my titties, but I'm not trying to seduce you. I'm trying on clothes. I bought some new things today with that twenty-dollar bill you loaned me."

"What I want to talk to you about. I have a lead, a young Mexican girl, slender, pretty, long hair. She's spent one or two of the bills. Bought ice cream with one. Now, what I want to know is what else might she buy? Say she's a street whore who's connected with the counterfeiter. She might be straight from Mexico's border or from the interior.

"Say she's fifteen to eighteen, never had much money before and now she has a hundred U.S. dollars. What would she buy? Where would she spend money?"

Ginny dropped on the bed beside him, making her breasts jiggle and bounce delightfully.

"Spend? Wow. First she'd get some clothes, I'd bet you that twenty-dollar bill. Some nice clothes, some underthings, maybe things that wouldn't show so her man wouldn't know she stole the bills.

"Then she'd buy some perfume. A cheap perfume and maybe a ring or two and a necklace. Yes, she'd buy a necklace, probably some fake gold chain or such with a cross on it, or a crucifix, since she must be Catholic."

Spur began to nod before she finished. "Yes, yes, good. And she might go back to a store where she bought something the first time, more clothes, different underthings, bloomers and such."

"Oh, yes. And then the other thing she would do with found money would be to gamble. Most Mexicans go head over applecarts about gambling. There are several places down in the south part of town where Mexicans do a lot of gambling. Most of the saloons down there are owned by Mexicans, and they want the Mexican business."

She turned and caught his face and kissed him hungrily. Then she let him go and moved his hands to her bare breasts. "Have I earned a little bit of attention? Don't think I've seen you all hot and sweating and about to come in two or three days."

"I've been neglecting you. Twice, then we get some sleep. Tomorrow you get up bright and early with me and we go buy you some new clothes, and we talk with the owners and clerks about a pretty young Mexican who seemed to have more money than she should."

The next morning they shopped. There were a dozen stores that sold women's clothing, and three seamstresses who might be open part time. Spur and Ginny shopped them all. Four of them knew Ginny, and she had to explain Spur as a family friend just down from San Francisco.

In the second store one of the clerks overheard them talking with the owner and came up.

"I sold some things yesterday, I think it was. The girl was Mexican, rather pretty. At first I thought she was one of the whores off the street, but she seemed nice and was quiet and well mannered."

"Did she wear a black blouse and a colorful Mexican print skirt?" Spur asked.

The woman smiled. "Now how could you know that? She did. I commented on the skirt, it was beautiful. She didn't speak much English. She bought bloomers and some underwear. That's when I decided she wasn't a whore. They buy things that show flashy and trashy on the outside."

"How old was she?" Spur asked.

"Sixteen, maybe eighteen. Hard to tell."

"Bangs cut across her forehead?"

"Yes, she did have bangs."

"Straight hair down to her waist?"

"We're talking about the same girl."

"Have you ever seen her before?"

"No, I don't think so. These girls come up from Mexico, trying to make a go of it here or earn some dollars to take home."

"So you have no idea where she lives?"

"Not a one."

"Thank you. It's highly important that I find this girl. I'm with the U.S. government on a special case here in San Diego. If she comes in again and buys anything, try to have some alteration needed on it, so you can ask her to come back the next day to pick it up. Then get word to me at the Horton House and I'll be here when she returns. This is vitally important."

"Goodness sakes, I'll be glad to," the owner said. "I'll be sure to tell the other clerks about this. I hope she does come back."

They found another women's wear store where the same Mexican girl had bought a pair of costume jewelry earrings and a cheap imitation gold chain with a crucifix on it. The clerk had no idea who the girl was or where she was now.

By then it was noon, so they went to the Anderson Cafe for lunch. Spur had bean soup and a cheese sandwich and Ginny settled for a piece of apple pie with ice cream.

"No sign of our girl yet," Mrs. Anderson said when she brought the pie. "If she shows up, I'll either grab her and hold her for you or follow her to where she lives."

"Thanks, Mrs. Anderson."

After that Spur said he had some banking talk to do, and Ginny should entertain herself for a time.

"Can we go to the concert tonight? The town marching band is going to play in its annual concert on the green down by the bay. It should be fun. We can take a picnic."

He nodded and left her looking in a jewelry store window while he went to see the closest banker.

The bank manager nodded when Spur had explained his theory.

"I'd say it's possible that such an individual would not bring his cash to us. That would be a rather large deposit for an individual and would be noticed. However, we'll look back through our deposits and see what we can find. It could take us a day, maybe two. We know what bogus money can do if it floods a small town like ours. We'll cooperate in every way we can."

Spur went to the other three banks in town. None of them had found any new fake twenty-dollar bills. All said they would search to see if anyone had deposited large amounts of money about once a month over the past five or six months.

That done, Spur went to see the sheriff.

Sheriff Raferty looked up from some papers he had been reading and scowled. "Any more bright ideas about how to nail Grundy to the outhouse wall?"

"Land office help any?"

"Yeah, forgot to tell you. There have been twenty-two different homesteads staked out on the land up those three valleys that Grundy claims grazing rights on. The land is open and available for homesteading. Not a one of those claims has been proved up, and none of them are now occupied. All have reverted and are ready again for homesteading."

"Figures. Homesteading started, when, in seventy-two," Spur said. "That's twelve years ago. Grundy's been a busy boy."

"Actually, the homestead act went into effect Janu-

Dirk Fletcher

ary one, eighteen hundred and sixty-three. That's
twenty-one years. So Grundy has been throwing
homesteaders off his land on average one a year. You
haven't had any citizen complaints?"

The sheriff frowned. "Yeah, a couple. But none
about anybody getting shot dead. Most of the homesteaders simply moved on to a different area where
they wouldn't have a son of a bitch for a neighbor."

"Any of those folks still around this area?" Spur
asked.

Sheriff Raferty shook his head. "Nope, I checked.
None of them stayed in the county."

Spur shifted in his chair. "Don't look at me like that.
Why should I risk my neck to be a homesteader for
you?"

"You're a lawman, and Grundy don't know you from
Mrs. Murphy. Besides, you can take care of yourself
and won't wind up getting killed."

"Right. That's why I'm working my counterfeiting
case. I see lots of election posters up. You running for
sheriff again?"

"Yep. Unopposed. Way I like it. No speeches, no
kissing babies. Just do my job."

"Which includes harassing visiting lawmen."

They both grinned.

"Hell, maybe when I get a handle on this bogus
money thing, I can lend you a hand. We'll see."

"'Preciate it."

Spur waved and left the sheriff's office. He was
down half a block when a man called to him from
across the street. Spur stopped, and the man ran past
a farm wagon and a team of oxen pulling a freight
wagon to cross the dirt street to face Spur.

"Mr. McCoy. Mr. Jefferson at the bank wants to see
you. I think we took in some more of the bad bills."

A short time later Spur looked at three more of the

bogus twenties and nodded.

"Yes, these are the bad ones. Who deposited them?"

The teller standing beside John Jefferson, president of the San Diego Trust bank, stepped forward.

"It was the one I couldn't remember before, the El Razza saloon. It's run by a man named Montez, Rico Montez."

"Have you had any trouble with him before?"

Jefferson shook his head. "No. Seems to be a fair businessman, holds down the fights in his place. Has a few girls but he works mostly the Mexican trade down in Southtown."

Spur took out his purse, extracted one twenty-dollar bill and gave it to the teller.

"This is for finding the bills. I'm confiscating them, so put through a charge on that account and notify him. I'm going down there right now to see Rico Montez and put some pressure on him. If he knows he's lost sixty dollars, it might help."

When Spur walked into the El Razza saloon a few minutes later, the small drinking establishment became silent and hushed. One man behind the bar frowned, then smiled.

"Yes, sir. How may I help you?"

"Looking for Rico Montez."

"That's me. You look like a lawman."

"I am. Did you make a deposit today at the San Diego Trust bank?"

"I did. Do it every day."

"Today your deposit contained three counterfeit twenty-dollar bills. Did you know that?"

"Counterfeit?"

"Bad money, bogus, fake. Not worth the paper they're printed on. No good."

Montez frowned again. "How you know this?"

"I'm with the United States Secret Service. We have

as our primary job defending the integrity of the U.S. currency. We didn't print these three bills." He spread the bills out on the bar.

Montez looked at them and touched one. "Look good to me."

"Check the serial numbers. They're identical. Good currency has a different serial number on each bill. That's how I know these are bogus."

"So?"

"So the bank has deducted sixty dollars from your deposit today."

"No, no. They can't do that. I'm a poor man barely making a living."

"Then help me. Tell me who passed these bills to you."

"How can I tell? So many customers."

Spur laughed. "Montez, how many of your poor customers give you a twenty-dollar bill for a nickel glass of beer?"

Montez sighed and nodded. "Sí. It was at the gaming tables, roulette. I worked the wheel last night myself."

"Who lost sixty dollars? That you would remember."

"Yes, I remember. I wondered where she got so much money."

"A pretty Mexican girl, long dark hair, bangs across her forehead, maybe seventeen, eighteen?"

"Yes, that's her."

"Do you know her name?"

"Sí. She is Consuelo. She used to work the street, but now she has a man she's living with. A gringo. I don't know who he is or where he live."

"Consuelo. Any last name?"

"The girls don't use last names. We hadn't seen her for five or six months, then she came in two days ago with money. She's been in twice now."

"Will she be back?"

"*Quién sabe?*

"I need to know. Has she been in today? About what time did she come the other two times?"

"Not today. She come afternoon, maybe three o'clock."

"Good, I'll be here at two."

"*Por favor*, not inside. You'll scare my patrons. You look like a *policía*."

"Guess I do kind of stand out in this crowd. I'll watch from across the street. If I miss her, and she comes in, you come outside your cantina and wave your arms. *Es bueno?*" The owner of the El Razza nodded.

"If you help me find where she lives, I'll make good on that sixty dollars you lost and any other counterfeit she spends. But only if I learn where she lives."

Montez thought a moment. At last he shrugged. "Sí, I can do that. It is against the law to make this bad money, right?"

"True."

"Then I will help."

Spur shook hands with Montez across the bar and went outside. He walked across the street and went in the first store he came to that had front windows. Inside, he went to the window and watched the El Razza saloon.

Rico Montez came out a few minutes later, looked up the street, then walked rapidly toward the main part of town. After the saloon man had passed the store where Spur watched from, Spur eased outside and followed him from well back. Montez did not turn around.

He walked a block, went over a block and then half a block down to an establishment that was easy to identify as a whorehouse. Montez was inside a short time, came out and walked half a block back the way he had come. He continued another half block and went into an old three-story house.

Another bordello, Spur guessed. The man must be hunting the girl Consuelo, but why? Did Montez want to warn her that the law was after her, or was he going to demand more money not to reveal where she lived? Spur had no idea. He would keep a watch on the El Razza every day from two until four. If the girl went back to gamble again, he would catch her.

He followed the saloon owner to one more house, but Montez soon left there as well. He looked up and down the street, then seemed to give up and walked quickly back to his cantina.

Spur went the other way. The banks. Maybe one of them had turned up a new bogus bill or had some information about big cash deposits on a regular monthly basis. Spur quickened his steps, anxious to get this case wrapped up.

Chapter Ten

Bernard Dennis settled back in the easy chair he had bought a week earlier and grinned at Consuelo. He waved a letter she had just brought back from the post office. He had established a fake name at the post office so Consuelo could go there and pick up his mail. That way he wouldn't have to be seen in public and he could get his mail quickly.

"Guess what I have here, my little Mexican sex queen?"

Consuelo wasn't sure what he said, but it was a question. She shrugged. "Don't know."

"It's another order. My good friend in New Orleans says that he can take another twenty thousand dollars' worth of my masterful printing. That and another order that came in yesterday means I'll be staying on in your beautiful little city longer than I expected.

"I could even run out of paper and have to take a train to San Francisco to find the best paper I can.

You'll go with me, of course."

"San Francisco? Consuelo go too?" She squealed and rushed to him, kissed him and stroked his crotch, then opened her blouse and put his hands on her breast.

"Much good," she shouted, and he laughed, grinning at her swinging breasts. He was a breast man, always had been. He loved to see a woman's breasts, any size, anywhere.

"Now calm down, calm down. I'll get you some new clothes in San Francisco. You'll like it there. We might stay awhile after I finish my work down here."

He kissed one swinging breast and eased her away from him. His hard-on urged him to make use of it, but he could do that any time.

"I've got some more work to do downstairs. Why don't you go out and see if you can find a new blouse to wear? I'm getting tired of those black and brown ones. Get some with lots of color."

He fished in his pocket for some money and came up with a twenty-dollar bill. He handed it to her. "Hell, spend it all. I just earned another six thousand, six-hundred in cold, real, genuine U.S. banknotes. Go on, get out of here. I'll see you tonight for some good eating. Maybe we'll even go out to that good Mex cafe you told me about."

He laughed at the delight on her face and went to the door that led downstairs.

He still had the trimming and weathering to do on the last batch of $3,000 worth of bills. That was the smallest order he would take. He'd been dealing with these people for only a few months, but he had six buyers now, scattered all over the U.S. The bogus bills must be driving the Bureau of Printing and Engraving and the Secret Service crazy. He knew they would be hunting him, but they didn't have a clue about where he was. He'd been too careful to give away his position.

Downstairs he trimmed the bills with a paper cutter. He cut only three at a time, making certain the measurements were precise so they would appear mint-made in a bundle. Precision work was his trademark.

He had a jig attached to the cutter so the measurements were the same on each bill. After forty bills he stopped and checked them and the jig placement. If any adjustments were needed, he made them, then went back to work.

Bernard Dennis was a happy man. He hummed as he worked. Sometimes he wondered what would have happened if the new supervisor had not taken a dislike to him? Possibly he could have been promoted into some kind of supervisory work. He certainly had been qualified.

Now he was qualified to become rich. He thought about the stacks of legitimate one-hundred-dollar bills he had in the safe place he had designed in the basement room. No one would ever find them, even if they knew the bills were stashed somewhere in the building. It was ingenious and at the same time so obvious that a hunter would never think to look there.

He hadn't counted his money lately. When he had counted several weeks ago he had just a smidgen over $10,000. Think of it, him, Bernard Dennis, printer, with over $10,000 in real U.S. currency. He grinned. All that money and a marvelously sexy little woman to satisfy his wildest sexual fantasies.

Maybe he should quit while he was winning. Simply ship the press back to the people he bought it from and ask them to resell it for him and hold the money. Then he and Consuelo would slip across the border into Mexico and find a fine little house down on the beach somewhere and he could learn to fish and swim and dive and while away the best years of his life in paradise.

Maybe. Dennis shook his head. Would he be happy without his printing work? Could he learn to set type and print in Spanish? It was an idea. He'd talk to Consuelo about it. He hoped that she had a good shopping spree. He should have spent more money on her.

Upstairs, Consuelo had not left yet. She looked at the twenty-dollar bill that Dennis had given her and her eyes went wide. She could buy so many things with it. She changed into the best blouse she had and a conservative brown skirt and clutched the twenty dollars in the small pocket in the skirt. It was safe. She hurried out of the old store, down the street two blocks and to H Street where most of the store were.

She stopped at a small Mexican woman's store, but they had nothing she liked. She moved on to another women's wear store and bought one blouse that was red and black in wild shapes and figures. She paid for it with the twenty-dollar bill, and the store owner eyed her suspiciously, then nodded, and Consuelo knew the owner figured that her customer was just another Mexican whore.

In the next store, she remembered she had bought some underthings there the day before. The sales clerk stared at her in surprise, then waited on her.

When she picked out two expensive blouses, the clerk asked how she would pay for them.

"Are you sure you have enough money . . . *dinero?*" the clerk asked.

Consuelo gave her a five-dollar bill she had received in change, and the woman nodded.

"I really should mend that place on the hem. Why don't you leave it with me and I'll repair it and have it ready for you first thing tomorrow morning?"

"Oh, no. Fine. Fine this way. I take now."

The clerk had frowned but at last agreed and took the money and watched as Consuelo left the store. She had to tell that nice Mr. McCoy something. She wrote him a note and asked a boy outside to take it to the Horton House Hotel and have it put in Mr. McCoy's box. She was sure he would be angry, but there was nothing else she could do. She was the only one in the store at the moment, and couldn't leave it unattended to follow the girl.

Consuelo stopped in two more women's wear stores and one stitchery shop, then bought some costume jewelry in a small jewelry store before going back home.

She always returned to the old store in a different way. Dennis had warned her repeatedly that it was vital that no one ever follow her home. If someone did, he told her they both could end up in an American prison. She had heard about prisons.

She took a ciruitous route through streets and alleys to the old store where they lived. The front of it was boarded up. They used a door on the side, partway down the sloping lot. The store had once been a tinware shop and there were still bits and pieces of metal lying around.

She made sure no one could see her, then slipped through the door and closed it gently. She threw two bolts on the door and sat down on the old sofa in what passed for their living room and spread out her purchases. She thought that Dennis would be pleased. He would enjoy taking the clothes off her before they made love.

She looked at the alarm clock on the kitchen table and knew it was time to start getting supper. He liked such strange foods. He gave her a list to buy, and she had learned to cook them the way he liked. Still, it was strange. When they were in Mexico she would teach him to like the local dishes, especially the abundant seafoods. Yes, soon they would be back in Mexico and living gloriously.

Dr. Brown wore a slight smile as he hurried along the street and then up the sidewalk to the Lothair Clinton house. It was a good one, set back from the street with a few struggling trees in front.

The door opened as he reached the steps. Mrs. Clinton rushed out, and he knew she had been crying.

"I think you're too late, Dr. Brown. Lothair had trouble breathing last night. Then this morning just after dawn he raised up in bed and coughed and wheezed, and he looked at me and told me he was dying. Then he lay back down and didn't say another word. He turned his face to me and smiled, and then he simply stopped breathing."

"How long ago?" Dr. Brown asked.

"Less than half an hour. That's when I sent for you. Thank you for coming so quickly."

Dr. Brown went into the bedroom and stared for a moment at the silent form on the bed. One side had been made up neatly. Lothair Clinton lay on his back. His mouth had stretched wide and his eyes were open.

The medic touched Lothair's throat and found no pulse. He pinched the man's nose, but there was no sucking of air into his lungs through his mouth.

For a moment, Dr. Brown hesitated. Then he looked up and saw the widow standing in the doorway. He shook his head. "Mrs. Clinton, I'm sorry. He's gone."

She burst into tears and left the room. He picked up his bag, heard the woman crying in the next room and headed for the front door. One more thorn in the side of the San Diego School District had been removed. The children would get a good education.

Dr. Brown closed the door softly and hurried down

the street. He had a medical practice to get back to. He kept thinking about other thorns in the community. There were several. One ran the biggest bordello in town. He called it a parlor house or some such. Trouble was, the man never got sick. Dr. Brown scowled. There would be another opportunity. One came along every so often. He had to be delicate and discreet.

Last night's city council meeting still rankled him. He had gone, as he usually did, as an observer. He enjoyed the democratic process. Six unlikely men got together to plot and plan and carry out a blueprint to turn the town of San Diego into the glorious city on the bay that it could be. He had great dreams for the town. Why couldn't others? They were too concerned about their own fortunes. Many times just how they made their money came in conflict with what was best for San Diego.

Dr. Brown had no such conflicts. What was best for San Diego was what he wanted. No quarter given.

The new councilman, Keith Edison, was a formidable man. Physically tall, strong, iron-willed, used to having his own way, he ran the hardware and plumbing store in town and urged the town to get a better water supply and sewer system. Dr. Brown supported him on both counts.

However, last night Edison had suggested that the council cut the San Diego Marching Band from the budget for the next year. He pointed out that they spent over $2,000 on the marching band. That money could go along with some other cuts to set up a better water distribution system, and start to bring in better water from the lakes and the new reservoir in the east county.

Dr. Brown had not said a word at the meeting. Often he asked to speak, but this time he did not. He knew at once that Keith Edison was a candidate for cleansing. Just how to do it and when was a problem. Edison used another doctor in town. Dr. Brown had never had any professional contact with him. He needed to learn more about the councilman, devise a plan that would work without fail, harm no one else, and that in no way could be traced to Dr. Brown.

The marching band was a symbol of San Diego. The volunteer players had performed in dozens of summer concerts. In fact, they were due to play tonight in an open space down by the waterfront. They had marched in Los Angeles and in Escondido. They were good ambassadors for the town.

Yes, he knew that better water for the city was important. But it was a matter of priorities, and in Dr. Brown's mind the marching band was even more important. He worried the rest of the way to his office.

When he stepped in the back door, his wife held a crying baby in her arms. She smiled that glorious smile that had won his heart twenty years ago and shook her head.

"No, the baby is fine, just hungry. It's his mother. I think she broke her arm. You better have a look in room one."

Dr. Brown took a deep breath, changing gears and moving into the work he loved. Here was a woman who was hurting and he knew how to help her. He nodded and pulled open the door to treatment room number one.

Spur McCoy checked with the California Bank just after Maybelle Jean Crowder had rushed in with a twenty-dollar bill. The bank manager checked the number against the one he had written on his notepad.

"I'm sorry, Mrs. Crowder, this isn't a fake bill. It's a real one."

Spur moved up beside the desk and checked the number on the bill.

"He's right, miss. This bill is real. No problem."

"But I saw her, the girl you described yesterday. She was a young Mexican girl, with bangs, pretty, and she gave me a twenty-dollar bill. I thought for sure . . ."

Spur smiled. "We thank you for your help, Mrs. Crowder. There are a lot of Mexican girls out there. This might be a different one than the one I'm hunting, or she might have got hold of a real twenty-dollar bill. Either way there's not much we can do about it now, is there? I thank you personally for being so helpful. Maybe next time it will be a fake bill."

Maybelle Jean Crowder took a deep breath. "Well, dad blame it. I thought for sure I'd be some help on this problem. Looks like I'm not. Yes, I'll still watch for her. The girl did buy a blouse today. Maybe it was just another one of the street whores. Goodness knows we've got plenty of them on the boardwalk come afternoon and evening." She raised her brows, nodded to the two men and walked out of the bank.

"She's really pissed," Spur said. "Sorry we couldn't make her a hero."

"Maybelle Jean'll get over it. She's a tough one. Now, about those deposit patterns you asked us to check. We just can't find anything. Learned something about our depositors, though. The only people who make any deposits over a hundred dollars are our merchant customers. They make regular deposits, some of them daily. But no non-merchant has made any regular monthly deposits over one hundred dollars."

"You did that quick."

"Interested to find out myself. I helped. Sorry we couldn't be any more aid to you."

"It will come. Patience is the name of the game now. We'll get to this guy yet."

Spur wasn't feeling all that positive as he left the bank. He visited the other three banks as well. One hadn't started the deposit checks. The other two had gone through enough time periods to see that they had had no pattern of deposits. Spur told them to call off that search and watch for the twenty-dollar bills.

"That will be our break when it comes," Spur said. "For now we just watch and wait. About all we can do."

Spur hated hearing those words come out of his mouth. There had to be something more he could do. As he walked down the boardwalk toward the hotel, he could think of absolutely nothing more he could do right now to dig out the counterfeiter.

He had no leads to work on.

He had no local suppliers or local distribution of the bills to key on.

He had one small Mexican girl who was passing some bills. But he wasn't sure even that was a lead that would work out. He checked his watch. It was nearly two o'clock. He had to go to the store across from El Razza and see if the pretty Mexican girl with waist-length hair and straight bangs decided that today would be a good time to gamble away another one or two of the bogus twenty-dollar bills.

Chapter Eleven

Lester Grundy rode back from town to the Bar G ranch feeling better than he had in months. He had done it! He had made a break with his father after trying for so long. No more did he need to practice the violin in secret and when his father was in town drunk or out on the range.

He had taken the violin that his mother had prized so and shown it to Mr. Kendrick in San Diego. The teacher had praised the quality of the instrument. He played it a few minutes and smiled.

"It's a fine instrument, Lester. Better than some of mine. I can see that it's been well taken care of. I do suggest a new bow. I'll order you one from San Francisco."

The lesson had gone well. His mother had started teaching him early on, five years ago. He had forgotten most of what he'd learned, but it was coming back quickly. The teacher had written out a series of scales and exercises for him to get his foundation down.

He was delighted with the arrangements. He had paid for two months of lessons in advance, over the mild protests of Mr. Kendrick.

"I want you to know that I'm serious about this and that I am going to spend most of my time practicing. I want to be a violinist in a symphony orchestra some day."

That was when Mr. Kendrick believed him.

Lester eased his mount up to the corral at the home place, swung down and took off the saddle. He looped it over the second rail of the corral and turned the bay into the enclosure. Then he took his violin and hurried into the house to start practicing.

He had made a chart that listed how much he practiced each day and what he had worked on. He wanted a complete record of his work and the progress he made.

Lester had just put his violin under his chin and picked up the bow when Josefina came in the doorway. Her eyes widened at the instrument. It was the first time she had seen it.

"You play?" she asked.

"I'm learning."

She nodded. Josefina wore a white blouse that was small for her and now stretched tightly across her full breasts. Her black skirt came almost to the floor. She stood there watching him a moment, then walked into his bedroom.

"Josefina . . ."

"I know, I know. But you are so tender, so gentle." She walked up to him and pressed her hips against his. "You are so kind and thoughtful." She paused and smiled her best at him. "Your father and all the hands are in the middle valley. They won't be back for hours."

She reached up and kissed him, long and softly, and Lester's eyes flared in surprise.

He eased away from her. "Josefina, I can't. You're only seventeen, a little girl. It's not right."

She unbuttoned her blouse and swung it open, showing both of her full, softly brown breasts with pinkish areolas and dark red nipples that now surged, filled with hot blood.

"Do I look like a little girl to you? Are these the tits of a small girl?"

She caught his hands and pushed them over her breasts.

"Oh, dear Lord," Lester whispered. Then his mouth found hers and he picked her up and laid her down on his bed and spread out on top of her, his hips pounding against hers.

"Wait, wait," she said. "Slow down. We have lots of time." She pushed him aside, sat up and gently undressed him.

"You are so hard and firm, such a handsome young man. Not old and flabby and sagging. I love you, Lester. I want you to love me."

She shrugged out of her blouse and quickly pulled down her skirt and petticoat and then her soft cotton bloomers until she stood naked in front of him.

"You like me?" she asked.

"Oh, yes. But I shouldn't."

"It doesn't bother your father. He fucks me and laughs at me. You are kind and gentle." She finished undressing him and pulled him on top of her, then she giggled and pushed him off onto his back and went on her hands and knees over him so her breasts hung down toward his mouth.

He kissed them, then sucked them and chewed gently until she shivered in excitement. She kissed him, then went back to her hands and knees.

113

"Right now, Lester. Fuck me from behind the way we did before. I love it that way. It feels so wild."

He had long before passed the point where he could stop. He got to his knees and came behind her, found her slot and eased forward into her as she yelped in delight.

She pushed back at him to capture all of him she could. He began to stroke at once, then caught the bend of her hip for a handhold and pounded harder.

Josefina climaxed, shivering and shaking and crying out in rapture. She paused a moment and then repeated the whole procedure until she climaxed again.

He caught up with her on the third climax and exploded inside her with a dozen hard, furious, desperate thrusts that left him bellowing in wonder and satisfaction.

They collapsed on the bed, still together, and rested. Later she moved away from him, kissed his lips gently and quickly put on her clothes.

"I must start supper," she said. "I have much to cook today. I loved loving you. I hope you are always here for me. Never leave me. If you did, I think I would die."

She bent and kissed his lips so gently that they barely connected and then she hurried out the door.

Lester rolled over and pounded the bed with his fists. He loved this girl. What the hell could he do? His father would never agree to his marrying her. He'd say you hire Mexicans, you work Mexicans, you fuck your Mexican cook or maid, but you never marry a Mexican girl.

In Chicago or San Francisco it wouldn't matter so much. Here it mattered, and Lester knew it. Another heartrending problem to agonize over. He knew he should tell the sheriff what his father had done to those homesteaders. But how could he? His father would be hanged if Lester testified against him. So he couldn't.

Just like he couldn't marry Josefina and take her away from the abuse his father heaped on her. He lifted his brows. Wasn't he just as bad as his father about Josefina?

No. She had come to him the first time. Every time they made love she had made it happen, like today. Still, he was having sex with an underage girl.

He stood and took out his violin. He would practice. He would practice until he was too tired to lift his bow. Yes, that's what he'd do. He would practice and practice until he blotted out all the bad things in his life. His music would solve all of his problems.

That same day, Spur McCoy watched the El Razza cantina from across the street in a small coffee shop where they served Mexican food. The coffee was good, and he ate two platefuls of a tasty cinnamon dessert he couldn't remember the name of. He had a good view of the saloon from the coffee shop.

He saw several women enter the cantina, but none of them had long hair. Two were much too old. One was a question mark. The owner did not come out and wave his arms, so Spur figured the right girl had not come.

By four o'clock, Spur decided that if this girl he hunted worked for the counterfeiter, she would be at his house cooking the man's supper. He might use her sexually, but almost surely the woman would also be a cook and shopper for him.

He snapped his fingers and left the coffee shop to find the closest store that sold food. It was a grocery store that had opened recently. It still had the grand opening signs on the doors.

Inside he found canned goods and baked goods, a

Dirk Fletcher

small section where cuts of meat were laid on chipped ice, and a produce section. It was a new kind of store for the area and had a lot of customers.

He asked who the owner was, and a young man with blond hair, a struggling blond mustache and a friendly smile came up and held out his hand.

"I'm Victor Copley, owner, manager, clerk and janitor of the Copley Grocery. How might I be of help?"

"I'm trying to find a young Mexican girl who may shop here. She would be buying gringo food, since she's cooking for one. Any idea if you've seen a young, pretty Mexican girl about eighteen with long hair and bangs across her forehead?"

Copley thought a moment and shook his head. "Afraid not. But I don't do much of the clerking. Why don't we talk to Elton, the young man who does."

They went back to a counter where Spur saw two women with lists and a man behind the counter filling their order. No one seemed to be in a rush.

Elton listened to the question and grinned.

"Hey, some of them little Mex girls are really cute. But with bangs? Most of them have lots of hair and keep it to the side. Bangs. Straight across? There was one girl had them, Conchita, I think someone called her."

"What about a girl named Consuelo?"

The young man shook his head. "Some of them look so damn attractive, you know? But then you see them with their mothers, and the older Mex women are about as wide as they are tall. Real fat."

"No Consuelo? I want you to watch for her. Pretty and with bangs cut across her forehead."

Elton grinned. "Hey, I'm the local expert on pretty girls, whites, Indians, Mexicans. No matter to me. A beautiful girl is a beautiful girl, right?"

"Yeah, Elton, I think you'll do, watching for her. Oh,

if you find her and notify me at the Horton House Hotel, and I get here in time to talk with her, there's a twenty-dollar reward."

That perked old Elton up. Spur figured if she came in that store he'd know it and run and find him. He could always count on the power of the good old American dollar.

Spur went to seven other stores that sold food and gave his story at each place. One man thought he'd seen her in his store a couple of days ago, but he wasn't sure. All said they would watch for the pretty Mexican girl with bangs and send him a message if they saw her.

The San Diego Marching Band's concert that night at the foot of H Street near the seawall was an outstanding success. Spur wore a string tie, white shirt and his best black jacket as if it were a grand opera opening night.

Ginny wore a low-cut attractive silk dress she said she'd been saving for an occasion. Spur had planned ahead and bought a pair of folding camp stools so they could sit in comfort during the performance.

The band played a number of marches and traditional tunes, then moved into popular songs, including "Little Brown Jug," "Silver Threads Among the Gold," and the brand new song, "My Darling Clementine."

During the intermission the band's ladies' auxiliary served punch and cookies for ten cents at a small stand. A sign assured that all proceeds would toward new music and instruments for the marching band.

After the concert, Spur and Ginny walked in the dusk toward the California Restaurant. It would be open until nine, and that left plenty of time for a leisurely late supper.

They dined on Washington crab and Oregon salmon rushed to San Diego in two days on the train. Spur saw some of the men he had talked to about the currency. They nodded and moved on. Spur was starting to worry that too many people knew he was in town and what he was doing. If the counterfeiter heard about it, he would hide in a shell, finish his work and quietly slip out of town on the train.

He told Ginny about his worry.

"But you said this man was a perfectionist. Didn't you say you figured his Mexican cook probably did the shopping so he wouldn't be seen in town? If he isn't seen, he can't hear what people are saying. The Mex girl won't understand enough English to pick up on the talk. I think you're safe for a couple of weeks at least."

After supper, they walked back to the Horton House and went up to their room.

"Race you," she challenged.

"Go," he said.

She won the contest to see who could get undressed and flat on the bed first. It was an interesting night.

The next morning at breakfast in the Horton House dining room, Spur looked up to see Sheriff Raferty steaming across the room toward him. He pulled out a chair at the table and sat down, scowling at Spur.

"Looks like you're off the hook, McCoy. I had word this morning from the land office registrar. He said a pair of brothers had just signed on for side-by-side homesteads. They checked the land carefully, he told me, and found an area with water at the near end of the Grundy homestead."

"They staked out their twin hundred-and-sixty-acre plots just west of the Bar G ranch. It's on the Jamul Creek that runs west of the registered homestead

118

boundary line of the Bar G tract. Of course, the brothers' homesteads are all on land that Grundy claims he controls."

"You warn them about the trouble out that way?" Spur asked, soaking the plate-sized hotcakes with warm syrup.

"Nope, but the land office guy did. Told them that the last homesteader out that way got himself and his wife killed. This man just laughed and said he and his brother knew damn well how to take care of themselves."

"They going in with cattle?"

"Land office guy said they have fifty head of pregnant brood stock, three range bulls and six horses. He said they'll sleep in their covered wagon until they can build a cabin for their 'improvement' requirement for the homestead."

"You going to ride out and visit them and tell them what they're up against?"

"Figured I would, if you want to make the trip with me. I don't know how many of Grundy's guns we might run up against out there in the east county."

Spur groaned. "You really have a way of spoiling a man's breakfast, Sheriff, you know that? Join me?"

A waitress brought him a cup of coffee to work on while Spur finished his hotcakes, eggs, bacon and orange juice.

"You figure on riding out this morning?"

"Figured."

"You providing the horse and the Spencer repeater with six tubes of ammo?"

"I will."

"Grundy won't even know they're there yet. Maybe two or three days from now would be better."

"They need to be warned. Their herd was about a mile out east of town this morning. They have a fifteen-mile cattle drive. We should catch them before they get there. Two miles an hour when driving fifty head of pregnant cows?"

"Two miles if you're lucky. Quicker we move, the less distance we'll have to ride."

They caught up with the herd about a mile past a settlement the local folks called Lemon Grove. The Hereford mix brood cows were in a four-across file obediently winding up a rise toward a low pass that would take them eastward and to the north of Mother Miguel mountain and then south of Jamul Butte and to the sometimes waters of Jamul Creek.

"Generally they'll be in the Otay Lakes area, which they can drive a herd to for water if they get desperate," the sheriff said.

Ten minutes later they came to the head of the line of cattle and found Oliver Harding. He looked competent enough. Maybe thirty-five, he sat tall in the saddle and looked Texas thin. He wore well-used range clothes and a Stetson that had served as a drinking fountain for his horse more than once. He had a round face and a smile.

"You'd be the sheriff—Raferty, I think the man said your moniker was. I'm Oliver Harding, and my brother Ira is chasing down a stray. Should be on our own land within six or seven hours."

They all shook hands, then kept pace with an old one-horn cow that led the pack.

"You know what you're riding into out here?" Raferty asked.

"Grundy, killer of homesteaders? Heard. Figured it was your job to take care of him. Brother and I can do the job if you don't feel up to it. We got a fresh start coming to us, and no old man is going to stop us."

"You have two guns, Grundy can bring up fifteen to twenty. Not good odds."

"If he gives us any trouble, makes any kind of sound at all in our direction, he's liable to have his ranch house burn down or his corral come open of a dark night. Lots of strange things can happen around a big spread like he has. None of them good."

"Mr. Harding, I just hope you'll be cautious around Grundy and his men. He can be polite as apple pie at times, and then I'd swear he can get killing mean. Trouble is, I can't prove that he's broken any laws. Know damn well he has, but proving it is another rope around a wild-eyed steer."

"Seen his kind before in Texas. Reckon I can handle him. If'n I can't, don't have no right to be staking a claim. Good talking with you gents, I got to keep these ladies moving to their home grass."

Spur and the sheriff sat astride their horses and watched the rest of the fifty head of brood cows move along to the east.

"I'd say the young men have been duly warned," Spur said.

The sheriff nodded. "Hope so. Hate to investigate another killing out there on the Bar G range."

"Killing, might be," Spur mused. "If it is, I wonder who it'll be, one of the brothers there or old man Grundy himself ready for a six-foot-deep plot of ground."

They rode west for a while back toward San Diego. About a mile along they came on a covered wagon followed by a string of six horses on a long lead line. A youngster no more than thirteen sat in the high seat clucking at the pair of mules that drew the wagon. He waved.

"You must have been talking to my brothers up ahead. I got behind a mite when I lost the horses back a ways. I'll catch up. My given name is Brody."

"Howdy, Brody," Spur said. "Looks like you have a man-sized job to do there."

"Yep. Been doing it for six months now. Reckon I can do it for a few more miles. I best be moving." He waved, slapped the reins on the mules, and they flipped their ears but moved ahead.

"So, there are three brothers on that ranch," Spur said. "Think that Grundy would wipe out a whole family?"

Sheriff Raferty frowned, then looked back at the moving wagon and its string of remounts.

"Just never can tell about Grundy. You for damn sure just never can tell."

Chapter Twelve

Consuelo sat in the bedroom and watched Bernard Dennis drink one glass of whiskey after another. She had never seen him drink this way before. He would usually have a shot of whiskey before he went to bed, but not this much.

He drank and then he cried. When the crying ended he had another shot of the cheap whiskey, then he cried again. He had been so happy all day working on his press, printing his bad money. At supper he had been sad and then started on the crying jag.

She moved, and he glared at her. "Don' move. Like your tits." He slurred his words now, and she could understand only a few of them. His head dropped forward, and he lifted it with an effort. Then he dropped the shot glass. She left the bed and picked it up. Then he started to sag forward on the chair.

She tugged and pushed and got him on the edge of the bed. One final push rolled him over on his back.

He was unconscious. Consuelo had seen lots of men drink themselves into dreamland. He would be out until morning.

She grinned. It had been two months since she had a chance like this. She dressed quickly in her flashiest blouse and wild skirt. Then she went down the steps into the half basement and found the newly printed bills that had been trimmed and weathered. They lay in a cardboard box, and she hoped he hadn't counted them. She picked out five, folded them and tucked them inside her blouse. Then she frowned at the feel, took them out and put them in the tiny pocket in her skirt.

She would have a wild time on the town, and Senor Dennis would know nothing about it.

She checked her appearance in a mirror, added a touch of color to her cheeks and lips, then hurried out, taking only a small beaded purse that had nothing in it.

Her first stop was El Razza saloon. She had not been back there since she lost the sixty dollars two days ago. They would be pleased to see her. She didn't know the man running the small roulette wheel. She bought twenty dollars' worth of chips from him and began to bet against the field.

By this time of night she knew the wheel would be rigged, so she bet against any large bet on the table. Soon she had doubled her money and was laughing. She wanted a tequila but knew that even one of the strong drinks would spoil her gambling sense. She had just won ten dollars on the wheel when someone came up behind her, stood close and whispered in her ear.

"Consuelo, it's time you had a conference with the manager of this fine establishment."

She knew who it was. He reached around her, put

his hand over one breast and gently turned her to face him.

"Move your hand, you bastard."

He slid his hand down to her waist. "No way to talk to a friend. I kept you out of jail—prison more likely. You know those twenty-dollar bills you've been spending in here? They are counterfeit. *Malo, muy malo.* Let's go into my office for a conference. Oh, bring your chips with you. We'll have a small accounting. You owe me sixty gringo dollars as it is. The U.S. Treasury agent refused to replace the bogus bills."

He led her to the back and through a door into a small room. It was part office, part bedroom, and he sat on the single bed against one wall and patted a spot beside him.

"Now, Consuelo. You have been a bad girl. You have robbed me of sixty dollars. That's more cash money than most of our people see in six months. What am I going to do with you?"

Consuelo lay down on the bed and lifted her skirt to her waist and spread her legs. "You can take it out in trade. At two dollars a poke, that's one every day for a whole month."

He grabbed her hair and pulled her up until she sat beside him again.

"I get all the poking I want. I want my sixty dollars back. What's in your purse?" He grabbed it and found only a comb and two hairpins. Consuelo moved so her hand covered the small pocket on her skirt. Montez noticed, pushed her hand away and dug into the pocket. He came out with four of the bogus twenty-dollar bills.

He compared the serial numbers.

"The same numbers. These are more of the counterfeit money." Rico Montez grinned. "Now we are making progress. You probably spent one of these tonight to get into the wheel, yes? So you owe me another twenty. That's eighty dollars. How can a whore like you ever repay me what you owe?"

Consuelo sat rigid, not believing what had happened. One moment she had been safe, secure, with good prospects and more money than she had ever seen. Now she was in dark trouble. It called for drastic action.

"I . . . I can go to the streets and work for you. All the money I make, you get. Just enough for me to eat a little and sleep here in your office. I can pay off eighty dollars. . . ." She stopped and opened her hands. "I have almost thirty dollars here. So I only owe you fifty. I can pay that back in two weeks."

Montez had a faraway look. He shook his head. "No, *puta.* I want more. Much more. I have heard of counterfeiting. You print the money and sell it to someone at half the value or less. Then you have good money to work with, to live off. This gringo you live with prints the money, yes?"

Consuelo nodded.

"So he must be selling it for real U.S. greenbacks. Does he use a bank?"

Consuelo shook her head.

"So this gringo printer has the real money stashed in his house somewhere, maybe a thousand dollars or more?"

"More. Much more. I can help you find where he has hidden it. We can steal it and run away to Ensenada where he will never find us."

Montez grinned. "Now you're talking sense, Consuelo. How come you're out of his house tonight?"

"He's drunk, passed out."

"Good, we will go out the back way and you and I will visit him and make him a proposition. He can tell us where he has hidden his treasure, or he can watch as I cut off his fingers one at a time. It is an effective argument."

He put the counterfeit bills in his pocket, stood and lifted Consuelo. Rico Montez hadn't been this pleased in a long time. He could sell his low-profit business here, take his thousands of dollars and go to Mexico and live like a prince for the rest of his life. When he tired of Consuelo there would be another willing girl for his bed. Yes, this could turn out to be the windfall of a lifetime.

They went out the back door of the El Razza saloon to the alley, down two blocks, over another two and then up another alley to the back of the old tinware store. The door to the half basement was locked from the inside. Consuelo knew it would be. She led Montez to the side entrance, and he nodded.

"Smart. Real smart to live in a wrecked store this way. And no neighbors to hear the press run." They went inside, and Montez checked the living quarters, saw the little man on the bed in a drunken stupor and smiled.

She led the way down the steps into the half basement. The room had no windows, so Montez carried a lamp to light their way. He lit two more lamps in the basement and stared at the sleek new printing press.

"I wouldn't even know how to get it started." He frowned. "But your man, Dennis you said his name was. He knows. Maybe we should keep him here awhile and print all the money he can. Those fake twenties look so good the people in Mexico would never question them. Yes, your man Dennis must print more money for us."

He looked around. "Now, where in hell would that little man with the half purple face hide the real money?"

"He didn't tell me. He never even let me come down

here. Where would he hide a lot of money? He showed it to me once and it was all in one-hundred-dollar bills. That's how it comes in the registered mail packets."

Montez's eyes lit up at the mention of so much money, and he began to probe around the old basement. For several years much of the basement had been abandoned and had been trashed by animals and riffraff. When Dennis had put in his press, he fixed up one side of the basement for his workroom, but half of it was still a clutter of boards, pieces of tin, old benches, one or two tin-bending devices and years of trash and garbage.

Montez concentrated on the cleaned-up section of the basement. He looked in boxes, under tables, in the floor joists overhead. He moved everything he could move that might contain a stash of money.

"Did you see the money in a box or bag of any kind?" he asked Consuelo.

"No. Only the packages as they came in the mail. Dennis likes to keep secrets."

At first Montez put back what he moved. As he became more upset with his search, he began to leave things jumbled.

He searched for an hour and then sat down in a chair and shook his head. "Where could that crazy man have hidden his treasure?"

Consuelo shook her head. She had been sitting on the table where the counterfeit bills had been weathered. The box filled with freshly crumpled and dirtied bills sat where it had been. She picked out a handful of the fake twenties and looked at them.

Montez came up behind her and grabbed them. "Leave them here. I also want you to give me any more of the counterfeits that you stole. We can't afford for any more of the bad bills to get in circulation. The man in town hunting Dennis is smart. We don't want him to find this place.

"Tomorrow when Dennis wakes up, we'll have a surprise for him. A big surprise. The first thing we want him to do is to complete his printing chores and print up all of the twenty-dollar bills. Then we'll find his treasure. Then with the good money and the counterfeit, we'll pack up and head for Ensenada or maybe even Mexico City and live it up. We'll have enough money to be safe down there forever."

"What about Dennis?" Consuelo asked.

"Might not be much left of him by the time we find out where he's hidden his stash of hundred-dollar bills. If there is, we'll just have to make sure that he can't send anyone after us. We might even have to put an end to that Treasury man's hunt, that man hunting you by your name. Yes, I think we should settle matters with Spur McCoy before he can upset any of our new plans. Tomorrow would be a good day to take care of him.

"Now let's get back upstairs and you watch your friend Dennis. I'll be back here at the side door tomorrow at six o'clock and we'll deal with Dennis. He'll do what I tell him to do when I tell him to do it, or he'll start losing fingers. As a printer, he needs those fingers. I think he'll cooperate. Let me out the side door, and I'll be here bright and early in the morning."

Spur spent the last half of the afternoon at the post office watching the clerks while they wrote up insured mail. Most of it was packages, a few letters. He assumed none of them bore the return address of the doctor up on Fifth Avenue, since none of the clerks signaled him.

He talked with the postmaster again.

"Not a lot more we can do, McCoy. We've cooperated in every way we can. If I think of anything else, I'll get in touch with you."

Spur nodded and left. There had to be some other way to work besides through the post office. Some way, somehow. He had to think of it.

He passed the office of the San Diego *Union*. The newspaper couldn't help him. The counterfeiter surely hadn't taken out an ad to announce his new business or given an interview to the editor about his upcoming endeavor.

What else? Find the girl. Somehow she had obtained some of the bogus bills and spent them. She probably didn't realize what repercussions that could have. If only she would spend more of them.

What now? He toured the banks again. None of the four had anything that would help him. No new bogus bills had shown up. He went back to the Anderson Cafe and talked to the owner.

Mrs. Anderson shook her head. "Not seen hide nor black hair of that girl. Maybe she gave up ice cream. Don't seem likely. If I see her I'll hog-tie her to a chair and send somebody after you. I ain't one to be subtle about things."

She looked at him with a slight frown. "McCoy, you got a woman?"

Spur chuckled. "Mrs. Anderson, I've had a woman from time to time."

She nodded. "Figures. Us widows got a right to ask a question like that. Hell, no pride. I miss my man." She shrugged. "You want supper?"

"Not yet. You find that girl for me and I'll eat up half your menu." He waved and walked out.

What now? He'd done everything he could for today. It was after four o'clock. He went back to the hotel and found Ginny combing her long blond hair.

"You look strange," Ginny said. "Tell me all about it."

He scowled at her. "How about you and me take off all our clothes and see what happens?"

She lifted her brows. "Really, Mr. McCoy. Is that anything proper to ask a lady?" She giggled. "Okay."

Out on the trickle of water known as Jamul Creek, the three Oliver brothers sat around a campfire and ate fried rabbit, biscuits and gravy. They finished with a can of sliced peaches. It was an hour to dusk.

"Rode up the slope this afternoon and looked over," Ira said. "That guy Grundy's home-place buildings aren't over five miles away. I could see the smoke."

"He might not know we're here yet," Oliver said. "Either way, I'll stand guard tonight. I can do a patrol sleep and have one eye open all night. Doubt if they'll challenge us today or bother us tonight. If they do, we'll be ready for them."

"Remington repeaters," Ira said. "I'll have four of them right beside my blankets. That's forty-eight rounds I can pound out without bothering to reload."

The youngest of them, Brody, thirteen, let his eyes go wide and his face worked with excitement. "I can shoot, too."

"I know you can shoot, little brother," Oliver said. "We just hope you don't have to. I'll be heading up there soon as it gets a little darker so nobody can see me coming. You two take your blankets and settle down fifty yards out from the wagon. Don't want you to be sitting ducks here by the fire."

Ira watched Oliver saddle his horse. "You be careful up there, big brother. Don't do nothing foolish."

"Hey, you know me. Cautious Oliver, I was known as. I'll be careful. We didn't come this far to be shot down like trespassers."

Oliver watched the darkness closing in, waved the other two off into a patch of brush along the creek with their blankets, and then mounted and rode quietly up the slope toward a small stand of scrub trees and mesquite on the ridgeline. He tied his horse just down the reverse slope, sat down against a tree trunk and watched to the east and south. The Grundy ranch lay in that direction.

For a moment he thought he saw a light far off. Then it was gone. Could have been a door opening, or the flare of a match a mile off. Strange how light penetrated the gloom of a clear night.

Oliver watched the cowboy clock in the sky as the pointer stars on the Big Dipper moved around the North Star. By three A.M. he figured there would be no visitors. He dozed and awoke and dozed again. By five-thirty, near daylight, he was back at the fire, stirring the warm coals and building a cooking fire.

His brothers soon straggled in for breakfast.

It wasn't until nearly midday, when the boys moved the herd into better grass downstream from their wagon, that Ira spotted a lone rider on a small ridgeline to the east. He told Oliver about it, and they kept up their short move of the brood cows and three range bulls.

The rider sat watching them for half an hour, then turned and rode fast to the east.

"We'll have company soon enough," Oliver said. "Best we get back to the wagon and make some arrangements."

They rode back the half mile, and Oliver made some preparations. Then he sent Brody and Ira into cover thirty yards up the slight rise behind the wagon.

"Find good firing positions and don't shoot until I give the word. Like as not, this will be a bluff and a warning. I'd guess he'll come with four riders backing him."

Oliver went around to the front of the wagon. A half hour after he figured they would, six riders came over the ridge to the east and walked their mounts down the slope.

When they were forty yards away, Oliver stepped inside the wagon and moved behind a four-foot-square sheet of steel in front of the opening. It had a firing port in it, and his rifle came out the opening.

"Far enough," Oliver bellowed. "Hold it right there. I can see you and talk to you. You're on my homesteaded land. You've got no right to be here. I'm asking you politely to turn around and ride east off my land."

One rider came forward five yards. Oliver put a rifle round into the dirt twenty yards in front of the rider. The round exploded two sticks of dynamite there in a shower of dirt and rocks. The rider on the big horse pulled his mount back and calmed her from the explosion. One of the horses farther back whirled and almost threw its rider and charged away from the explosion.

"No cause for gunplay," the rider out front called. "I'm Archer Grundy. I own this land. You're on range of the Bar G ranch. This land can't be homesteaded. You've moved into the wrong range."

"Not so. Land office in San Diego showed me exactly where your homesteads begin and end, mostly along the waterways. This was free range until today. You could use it. Now I own it, and you can't use it. I'm advising you to have all of your stock off this pair of one-hundred-and-sixty-acre homesteads before sunset tomorrow night."

"You lie. I own this land."

"Your homestead is all you own, old man. Now turn around and get your bully boys off my land."

"Or you'll do what?"

"There are four more rifles trained on you right now. Don't look, you won't see them. If I give the word, old man, you'll be the first to die, with at least three more of your riders falling dead off their mounts. The law is on my side. So turn and ride, or be prepared to die where you sit."

"We're not shooting. We obey the law," Grundy shouted.

"Then have the sheriff come out and throw me off this land. He'll tell you exactly what I told you. Now git."

Oliver was close enough to see the big, gray-headed man's face working in anger. He looked at his men, shifted in his saddle. His hand came close to the rifle in his scabbard. Then Grundy exploded, venting his anger with one word, and slowly turned his horse. The men behind him did the same.

At the top of the ridge, the tall old rider turned and looked down into the valley.

Oliver stayed behind his steel barricade until the men moved over the hill. Then he signaled to Ira, who ran around the lip of the ridge so he could watch if the men continued back toward the Grundy ranch.

Ira waved when he was in position, and a half hour later he came jogging down the slope. They called in Brody.

"They're gone," Ira said. "Watched them for a mile and a half. They aren't coming back today."

Oliver nodded. "Get the mules. We've got to saddle up and move the wagon into a spot where they can't find it without a lot of looking. We passed a little wooded ravine about a mile back. It's well off our land but will be good to hide the wagon. We'll make that our home base for now. You and Brody get it done and take the spare horses back there as well. We'll keep just our three best mounts here. We'll find positions where we can defend the herd, if it comes to that."

Oliver frowned and rubbed the back of his neck. "Meantime, I've got some planning to do."

What do you mean, Oliver?" Brody asked.

"Tonight I'm visiting the Bar G ranch and we're going to have a bonfire. Might be the barn, might be the ranch house. I'm giving notice that we'll fight to keep what's ours. If he wants to fight, we'll be glad to take them on."

"But he could have twenty men over there with rifles," Ira said.

"We'll see how many of them want to die for thirty dollars a month and found. Bet your bucket that his twenty will shrink to a quarter of that when he tries to launch an attack. Grundy's been running things here for so long he thinks he can get away with anything. I'm the one who's going to stop him."

Chapter Thirteen

Spur McCoy had spent two hours during the night worrying and wondering. The more he thought it through, the more it seemed that the post office should be a key to finding the counterfeiter. He was using it to make all of his contacts. Why couldn't he figure out the key?

Sometime before dawn he had the idea. He was up at six, left Ginny sleeping nakedly beautiful on the bed, shaved and dressed, had a quick breakfast at Mrs. Anderson's, then sat on the front steps of the post office until the workers showed up. The postmaster was the third one to report for duty.

Fogiletta stared at Spur for a moment, then nodded. "Looks like you got another wild-eyed idea. Come on into the office while I make a pot of coffee and we'll talk about it."

When the coffee was boiling on a small heating stove in the back room, Spur laid out his idea.

"Somehow the counterfeiter mails his goods from here to his customers. Fine. We almost had him but we missed. By the same token, he must *receive* his mail through this post office as well. How does he get it? You don't have free mail delivery here yet. It's supposed to be authorized in towns of ten thousand or more in eighteen and eighty-seven. Three years from now. So how do the locals get their mail?"

"Most of them by general delivery. You've seen the clerks outside with the letters over their windows. You go to window three if your last name starts with G, H, I or J. And so on."

"Does everyone get mail that way? All ten thousand souls?"

"Not every household gets mail every day. When we get our free delivery here, we're going to have to hire two or three dozen men to carry the mail out to the houses and businesses. Going to cost a lot."

"What about the businesses? Do they get their mail in some kind of locked boxes here in the building? I saw one town where they had boxes that the addressee unlocked to take out his mail. Little square boxes six inches or so."

"Seen them in some big towns. We haven't been authorized to use them yet. That certainly would be a help."

"How do you deliver a registered letter?" Spur asked.

"That's different. We put a notice in the general delivery mail. The clerk spots it for Spur McCoy. It's usually a colored card that says 'Registered Mail for,' and then there's a line where the name is written in.

"The clerk gives you that card and you go to the service window where they sell stamps and postal money orders, and next year there will be Special Delivery. There the clerk takes the card, goes to the registered mail lock box, opens it and takes out your package or letter."

"Then I have to sign for it, right, to prove I'm the one it says on the registered receipt?"

"Right."

"How do I prove who I am?"

"Many of the people in a town this size are known by sight to the clerks. Those need no other identification. A stranger would need a letter addressed to him at the same address shown on the registered mail. Maybe a bank book with his name in it. Any kind of a picture of himself on a card or poster, that sort of thing."

"Is that how our counterfeiter gets his registered packages back with the real greenbacks in them?"

"I would imagine. Only we don't know his name, so we can't check on him and tell you when he comes."

"You might be able to."

"How?"

"I'll help. We go back over the registered mail records to see who has received at least five registered mail packages with a certain higher-than-normal amount of postage on them in the past six months. Then we narrow down the field by eliminating those you know. The banks, lawyers, officials, probably some of the business firms in town. That way we should be able to come up with a dozen or so individuals who have received that many registered packages."

"What can you do then?"

"Then the work starts. I'll be a postal inspector checking on the delivery service, speed and quality of service of the registered material. That way I can get into the houses or stores of the suspected people and nose around a little. Best plan I've come up with yet. What do you think?"

The postmaster shrugged. "I can give you one clerk to help on the records search. It won't be easy."

"Much obliged."

The mail clerk named Toby showed Spur the registered mail forms and pads and copies they kept. Then they started working.

"We pick out the ones who paid a dollar or more in postage and fees," Toby said. "That should give us a good sample. Let's start with the ones that came in today and work backward."

By ten o'clock that morning they had found twelve names that had received registered packages. None of them were repeats. They had covered almost two weeks of time.

They kept working. By noon they had worked back another three weeks and had uncovered twenty-one more registered parcels that cost over a dollar in fees. Two of them were repeats of the names they had first found.

"You know either of these two names?" Spur asked Toby.

The young clerk nodded. "Yep. One of them is the district attorney, the other one is a store owner here in town. Been around as long as I can remember, and I've been in San Diego for ten years."

They had a quick lunch, with Spur buying at a nearby cafe, and went back to work on the registered mail forms.

They stayed at it until six o'clock and had worked back to nearly six months ago.

"No need to go any further," Spur said. "If he received anything before this it couldn't have been a payoff. Let's look at what we have."

They had been writing the name and address of any package that cost more than a dollar to ship on separate slips of paper. They had over sixty of them. They

139

laid them out in alphabetical order on a big table. Slowly a pattern developed. Six or eight business firms in town had frequent registered documents. Two were lawyers, one a builder. Toby assured Spur that all eight were legitimate, longtime firms.

They found five that had three registered packages and seven with five. That was the fruits of their labor.

Spur laid out the seven slips of paper with the five registered parcels and let Toby look at them.

"No, sir, I don't know any of them. Heard of a name or two, but I couldn't say how long they been in town. When you work the will-call mail windows you get to know a lot of folks."

Spur yawned. He was hungry and as tired as if he'd been on a twenty-mile ride. He thanked Toby for his help, gave him a ten-dollar bill for his overtime work and headed for the Horton House. He wanted a big supper, then a long sleep with no thoughts of a delightful young body lying beside him.

Earlier that morning, just after eight o'clock, while Bernard Dennis worked below in his printing shop, Rico Montez slipped in the side door of the old tin-smith store. Consuelo saw him and motioned for him to be quiet. They went to the door that led downstairs, and Montez took out a six-gun and checked the rounds.

"Don't worry, I won't shoot him. We need him to finish the printing. Then we find the real money, take it all and vanish across the border and head for Mexico City and a life of luxury."

He pointed to the door that led down the steps. "Does he lock it from below?"

She shook her head. There had been no need. He had told her never to come down there, and she hadn't, except when he was drunk.

Montez lifted the six-gun and pulled the door open slowly so it would make no noise. Then he ran down the steps and grinned when Dennis looked up from his press.

"Who the hell are you?" Dennis blurted.

"Me, Bernard Dennis, master counterfeiter? I'm your new partner." He brought the six-gun around and covered the small man and grinned. "This is such a fine business I decided to join you. How much more paper and ink do you have? How many more of the counterfeit twenty-dollar bills can you print?"

Dennis crossed his arms in front of him and scowled. "I'll share nothing with you, and print not another bill if you think you are going to be involved."

"Involved, my gringo friend? Involved? I am in charge. You will do exactly what I tell you, when I tell you, or you will find yourself dead and buried in a shallow grave down here in this deserted basement. Is that clear?"

Dennis made a try for a pistol he kept under a counter nearby, but Montez was younger and faster. He beat the printer to the shelf, slammed the six-gun down across Dennis's head and knocked him to the floor.

Dennis sat up, holding his head and trying to stop the blood that poured from a gash on the side of his head.

"Consuelo," Montez called. "Bring some bandages down here and some towels so we can mop up the blood that Senor Dennis is spilling. We have to keep him healthy and working."

Montez found the gun, took it and checked other places around the room, but discovered no other weapons.

Consuelo came and stopped the bleeding with compresses and taped-on bandages. Dennis looked at her with wonder, then surprise that turned into anger.

"You told this . . . this Mexican? How could you do that? I've been good to you. How could you do that?"

"For the money, Dennis. The money," Montez answered for her. "You're going to have to tell us where you hid the fifteen thousand dollars that you got back in the mail."

Dennis smiled through his fear and anger. "That real money you'll never find. You can hunt for months and never find it. All you have is counterfeit. You try to spend it and Treasury agents and police from all over will jump right astride your backs and ride you into a federal prison for twenty years."

"I don't think so, Dennis. I have a plan. First, how much paper do you have left to print the twenty-dollar bills on?"

Dennis sat on the floor where he had fallen. He slowly shook his head but said nothing.

Montez squatted near him and held a gleaming six-inch stiletto. "Dennis, for two years I was the enforcer for a famous man in Mexico. I have training in pain and can make you tell us where your mother's jewels are if I want to. For now, you will stand up, answer my question, or I will beat you until you can't stand. Then tomorrow when you can stand we'll go through the same ritual again. This lasts until you die or you do what you are told. Do I make myself perfectly clear, Senor Dennis?"

Dennis was no hero. He nodded, struggled to his feet and dusted off his clothes. Then he went over to two boxes and opened them. He riffled through the sheets of paper inside.

"My guess is that I have enough paper for another three thousand bills. That would be sixty thousand dollars' worth of currency. It's a lot more paper than I thought I brought."

Montez smiled. "Now, that wasn't so hard, was it? Life is precious to most people. It's surprising what most men will do to keep from dying. Now, what were you doing when I dropped by?"

"Working on the press. I'm doing the back side of the bills first. I work on two hundred at a time. After they are completely dry, I print the front of them. It's precise work, and I will insist that it be done correctly."

Montez put the six-gun away in a holster on his hip.

"That is good. A workman proud of the quality of his work. I like that. Also it will make the bills easier to pass in Mexico City. So, shouldn't you be getting back to work on the press, Senor Dennis? I'll watch."

Dennis looked up. "You can't watch me all the time. Sometime you must sleep."

"That's true, Senor Dennis. But you see, there are two of us, Consuelo and me. There is just one of you. Now, back to work. How long will it take you to print the rest of the bills?"

"This is not work that can be rushed. It must be done precisely."

"How long?"

"A month, a month and a half."

"You must work faster. You have three weeks. That's all the time there is left to print the rest of the bills. How many do you have on hand?"

"Only this batch, this two hundred that I'm working on. The rest have been shipped to customers."

"We're your new customer, Dennis. Get back to work." The last words came with a whip crack to them. The soft gloves were off, the blacksnake was out and it would be used. Dennis bent to his work.

Oliver Harding got the covered wagon hitched and the mules ready, then reconsidered his plans.

"Don't think I'll go over to the Bar G tonight. I'll help get the wagon and horses moved, and make sure we're inside where it would take a bloodhound to find us. Tomorrow night will be time enough to go calling. That way I'll be able to see what Grundy tries to do to us tomorrow."

Later Oliver was glad he had waited. The brush and trees proved to be thicker than he had judged, and it took some cutting and a tight squeeze between two trees to get the wagon deep enough into the copse to hide it completely. They got it placed just before dark and had a late cold supper but planned on a big breakfast.

Tomorrow they would work out a defense for the wagon and another for the brood cows. Before long the cows would start to wander and spread out. They had a half section of homesteaded land to graze. It wouldn't be enough, but there was unlimited land stretching up to the hills to the west and north. He would do as other cattlemen had done, homestead land and graze on the free range around it.

That is, he would if he could keep Archer Grundy and his band of pistoleros in check. He'd worry about that tomorrow.

The next morning, Spur McCoy came awake to find a beautiful naked woman lying half on top of him. Her breasts brushed his face and he captured one. Then he realized that he had an erection from her ministrations while he had been sleeping.

"What a glorious way to wake up," he said, rolling her over on her back and entering her at once. He pounded hard and fast and beat her climax by only a few seconds. He pushed away from her and sat up.

"Two more times," Ginny pleaded.

Spur shook his head. "I've got seven prospects to

talk to today. Prospects that could develop into one suspect. One of them could be the counterfeiter."

"You're a beast. You have no awareness of my needs, of what I want from a man. You poke me and run. A woman isn't made that way, Spur McCoy."

He bent and kissed her gently, then pulled away. "You know I know that, sweet maiden. I'll play with you and satisfy your every wish and fantasy, but at another time. Important business to get done today."

He pulled a sheet over her and tucked her in. "You have another nap, three or four hours, then have breakfast downstairs and go and buy yourself a new blouse. Something low-cut and sexy." He dropped a five-dollar bill on the sheet and went to shave and dress.

An hour later, Spur was talking to the first suspect on his list. The man had just opened a legal office over the bank, had few clients and was going broke. He got the registered packages with cash in them from his mother in New York City, who was worried about him.

"She even sent me a pair of socks when she thought I would be cold," the lawyer said.

Spur thanked the man and went to look for the next address on his list, 125 H Street, on the busiest thoroughfare in town, where most of the businesses were located.

But there was no 125 H Street. The store next to 121 H Street was 131. He looked at the name on the return: C. J. Herez. Strange. How could there be someone here when there was no building?

He went into the store and showed the address to the owner of the building. He was an older man with white hair and a slight tremor of his hand as he held the paper to read the address. He shook his head.

"Sorry, no such number. Nobody could have that

number. I use up from one twenty-one to one thirty-one. Arranged it that way with the city planners. No number one-twenty-five."

Spur thanked him and left. The other five names and addresses checked out as legitimate people with believable reasons to get registered mail. In response to his survey blind, all said they were well satisfied with the service.

He went to the post office, told Toby what he had found, then talked to the postmaster in his office.

"So it's a phony address. Probably a fake name as well. That means someone comes and asks for mail under the name of C. J. Herez."

"If there's no mail, that person leaves," Spur said. "He would only come in when he expected a package to be coming for him. Might come in five or six days in a row."

"Right. When there's a registered mail item, the card goes in the H basket, the clerk finds it and gives it to him, and he takes it to the service window, shows identification and signs for the registered item."

The postmaster frowned. "He's worked out a fool-proof way to obtain his money through the mail without getting caught."

"There's a flaw," Spur said. "Let's say this guy made up the name C. J. Herez. That's a Mexican name, right? We figure the counterfeiter is a white man. So that means he has someone else pick up the mail, further insulating him from getting caught. He could even be using Consuelo to get the mail. C. J. could be Consuelo Juanita, for all we know."

"So how do we catch her or him?"

"We red flag the name C. J. Herez. When anyone comes to the H window and asks for C. J. Herez's mail, it sets off our alarm, and you have one of your postal employees follow him or her back to wherever their home base is. A house, more than likely."

The postmaster nodded. "It certainly could work. The Herez person would have no reason to suspect that anyone was following, so wouldn't check behind."

Spur grinned. "It's worth a try. That last shipment went out three days ago. The return letter with the real money in it couldn't be due here for three or four more days, depending on where the counterfeit bills went."

"Chicago takes about three days," the postmaster said.

"So make up a red alert card and warn everyone who clerks on that H window. Designate someone to follow anyone claiming to be Herez. Let me have him for three or four hours and I'll train him how to follow a person without their knowing it. Can we do that right now?"

"Yes."

Chapter Fourteen

At a lunch meeting of the San Diego Merchants Association, the board of directors met at the Horton House banquet room to plot out the July Fourth celebration. They wanted to do something bigger this year that would get most of the people in San Diego to turn out. There were a lot of suggestions.

Dr. Philip Brown had been a member of the association since he first came to town. He was the only doctor or dentist in the group and maintained that he had as big a stake in the welfare and promotion of San Diego as any of the retail merchants.

Two years ago he'd been elected to the board of directors. Today he made an effort to agree with Keith Edison, the city councilman who had led the move to disband the San Diego Marching Band.

"I think Keith has a good point about extending the celebration to the smaller towns growing up around San Diego as well," Dr. Brown said. "We could make it a county-wide celebration."

Edison gave Dr. Brown a big grin and launched into more details of his plan.

Dr. Brown settled back in his chair and worked on his salmon steak. He had firmly established that he had no problems in getting along with Edison, the hardware and plumbing store owner. Avoid suspicion was his first rule.

That afternoon he went into his laboratory and closed the door. No one, not even his wife, came through his laboratory door when it was closed. He took down a special box of chocolates and removed two of the largest. He selected the drug from his shelves with care. It had to be something that would work quickly and irreversibly.

He rejected two drugs as developing too many symptoms that could be recognized. Then he found what he wanted, a little-known poison from South America he had been evaluating. He had found that when it was combined with certain other ingredients it had a stabilizing effect on the pains of rheumatism.

Dr. Brown nodded and smiled as he took a new kind of syringe and drew a half cubic centimeter of fluid from the vial and carefully injected half of it into each of the two chocolates. He pierced the outer shell from the bottom in a spot where a small imperfection had been created by the surface on which the dipped chocolate had been left to cool. No one would notice the deeper impression of the needle.

He put the rest of the box of chocolates high on a shelf. They were common enough that anyone in town might have some. Anyway, the evidence would be gone, all eaten up. He had spent several hours discovering the hardware man's likes and dislikes. Edison had a weakness for children, with seven of his own, and he went absolutely crazy for dipped chocolates.

Dr. Brown wrapped each of the doctored chocolates in white tissue paper and put them in a small box. Then he wrote a note, making it look like a child's printing.

"Mr. Edisen," he began, deliberately misspelling the name. "Thanks for fixing my wagon. Works fine. Ma couldn't do it. I give you present."

He didn't sign a name. At the bottom of the sheet of common tablet paper he put on a smudged pencil mark, erased it and wrote another word, and then erased most of that. He nodded. Just about right.

Next he wrapped the small box in red and white paper and tied it with a string, doing a childish job of it. The note on a second piece of tablet paper said in pencil: "For Mr. Edisen."

He put the box in a paper sack, put on his suit coat and went out the back door. He walked to the hardware store half a block down and, holding the sack at his side, went in and asked a clerk for half a pound of sixpenny box nails.

While the clerk got them, and when no one else could see him, Dr. Brown took the wrapped box out of the sack and edged it half hidden onto the counter. He moved to another part of the store, and when the clerk called, he went back, paid for the nails and left.

The trap was set. He was sure that when Keith Edison saw the chocolates he would think some small boy had brought them in thanks for repairing a wagon. He often did that for children. He wouldn't share the chocolates. He'd eat both of them at once and pat himself on the back for being a kindhearted helper of children.

After that it wouldn't take long.

Dr. Brown smiled as he entered his clinic by the back door, took off his suit coat, put on his white smock and checked with his wife. Two patients were waiting. Good. There was nothing he enjoyed more than making his patients well and reducing their suffering.

Spur McCoy was as nervous as a long-tailed cat in a room full of busy rocking chairs. He had breakfast, then spent an hour watching the clerks at the General Delivery windows hand out mail. He paid special attention to the clerk at window three for people with last names starting with G, H, I and J.

Spur had looked over the trays of mail set behind the clerks. In the H, tray he found the red-flagged piece of cardboard bearing the name C. J. Herez and instructions what to do. First the clerk was supposed to stall the patron with some excuse about not all the mail being put up yet. Then the clerk should notify his supervisor and the postmaster at once.

The postmaster would have the designated clerk identify the person at the window and then follow that person when he or she left the post office.

Spur sighed. Damn. Nothing to do but wait. Maybe he should have taken out a homestead out on the Grundy range. At least he'd have something to do.

He went back to the hotel and cleaned and oiled his Colt, then did the same for the spare Colt in his luggage. No call came from the post office. No one might check on that name for four or five days, maybe a week.

Should he ride out and see how the homesteaders were getting along? He though about it, then shook his head. The oldest one looked like he could take care of himself.

He went out and walked up and down the street, watching for a pretty Mexican girl with long hair and bangs. Most of the slender senoritas had long black hair, but none of them had bangs cut straight across their foreheads.

Oliver Harding herded some stray brood cows back toward their small valley and watched to the east. He saw no riders, heard no shots. All was quiet. Perhaps too quiet. He went back to the wagon in the brush and trees about four o'clock and began making preparations for his ride that night.

He took six sticks of dynamite, each with a detonator pressed into the stick and with a foot-long fuse on it. He wrapped these in a cloth and put the bundle in his saddlebag. He filled a gallon can with kerosene, capped it and set it aside. Then he cleaned his favorite Spencer rifle, checked the action, made sure there were no problems with the rounds feeding through the tube that went through the stock. He loaded two extra tubes, wrapped them and put them in the saddle boot next to the Spencer. He made sure that the extra tubes were tied in so they couldn't bounce out of the boot.

They spent an hour picking out the site for the cabin. One of the requirements of the Homestead Act was to build a dwelling on the land and make other "improvements." On cattle land these improvements didn't include planting, clearing or other farm-related activities.

The three brothers picked a spot near the creek on a little flat area at the side of the rise where the land rose up into a range of hills. They laid out points for the foundations. The next day they would build a framework and put up their ten-foot-square tent as temporary quarters.

Back at the wagon that afternoon, Ira stared at his older brother at the small cooking fire.

"You still going over to that ranch? You could get

in trouble over there, maybe even shot dead."

"Don't aim to let that happen. They'll be so confused they won't know what hit them, and I'll be careful not to kill anybody. Now quit worrying. We been through worse than this and survived."

A few minutes later it was dusk, and it would be long dark before Oliver rode anywhere near the Bar G ranch. He took the can of kerosene, mounted and rode.

A little over an hour later, Oliver could see the ranch buildings ahead of him. Lights showed in the bunkhouse, in what he figured was a harness shed, and in the main ranch house.

He studied the buildings from horseback for ten minutes while he made his plans. Then he tied his horse to some brush near a small creek and carried the gas can and the package of dynamite bombs toward the buildings.

When he got within fifty yards of the corral, he bent low and ran to where he had planned to be, thirty feet to the left of the corral. There he readied his tools.

He turned away from the buildings and, shielding with his body, lit one of the foot-long fuses and threw the dynamite stick toward the barn. He lit another stick and threw it toward the well, then he lit a third and dropped it where he was. He grabbed the last ones and raced past the well across the ranch yard, past the bunkhouse and behind the ranch house.

There he paused, panting from the run. He eyed the house itself, which had been built on pier blocks slightly off the ground. He opened the can of kerosene and sloshed it along the baseboards of the frame house. He had wet twenty feet of the back of the house when the first dynamite bomb went off near the barn. It brought some screams and yelling. Lights came on in two more of the ranch-house rooms. He heard a door slam.

Somebody in front of the house began yelling orders.

"Who the hell did this? Get your guns, men, we're being attacked. Don't just stand there, get your guns and—"

The rest of his sentence was smothered by a second explosion, and before that died down, a third.

The confusion seemed to increase. Two men began screaming orders.

Oliver dumped the rest of the coal oil along the ship-lap, struck matches and ignited the fluid in two places, then slid backward away from the fire.

The kerosene burst into flames. The flames ate greedily at the dry wood of the ranch house, which hadn't been painted for ten years.

Oliver ran into the night, circled around and came in behind the barn. It was then that he heard someone yell, "Fire!"

He saw men stream from around the corral and barn and race toward the house. A bucket brigade started from the well, but the water was thirty yards from the fire. Now Oliver could see the glow from behind the house. The flames had a good start.

He lit the two remaining dynamite bombs and threw them into the yard.

A voice bellowed in anger, and two shots thundered into the night. Evidently someone had seen the flare of his match. Both shots were short or wide. Oliver turned in the blackness of the night and jogged back toward where he had left his horse due west of the buildings.

Five minutes later he mounted his mare and turned her so he could look at the ranch buildings. The night had taken on a brilliant glow where the Bar G ranch house stood. By that time it was engulfed in flames. There was no way they could put it out.

He heard two riders coming toward him. Before they reached the brush of the creek, they turned and continued in a wide arc around the ranch buildings, evidently looking for the attackers.

When they had vanished into the night, Oliver turned to the west and began his ride home. He let the mare go at her own pace. Neither of them was in any hurry now. It gave Oliver more time to wonder what Grundy would do come morning. He was sure that the rancher would come at them with guns.

What would Grundy's target be? Oliver worried about it for a time, and decided it would be the easiest target to find, the brood cows. Without them their ranch would be worthless.

With first light he and his brothers would round up their ladies and bring them into the graze where the three of them could set up a defense with their rifles. It might not be enough, but Oliver had taken all the pushing around he would take. From what the land office said, Grundy was long overdue to have someone take a stand against him. Oliver knew that he himself was the man to challenge the big rancher.

Just before noon, Ira signaled from his vantage point on the west ridge that riders were coming.

"How many?" Oliver called.

"Ten, maybe twelve."

Oliver settled down behind his firing position on the east ridgeline. He had dug a pit two feet deep behind a large rock. He could stand in the hole and fire over the top of the rock with good protection. He was 100 yards from the herd and 200 yards from Ira. Brody was 200 yards back up the valley and out of the danger zone.

Oliver wondered if the small army would come

looking first for the herd or for the wagon. He bet on the herd. He levered a round into the Spencer and waited.

Fifteen minutes later, he could hear the pounding of the ten to twelve horses as they came up the far ridge. Ira should be back about fifty yards in brush and stunted trees, so the riders would skirt around his position.

When the twelve riders came over the ridgeline, they paused a moment, saw the cows and headed for them. Half the men had their six-guns out and fired into the air. Oliver sent two quick rifle rounds crashing over their heads. The men could tell the difference in sound between their rounds and the rifle slugs slamming through the air.

Half the riders pulled up. Three of them ducked and rode ahead faster. Two riders slowed but kept moving ahead.

The defenders had worked out their strategy earlier. If the riders tried to run off or harm the brood cows, the brothers' rifles would be aimed at the men's mounts, not at the cowboys.

Now Oliver zeroed in on the lead rider's horse. A big man rode the gray, and Oliver figured he was Archer Grundy. Oliver led the animal a fraction of an inch and fired. While he levered in a new round he saw the big gray stumble and fall, pitching the rider into the dust. Grundy hit the ground hard, rolled, then screamed in agony.

Rifle rounds came from the other two positions. The second horse went down suddenly like it had a round to the head. The third rider in the advance group turned his mount and rode for the ridge. The other riders took the cue and rushed back over the ridgeline as well. The defenders stopped shooting.

The two cowboys in the dirt sat up and stared

around. The rider from the gray shouted at the others.

Oliver lifted up over his firing position and bellowed at Grundy.

"Enough, Grundy. You get your men and horses off my property and don't come back. Next time we'll aim at your cowboys and at you and not just your horses. Now get moving."

"Broken leg," Grundy bellowed back.

Oliver grinned at the news. Now Grundy wouldn't be riding for a while. Oliver was pleased by how well his voice traveled in the clear mountain air.

The second downed cowboy ran up to his boss, talked a minute, then jogged up the slope the riders had vanished over. He stood on the top and waved. Soon two horsemen topped the ridgeline and talked with the cowboy. A few minutes later, the three men rode down to where Grundy lay with his broken leg. One of the men made a crude splint for the leg, and the three men lifted Grundy onboard the biggest horse. He sat there unsteadily for moment, then turned toward Oliver's position.

"I'll be back, you damn squatters. This is my land and always will be. We'll all be back."

"I'm filing a complaint against you with the sheriff, Grundy. I'm charging you with harassment, with assault, with threats of great bodily harm, and anything else my lawyer can come up with. I'll see you in court, you old bastard."

Grundy shook his fist at Oliver's position, then one man walked and two rode the second horse as the trio walked slowly up the rise away from the brood cows and over the ridge.

Minutes later, Ira came out of his brushy hiding spot and walked down to the wetness of the small creek.

"Gone," Ira said. Oliver came down and so did Brody.

"Yeah, gone for now, but how long will it be before they come back? We surprised them today. The next time it won't be so easy."

"That true about you going to charge him?" Ira asked.

"Absolutely. I'm riding into town this afternoon and talk to the district attorney while Grundy is getting a bumpy ride into town to go to the doctor to get his leg set. He won't try anything else for a week at least. By then we can have better firing positions, and maybe put the brood cows up higher in the hills where they won't be so easy to find.

"We won't start moving them up that way for a while. Not enough water up there for more than a day or two. We'll work it out. Let's get back to the wagon so I can put on a clean shirt before I go to town."

Chapter Fifteen

Lester Grundy stood beside the cold ashes of the ranch house on the Bar G ranch and kicked them. A blackened piece of a board broke loose and fell into the white ashes, vanishing into the powdery remains of his home.

Gone. A lot of bad memories were gone that he had lived with for years in that house. Some good ones too, but mostly bad.

He was glad it had burned down. He had lost a lot of things that couldn't be replaced, books and souvenirs and some music scores. But he had saved all of his violin music and the scores his mother used to play. He'd rescued his violin, as well. He had wrapped it in two pair of pants and a shirt and run through the edge of the blaze into the yard. Then he had gone back to his room by another route and brought out his violin music.

He had claimed a corner of the barn as his own,

hung up his two pair of pants and shirt and found a milking stool to use as a chair and a cardboard box to put his violin in. The case had been burned.

Lester walked over to meet a dozen riders who came into the ranch yard. Two of the horses had double riders. Something had gone wrong. Then he saw his father leaning on the neck of a horse he usually didn't ride.

Lester ran to help the men lift his father off the horse and set him on the ground.

"The horse and buggy, damn it," Grundy bellowed. "Get out the buggy and harness. I got to get to town so Doc Brown can set this busted-up leg. Don't just stand there, idiots. Go bring the damned buggy."

Archer Grundy looked at his son, who sat in the dirt of the yard a few feet away, facing the older man.

"Something go wrong, Pa?" Lester asked. "You was aiming to cut them upstart squatters down to size this morning. You figure they burned down the house?"

"Know damn well they did. Sneaky trick. We would have had their brood cows, only the bastards got lucky and shot my horse. Then the fall broke my leg, and I decided to come home. Get the bastards later. Fucking bastards. I hate them cheating, swindling, house-burning bastards."

Lester grinned. "Pa, you sound a mite bit upset. Not used to having things go against you, are you? First the house getting torched, now this homesteader who's willing to put up a fight. I admire them, whoever they are."

"Admire them? I should horsewhip you. How dare you say a thing like that? What's the matter with you?"

"Not a thing, Pa. I finally learned that everything you do is not etched in stone or comes down from heaven. I've seen you kill a man and a woman for no good reason. And now I'm free of you. I'll be moving in to town as soon as I can find a place to stay."

"Oh, yeah? How you going to support yourself? You won't get free room and board and expenses. I'll cut you off without a dollar."

"That's what I expected. I'll get by. I can find a job. I won't need much. There's certainly no place to stay here at the ranch, except the bunkhouse."

"It's good enough for me," the older man said.

"I just want to move to town."

"We'll talk about it later. I'm going to see Dr. Brown. You best be here when I get back."

The buggy drove up and stopped a few feet from the ranch owner. Two of the biggest men in the crew came and lifted him into the buggy. He screamed in pain when his broken leg hit the side of the buggy. Then he swore as the rig moved toward the lane leading to town.

"Easy, stupid!" Grundy bellowed at the hand driving the buggy. "You want my leg to break in half and fall off?"

Soon the rig was far enough away that Lester couldn't hear him anymore. He thought about what his father had said. Maybe the old man would relent and give his only son some money before he went to town. He just might.

It would be helpful to have a few hundred dollars to live on while he practiced. Too, that would give him more time to work on his music. Yes, he'd wait. One more day wouldn't make that much difference.

Lester went to the barn, took his violin out of its cardboard box and went out by the creek in the shade of a sycamore tree and began to play. He was still at it when the cook rang the triangle announcing the evening meal.

* * *

Keith Edison opened his hardware and plumbing store as usual, swept the floor, put some items he was pushing outside on the boardwalk, came back in and put the change in the cash drawer he had built into a small counter near the back of the store.

He didn't feel well this morning. Gas, he decided. As he cleaned up the counter he noticed a small red paper-wrapped box half hidden behind a display of gopher traps on the counter. He pulled out the box and saw his name in a childish scrawl on top.

Edison grinned. Some small child had left him a present. He spent a lot of time fixing bicycles and wagons and other small things when the boys' own fathers didn't or couldn't. This must be another of the little gifts to say thank you.

He smiled at the poorly tied string around the box. This one had to be from a boy. He pulled the string away, took off the lid and saw the small items wrapped in tissue paper. He opened one and found the chocolate inside. He picked it up and eyed it.

Then he popped the whole thing in his mouth, closed his eyes in delight and chewed the delicacy. There was a small aftertaste that seemed strange, but just the idea of having a chocolate of this quality touched him. Eagerly he looked in the box and unwrapped a second chocolate. This one he bit in half and ate. No bad taste.

Edison grinned, glad that his clerk Harry hadn't come to work yet. He would probably have shared the chocolates with him if he'd been there. He ate the second half of the chocolate and noticed the bitter taste again.

Then things went strange. He saw Harry come in the front door and say hello, but then the room turned around and he clutched at the counter to catch himself, but he fell. He knew he was falling but didn't notice when he hit the floor.

The worried face of Harry hovered over him.

"Mr. Edison! Mr. Edison, are you all right? You just collapsed. What's the matter?"

Edison heard the words, but they made no sense. Pure gibberish. The ravings of a fool. He had to get up and get the store open. Couldn't lay there all day.

Then the pain hit him in the head and he cried out, a roar of fury and agony and wonder all wrapped up in one burst of sound.

The face wavered over him again, then the pain vanished. He thought the lights had been blown out, but it was daytime. His mind functioned slowly for a moment, then the blackness closed in on even that and he had only one last fearful thought. He was dying. He knew he was dying. A gentle peace settled over him, and he tried to smile. Then his lungs refused to work, a last ragged whoosh of air came out of them, and Keith Edison ceased to exist.

Harry wanted to scream. He couldn't believe it. He pinched Mr. Edison's nose but his mouth didn't open to suck in vital air. Keith Edison was dead.

Harry rushed to the front of the store, snapped the inside lock on, closed the door and ran to Dr. Thatcher's office. The man had been Mr. Edison's doctor for years. If there was anything to do for Mr. Edison, Dr. Thatcher could do it.

Oliver Harding stopped at the first lawyer's office he saw in San Diego. The sign read "Milton J. Oxe, Counselor at Law."

Harding went inside and found himself looking at the prettiest girl he had seen in months.

"Yes, sir, may I help you?"

She was dark-headed, with bright dark eyes, a pure

white blouse to her neck and wrists, and sat behind a desk protecting two doors.

"Uh, yes, I'd like to talk to Mr. Oxe."

"Did you have an appointment?"

"Nope, just got into town."

"Let me see if Mr. Oxe can see you. Won't you please sit down?"

He sat on a chair as he watched the sleek young woman rise, go to the door, knock twice, then slip inside. Just as she closed the door she glanced at him.

A moment later she came out followed by a medium-sized man with a short full beard, mustache and spectacles perched on his nose. The man came forward with his hand out.

"Good afternoon, I'm Oxe, how can I help you?"

"I want to sue a man. You do that?"

"Certainly, come into my office."

A half hour later the two men shook hands.

"Mr. Harding, I'll draw up the papers tomorrow and file them with the court. We'll be suing Archer Grundy for twenty thousand dollars for damages to your cattle, and to you and your two brothers in his reckless and unprovoked attack on your herd of brood cows yesterday. We'll ask for the cash payment to cover your grievous pain and suffering after he and ten of his men charged your cattle, firing weapons with the intent to do great bodily harm on your livestock and on the three defenders.

"Should be an interesting case. We might not win it all, but it certainly will get Mr. Grundy's attention. I've been wanting to get something aimed at him for two years."

At the door they shook hands again, and Oxe waved a paper he carried. "This agreement states that you will be charged nothing unless we receive a judgment from the defendant. In that case you will pay me twenty percent of the judgment."

They grinned at each other, and Oliver Harding left the office, had a beer at the closest saloon and then rode for his new ranch, hoping to get back before dark.

Spur McCoy checked the post office just before it closed at five o'clock. They had nothing to report at the call window on C. J. Herez.

"We've got to get lucky sometime," Spur said. "He sent out that last shipment, what, three or four days ago. We might get a quick response anytime now. At least he should be checking at the window tomorrow or the next day. Damn, I hate this waiting."

He went back to the hotel and found Ginny ready to go out for supper.

"Let's go to that little Chinese restaurant down on Fourth Street," Ginny said. "I've only had Chinese food once, but I really liked it."

They ate Chinese. After supper, they walked the business district until it began to get dark, then went to the hotel and Spur took a bath. They had a room with a bathtub and hot and cold running water.

Ginny confessed that she loved the tub.

"I've had a hot bath almost every day that we've been here," she said. "I think the maid believes that I'm selling the towels, I use so many."

That same evening, Bernard Dennis looked up from where he sat beside the paper cutter in his downstairs printing shop and shook his head.

"No use. I can't do any more tonight. My hand is so tired I can't keep it steady. If these bills aren't cut precisely, the rankest beginner could spot them. If you want to be able to spend any of this batch, you better let me rest. I'll get back on it first thing in the morning."

Rico Montez burped from the beer he had just finished and looked over at Consuelo. She nodded.

"True," she said in Spanish. "Often he works just half a day because the work is so taxing, so draining. He's right about the size of the bills, and the printing. It all must be done with precision."

"What the hell does a whore like you know about precision, pretty little Consuelo?"

"A lot. I've learned from Dennis. I watch and learn quickly. I can learn a lot."

Montez belched and nodded at Dennis. "Okay, old man, quit for tonight. Then I'm gonna put the chain round your leg just like last night. Don't beef about it or I'll put one on both your legs. You ain't going anywhere. Not until you get those bills all printed."

Montez yawned, then grinned at Consuelo. She shook her head.

"Not again tonight, Rico. I'm still sore from this afternoon. You get too rough."

"Way you like it, *puta*. Way you like it." He let his chin drop down to his chest. He had wrestled a big, soft chair down the steps and now spent most of the day in it, watching Dennis work. He took a long breath and his eyes closed again. This time he slept soundly.

Consuelo went over to Dennis and showed him where to sit down. He slept on a mattress on the floor at the end of the room. The chains and locks were there, and she slipped the steel band around his right ankle and snapped it in place, then closed the padlock holding the steel band to one end of the chain. The other end had been padlocked to a vertical post holding up the second floor.

"Consuelo," Dennis said softly. "I need to talk to you a minute."

They were thirty feet from the snoring Montez.

"I told you, now I have a new man. Montez will take care of me."

"Consuelo, how would you like to earn five thousand dollars? No strings attached. A simple task and then you would be free to take your money and fly across the border and live like a queen for ten years."

"I don't understand. Five thousand dollars?"

"Yes, real U.S. banknotes. Then take what I've printed up so far, another three thousand in counterfeit."

"How could I do that?" She took a quick look at Montez. He snored on. They were too far away for him to hear them talking.

"Quite easy. First you unlock my ankle. Then you hold the pistol as I take an iron bar and hit Motez on the head to knock him out.

"Next I tie him hand and foot. After that I give you the five thousand in good U.S. currency and let you out the side door. I will take what money I have left, the plates, the counterfeit bills if you don't want them, and my paper and ink and catch the next train north. We will leave Mr. Montez here to regret his grievous sins and wickedness."

Consuelo frowned, then looked at him closely. She wasn't sure she understood his English. "You mean it? You give me five thousand U.S. dollars just to let you get free?"

"Indeed I will. Montez will kill me when the printing is done. I know he will. He has the gun. Then he may kill you as well. What more will he need you for? He will have the money and the plates. He can find a woman to poke anywhere here or in Mexico."

Consuelo looked at Montez and scowled. "I never trusted that man. He is a snake and I don't like him. When do we do this?"

"I have several more days of printing to do. I want to print up as much as I can. Then too, the payment of three thousand good U.S. dollars should be coming in to the post office tomorrow or the next day. We'll get that and split it in half as well. You could have six thousand, five hundred dollars all your very own."

Consuelo thought about it. She was quick, a fast learner. One thing she had learned about men was that they took what they wanted and left the women behind. Montez would do the same thing no matter what he said. He would claim all the money, she would be left with nothing.

Slowly she nodded. "Yes, Dennis. I think you right. Montez will leave me when he not need me to cook or to poke. Then he will kill you and take all the money.

"Yes, I'll help you to get away when you say the time is ready. Until then I not treat you kind, so Montez not get suspicious. It will be our secret."

Consuelo left him then and went to Montez. She unbuttoned the fly of his pants and slowly began to arouse him. He groaned in his sleep, tried to move her hand, then relaxed and began to grind his hips. She unbuttoned her blouse and let one breast fall out and rubbed it across his mouth. It opened and he licked her, then gulped in a mouthful.

Montez awoke with a start. He spit out her breast and brayed in delight.

"You little whore, you *puta* with an itch. Why didn't you say you wanted to get fucked again good before we go to bed? I'll take you right here so old man Dennis down there can watch. Right here on the boards, and I want you to make some noise to show me how much you enjoy it."

Consuelo pulled up her skirt, kicked out of her bloomers, lay down on her back on the floor and made more noise during a poking than she could remember ever doing before. Dennis watched her and yelled at them to stop. Montez laughed and took her again, moving closer this time.

Bernard Dennis watched them mating like a pair of animals and worked up a secret smile. In three or four days, Montez would be the one screaming for mercy and to be unchained. Dennis realized how totally exhausted he was. He had put in a ten-hour work day. He would follow through on his promises to Consuelo. She would have half the money he had earned on this venture. That was better than being dead at Montez's hands. He had no doubt that Consuelo would do as he asked her to do. She knew what kind of a liar and cheat Montez was.

Yes, it would work. Now all he had to do was finish the printing and weathering of the bills, then decide just where he would set up shop again.

The next morning Montez woke up early and had Dennis fed and at work by seven-thirty. He brought up the chains and leg iron and locked Dennis to the base leg of his press.

"I got to go to town to take care of a small item," Montez announced. "This one can't wait. We can't afford to let some nosy federal lawman mess up our plans.

"This morning I'm going to go out there, find Spur McCoy and kill that bastard just dead as all hell."

Chapter Sixteen

Spur McCoy admitted that he wasn't good at wasting time. He would rather have too much to do and not enough time to get it all done. Now he was forced to sit and wait. The post office was the key. The counterfeiter would not sit by and not even try to collect the package with one, two or three thousand dollars in it in hard cold cash.

This was the payoff for all of his work. He'd be there. It was simply a matter of time.

Somebody told Spur it was good fishing now in the bay. There was a run of bonito and barracuda that would strike at anything. He wandered down there and found a boat owner who would take him out to the best fishing area of the fifteen-mile-long San Diego Bay. He was a small Mexican man who spoke little English but said he knew the fishing grounds.

"Long time fish," he said. "Have bait. Good bait. You come."

Spur paid him two dollars to use his poles and line. He had a simple reel on one pole to wind the line in. The bait was live anchovies kept in a pair of buckets let over the stern of the eight-foot rowboat. The buckets had small holes to let fresh sea water in and out to keep the fish oxygenated and alive.

The Mexican fisherman rowed the small boat out from the foot of D Street across from the railroad station and went north to some pads of seaweed.

"Kelp," the guide said. "Usual not grow here. Now grow. Fish like."

Spur hooked one of the anchovies the way the guide showed him under the small bone along the bottom of the gill. That way there was almost no damage to the fish and it would swim like crazy. Both bonito and barracuda loved to eat live anchovies. Dead ones they passed up.

The anchovy hit the salt water of the bay and shot off away from the boat, swimming strongly and towing the line into the deeper water. A moment later Spur felt a jolt on his line. The bamboo rod bent and the line whined off the small reel. A moment later the reel stopped spinning, because it had come to the end of the line.

"Pull up on pole," the guide suggested. "Pull up and reel in line as you let pole down slowly."

It worked. Spur could feel the fish tugging on the line, swimming one way and then the other, trying to get free. Then he pulled upward on the pole, bringing the fish closer to the boat. He guessed there was about twenty yards of line on the small reel. He had no idea how big the fish might be or how strong the line was.

He simply kept pulling up on the pole and winding in on the reel as he lowered the tip of the pole toward the water.

"Yes, there!" the guide shouted. Spur looked and

saw a fish break the water and dive back deeper. It was a flash of silver and white, and the guide grinned.

"Bonito, grande bonito," the guide announced.

A half dozen more lifts with the pole and stronger reeling-in by Spur and the exhausted fish came alongside the boat. Spur reached down, caught the line a foot from the silver and blue beauty and lifted the fish out of the water.

It was a four-pound bonito. Spur looked at the guide. "You eat?" he asked. "*Alimento, comida?*"

The guide nodded, lifted the fish off the hook and promptly pulled out a long slender knife. He filleted the fish while it still flopped around.

"*Bueno comida,*" he said. It would be a good dinner for the guide and his family.

Spur baited another anchovy on his hook and threw it out. He let the three-inch fish run a moment, stopped it with a tug and then let it run again, pulling line off the reel.

After two minutes without a strike, the guide motioned for him to bring in the bait. It was dead. Spur put on a new one, and it had barely hit the water and begun swimming when a silver streak slashed partly out of the water, gulped down the anchovy and dived.

This time the end of the line came quicker and Spur had a tougher fight. He battled for ten minutes before he landed the fish. Twice he had it up where he could see it, a long narrow fish with rows of needle-sharp teeth.

"Barracuda," the guide said on the second sighting. When Spur at last pulled the fish to the surface next to the boat the third time, the guide caught it in a hand net and lifted it on board. It was an eight-pound barracuda over three feet long.

"*Mucho comida,*" Spur said. The guide grinned and cut the fish's head off and threw the sharp teeth into the bay. A brown pelican swooped down and grabbed it before the seagulls had a chance for it. The guide filleted the barracuda and produced two long, thick slabs of boneless meat. He put the fillets with the others in a bucket of cold bay water to help keep it fresh until it hit his frying pan.

Spur caught six more fish that afternoon. The guide kept two more for his neighbors, then they released the rest. By the time the guide rowed back toward the dock, it was late afternoon. Spur felt relaxed. He had enjoyed the time away from the case.

The boat was twenty feet from the dock when a man stood up and fired three times at the boat with a six-gun. One round grazed the guide's arm. A second one dug through Spur's left upper arm. He drew his own revolver and fired twice. The bouncing boat made him miss, and the man on the dock ran down the fifty feet of dock to the shore.

The guide pulled the boat into the wooden dock, and Spur jumped the last three feet and pounded down the wooden planks after the bushwhacker. His left arm hurt, but he figured the round had gone through the fleshy part. No big damage. Just sore as hell for a week.

The man Spur chased wore a blue shirt and dark pants. There were few building this close to the water. At the end of the pier, Spur saw the man running between two small buildings where fish were displayed to be sold.

Spur surged between the buildings with his Colt fisted and ready for action. The man hid at the corner of a building twenty feet away and snapped off a shot as Spur blasted around the structure. The round missed. Spur returned the fire with one round, thought he hit the man in the leg, but he vanished around the corner.

Spur ran to the corner of the frame store and stopped and squatted, searching the area. There were lobster pots, nets, an old fishing boat, a rack of oars and dozens of wooden boxes to hold just-caught fish. He scanned each area where a man could hide, then went back over them again.

Something moved. The third wooden fish box on the left. Spur watched it. It moved again, and this time a hand came out beside it holding a .44. Spur angled his weapon toward the spot, and the moment a face appeared around the side of the box, Spur fired twice. Once would have been enough. The first round caught the man flush in the forehead, drove into his brain and slanted upward, blowing off a four-inch chunk of skull and splattering gray matter, bone and blood over the side of the building behind him.

Spur went to the spot and stared at the man. He was Mexican, maybe twenty years old, thin, and his clothes were ragged. A hired gun.

Two curious men came from the fish market, and Spur sent one of them to get the sheriff.

It was almost an hour later when Spur finished his report to the sheriff. The fishing guide gave a statement as well about the unprovoked attack from the dock and the subsequent chase.

"You do liven up a town, McCoy," Sheriff Raferty said. "I can say that for you. Any idea who he was and why he wanted to kill you?"

"No idea who he was. My only idea about motive must be that the counterfeiter knows I'm in town and decided to eliminate me. That would solve his problem long enough to finish his work here and move on to a new location."

"Well, we'll leave the case open for a while and see if there are any notes to add to it. My inclination is that you're right. This man was a hired gun, which

174

means there could be more out there looking for you, waiting for you and trying to gun you down for their fifty-dollar payday."

"Only fifty dollars? A man's life isn't worth much in your town, is it, Sheriff? If you find anybody else who wants to kill me, let them know that I'll pay them seventy-five dollars not to kill me. Wonder if I'd have any takers."

Spur left the jail by the back door, went down the alley, over a block to another alley and up to the back door of the office of Dr. Brown. There was only one person in the waiting room.

A woman came out, saw the blood on his arm and rolled up his shirt sleeve.

"Doctor will be with you in a minute. Let me get the blood cleaned off so he can see what the damage is. We'll have to report to the sheriff about your gunshot wound."

"He already knows about it," Spur said.

Ten minutes later he was bandaged and out the front door. The bullet had bored through an inch of flesh on his arm and missed the bone. Be sore but wouldn't slow him down much.

He went on to the Horton House Hotel. He rousted Ginny out of a nap and made sure she was awake.

"We're moving. The counterfeiter knows I'm in town and why I'm here. He just hired a man to try to blow my brains out. I'm moving to a different hotel under another name, and you're going back to live with your mother. It's too dangerous for you to be around me this much."

"I won't go. I'll scream and cry and yell that you raped me. I'll do it in the lobby downstairs where I'll have a dozen witnesses."

"You try that and you'll wind up dead when the assassin tries for me, misses and hits you. You don't understand, do you? Remember Los Angeles, where you almost got a bullet through your pretty little head?"

She frowned and nodded.

"The same thing can happen here. Now, get your things together. I'm going down to settle my bill. You're going out the side door alone and back to your mother's house. I can't have you on my conscience, and you're too pretty a girl to get killed."

She kissed him, her shoulders slumped, and she gathered her belongings and clothes in a new carpetbag.

"I don't want to go, but I will. Where will you be?"

"I don't want you to know. That would get you killed."

"When it's over, will you find me?"

He paused and she looked up, pleading with her eyes. "Yes, yes, I owe you that. I'll find you and say good-bye."

"That's something. I'll be gone when you come back from the desk."

He packed his carpetbag and carried it downstairs. He had a pocketful of cash from his moneybelt. After the clerk totaled his bill, Spur paid it and checked out.

Half a block down from the hotel in the growing dusk, someone hurried up behind him and called his name. A woman's voice. He turned slowly, his right hand near his Colt, his left holding the carpetbag.

The woman came up to him. She smiled. "Mr. McCoy. My name is Natasha. I'm a reporter for the San Diego *Union*. I know who you are and why you're in town. Now with the murder attempt on you, we don't need to sit on the story any longer. I'd like to buy you supper and talk with you."

He shook his head. "I'm sorry, Natasha, but I'm not authorized to talk to the press. One of our rules. You'll have to talk to the home office in Washington, D.C."

She laughed. "Fine chance I'd have of getting anything out of them. I know most of it. We're going to run a story with or without your help. Wouldn't it be better if you checked my facts so I can get the story absolutely accurate?"

He smiled. She was over twenty-one, had a cute face with green eyes and soft brown hair that curled around her ears and her shoulders. She was slim, and energy seemed to burst out of her young body.

"Accurate, that would be nice. I would like that, but like I say, we are prevented from granting any interviews to the press."

"Oh, I figured so far from the boss you might give me a small favor and talk just a little." She frowned, and the lines on her forehead spoiled her pretty face.

"Tell you what. I'll still buy you supper and we can pretend you have escorted me out. That way it won't be an interview, it will be a social occasion. I bet the home office doesn't restrict you when it comes to your social life. Right?"

Ten minutes later they sat at a booth in one of San Diego's better restaurants. They both ordered the roast beef dinner, and Natasha started to talk.

"I understand that five of the counterfeit twenty-dollar bills have been found right here in San Diego. Do you think more will show up?"

Spur grinned. "I really couldn't say. You never did tell me your last name. Are you married? You're not wearing a ring."

Natasha laughed. "I'm supposed to be the reporter here, not you." She lifted her brows. "Okay, I'm Natasha Spooner. I've worked at the *Union* for just over a year and I'm only a part-time reporter. Usually I write the obituaries and help them on circulation. Now you know my secret. If I can turn in a really good story on this counterfeiting, it'll help me get a full-time job as a reporter."

"If I tell you everything I know about the case and the counterfeiter, he'll know that I know and he'll be on the train in the morning, and the next time we hear about these bills he'll be in Seattle, or Bozeman, Montana, or Atlanta or maybe Dallas, Texas. That's why I can't tell you anything."

"Oh," she said in a little-girl voice. She sipped daintily at her soup and then looked up at him.

"Are you always this tough on reporters? I mean on other reporters, men or women?"

"I'm going easy on you. It's not every day a pretty young woman asks me out to dinner."

She ducked her face behind both hands and took a deep breath. "Usually I'm not all this forward, except when it comes to a great story. Most of the time I'm quiet and shy."

"Most of the time."

She grinned. "Well, you looked nice, and approachable, and I figured since you were a lawman I was safe as in jail. So I screwed up my courage and asked the room clerk to point you out to me when you came in. He did."

"I had an arrangement with him," Spur said.

"So did I. Mine was a dollar more than yours."

They both laughed.

They talked about other things, about San Diego and the newspaper and how times were still tight.

"We need more people here, and some businesses and some industry where people can work. More shipping. We'd have a great port if we had some better docks. Those spindly things sticking out into the bay are not the answer."

As they ate their ice cream, Spur offered her a deal. "I'll give you the whole story that you can print as soon as I get it all wrapped up. You get the story and only you. You can tell your editor that. But until I capture this guy and his engravings, I hope you won't print anything."

She frowned. "I won't print anything that isn't public knowledge. Like the five counterfeit bills that were discovered because they all had the same serial numbers on them. And that there is an attempt at the post office to track down the counterfeiter."

Spur held up his hand. "Please, not the post office. Please don't mention them. That's the one chance I have to nail this guy, but I can't let him know that we have a way at the post office that we might be able to track him down."

"No post office?"

"No post office. Whatever else you know, but nothing about the post office. Otherwise he's on the train and out of here by tomorrow."

She lifted her brows and nodded. "Okay, nothing about the post office. I won't have much left."

"You'll have the whole thing once I get it solved. I do need some more time. Three or four days."

Outside it was dark. He asked her where she was going and she said home. He walked with her.

"You don't have to walk me home. I'm perfectly capable of finding my house."

"True."

"So why are you coming?"

"I enjoy talking with you, walking beside you. So sue me, you're a pretty, charming young lady. I happen to enjoy being with pretty, charming, humorous, friendly young ladies."

"A lot of them, I bet."

"No, not a lot."

"But you're not married."

"True. I do too much traveling."

179

She lived ten blocks from the downtown section with her widowed mother. There were three steps up to the porch, and on the last one she stumbled and pressed against him. He caught her and their faces were close together. He bent in slightly and kissed her gently on her trembling lips.

He held it only a moment, then eased back and helped her get on her feet again.

"Thank you for catching me." She looked at him. "You kissed me."

"Right again. It didn't seem like you minded."

"Oh, I did mind. I liked it a lot. It's just a good thing this isn't the eighteen sixties or my father would have made you marry me."

"The good old sixties. Yes, things are a bit more relaxed now, easier, less restrictive."

"I know. I like it this way." She smiled and looked up at him. "What would you say if I told you that I stumbled on purpose and fell against you just hoping that you might kiss me?"

"What would I say? I'd say you're an extremely wise young lady. I enjoyed it too. Want to try it again?"

Her eyes widened in the soft moonlight and she nodded. He put his arms around her and kissed her with more authority this time and held it until she moved. He came away from her lips but still held her.

"Oh, my, Mr. McCoy. Now that was a real kiss. I . . . I better get inside before Ma starts to worry about me."

She frowned slightly. "Mr. McCoy, you can take your arms from around me now."

"I forgot." They both laughed softly.

"About the story. I'll wait and get the whole thing first. I wouldn't want to impede the course of justice here. Drop by at the newspaper when it's all over."

She smiled, touched his shoulder and slipped into the house.

Spur still carried his carpetbag. He went back downtown and found another hotel, the President Grant, and took a room under the name of Charlie Breen.

Upstairs he found room 23 and went in, hung up his good jacket and a pair of pants, then dropped on the bed. It had been an interesting day, but he didn't know a thing more about the counterfeiter now than he had yesterday. Maybe tomorrow. At least his arm didn't hurt much. From experience he knew it would hurt ten times as much tomorrow.

That evening, just before dark, Rico Montez stormed into the old tinware store and dropped down the steps into the basement. He was drunk, angry and ready for a fight with anyone.

"Got the rest of those bills printed yet, old man?" Montez thundered.

Bernard Dennis knew a wild, angry drunk when he saw one.

"No, sir. Not quite yet. May take another two days, depending how fast the ink dries. We get these clouds and wet fog and it makes the ink dry slower."

"Well, hurry up. I'm in a rush to get to Mexico. Didn't even get my job done today. Damn McCoy is still alive. Man I sent to shoot him dead is now a corpse himself. Nobody told me that this McCoy was a fucking gunslinger. He's good and he's fast." Montez slumped down in the big sofa.

"Oh, hell, you got anything to drink around here?"

Consuelo had been staying out of the line of fire. Now she came forward with a bottle of whiskey, and when Montez saw it he yelped and grabbed it.

An hour later he had drunk himself into a stupor. Consuelo spread a blanket over him where he sat in the big chair. He'd be sore and furious come morning.

Dirk Fletcher

She talked with Dennis in low tones. They decided that tonight wasn't the time to shackle Montez.

"I need another two days of printing and trimming and weathering to get the rest of the sixty-five thousand dollars' worth printed and ready. Then we'll pick our time and do it. I have another gun hidden I can get. We'll plan on it later. Maybe tomorrow night if he gets drunk again. Then let him bellow and rage for a day chained up like a barking dog."

Consuelo nodded. She had been wondering about half the money. When Dennis dug it out of its hiding spot, she could shoot him with the weapon she would have, take all of the good bills and leave the rest and slip over the border with more than $10,000.

She half closed her eyes thinking about it. The things she could do with $10,000! She could live like a queen for the rest of her life. She could buy a good business and hire someone to run it. She could go to Mexico City and join the quietly rich. The more she thought about it, the more she liked the idea.

Chapter Seventeen

The next morning, Consuelo fixed breakfast for the two men. Dennis remained chained to the post downstairs, and when she took his food down he pleaded with her to help him.

"What do you know about this man? He'll take advantage of you. He'll take everything and leave you nothing. You simply can't trust a man who acts the way he does. If you help me, I promise to make you a rich lady. You'll be able to go back to your village and live like a queen."

"He is one of my people. We are alike. He take care of me. He help me in the past." She spoke loudly, hoping that Montez was listening. She winked at Dennis. They would fool Montez up to the last moment. She knew Montez would turn against her when he had the money. Montez was only a pimp, and he would cut her off and abandon her quickly if he thought it would benefit him. Surely he would not give her half of the money when they found it.

Upstairs, Montez demanded more *huevos*, so she fried him three more sunny side up and buried them under country fried potatoes. At last she filled him up.

"This morning check the post office for the package," Montez said. "The old man said it would be coming today or tomorrow or the next day. Let's get it and then get the money printed and we can get down to Mexico. We'll live like royalty."

"Can't go this morning," Consuelo said.

He glared at her. "Why the hell not?"

"The mail is not sorted and ready for delivery at the window before noon. The mail we want comes in on the train from Los Angeles, then has to be sorted. Dennis explained it all to me. I always go just after our noon meal."

"All right, all right. I'm going downstairs and get the old man to work again. He says another day or two on the printing. I'll see if I can find where he hid the money. Shouldn't be that hard to find."

Downstairs, Dennis toyed with the idea of printing the money with wrong colored ink. Then Montez or the girl wouldn't have a chance to spend it. But his printer's professionalism took charge and beat down the idea. Anything that Bernard Dennis printed was going to be the best in the world. Absolutely the best. He couldn't stand sloppy work, and certainly not intentional mistakes.

He went back to printing the final 500 twenty-dollar bills. He never thought it would end this way. He had more money than ever before in his life, but he couldn't even spend it. Now Montez would surely kill him. Montez would have no need of a printer who could identify him. Then there would be nothing to show for his big strike against the government and the

Bureau of Engraving and Printing. What did his life stand for? What had he accomplished?

Thinking that way had always made his head hurt. It did so now. Dennis shook his head to stop the pain, then went back to the work he loved, printing fine paper money. Right then it made no difference to him that it was counterfeit. He would do the best possible printing job. It was simply the way he functioned.

Consuelo arrived at the San Diego post office a little after one o'clock. When she asked at the H window for the mail for C. J. Herez, the clerk turned to his trays of mail behind him, found the H and the Herez red card. There was no mail, but he knew what to do. He turned back to the counter.

"Miss, there's still some mail to be sorted. Let me take a quick look and see if there's anything there for you." She nodded, and he left his window and found his floor supervisor. The supervisor told the postmaster that a call had come for the C. J. Herez file.

Postmaster Fogiletta grinned and called Phil Blake from the sorting room. "Remember when you were told how to follow someone? The time is now. A young Mexican woman. She's the first in line at the H window. Go out now and get a good look at her, then follow her and find out where she lives or works or where she goes back to. Understand?"

"Yes, sir," Phil said. He went through the side door into the main reception area of the post office and watched the H window. The girl there was slender, with waist-length black hair. She turned, and he saw a pretty face with black bangs cut across her forehead. He had her.

She said something to the clerk at the H window, then turned and left. The chase was on.

Phil followed her down H Street. She seemed to be in no hurry. She looked in the windows, stopped in a grocery store a moment, then came out and went on down the street. Twice more she went into stores. These times he followed her in, watching her without seeming to.

The third time she went into a store, he couldn't find her inside. He asked a clerk, who said he had seen her go out the back door to the alley.

Phil charged out the same door, but she wasn't in the alley. He chose the short way to the cross street and ran hard, but when he got there he couldn't see her anywhere. He ran the other way, then jogged along the street half a block over. He couldn't see anyone who even looked like the girl. After another half hour of fruitless searching, he went back to the post office and told the postmaster what had happened.

"Don't worry, Phil, you tried hard. She may have noticed you following her, or she just might do this every time in case someone does try to follow her. We'll get her the next time she asks for mail."

The postmaster sent a note to Spur McCoy at the Horton House Hotel, but the boy came back with it, reporting that Mr. McCoy didn't stay there anymore.

Less than an hour later, McCoy came in the post office and asked to see the postmaster, who explained what happened.

Spur jumped up and paced the office. "You had her in your hands and let her get away. Phil may even have been spotted. She might not come back to that window again. The counterfeiter might not let her if he thinks she was followed. I should have been here watching. You can bet that I'll be here as soon as the mail's ready to be picked up. What time is that?"

"Usually by twelve o'clock we're ready to deliver at the windows."

"Good. I'll be here, in back or in front, but here watching. You can count on that. No more mail comes in today from Los Angeles?"

"Actually, we get some mail on each train, but it's not enough to put a crew on to sort it. We do that tomorrow morning when the big shipment comes in."

"And have it all ready to be picked up at noon?" Spur asked.

The postmaster nodded.

"Good. I'll be here tomorrow."

"How's your arm where you were shot?"

Spur looked down and saw that he was holding his left forearm with his right hand to take some of the strain off of it. Now that he thought about it, the gun wound hurt like hell. Better he didn't think about it.

"I'll live, just a puncture wound. Didn't even hit a bone."

"Glad he hit only your arm. You watch yourself."

Spur mumbled a thanks and walked stiffly out of the office. He walked down the street, berating himself. If he'd been at the post office two hours earlier he could have had this case wrapped up and the counterfeiter in jail by now. Damn it!

Someone brushed by him on the boardwalk and bumped his left arm. Pain shot through it, and Spur groaned. Maybe it was time to get the arm looked at again.

Five minutes later in the clinic, Dr. Brown put some ointment on the two wounds the bullet had made and wrapped his arm with a clean bandage.

"No real trouble. Healing fine. Just don't get in any bare-knuckle fistfights."

Spur said he wouldn't. He paid the nurse a dollar for the visit, and she seemed surprised.

"We don't charge for follow-up calls," she said.

Spur nodded. "I usually don't make follow-ups. It's worth it to know that the wounds are healing." He went out the door and the woman smiled.

* * *

Dr. Brown wasn't in such a good mood. For a change he had no one else in his waiting room. He'd been thinking a lot lately about Bovary Walker, the madam who ran the bawdiest brothel in town. Worse, she ran it wide open and with half-naked girls sitting in the second-story open windows in the best part of town on H Street. She had been asked to move her girls back a block or two, or down where two more houses were situated. She had refused.

The city council took up the matter, but the city attorney cautioned them about trying to legislate morals, saying Bovary Walker could challenge any law and tie them up in Superior Court for years trying to get the situation resolved.

They were stymied. Dr. Brown had sat in on several public sessions of the council. He had worried about it for six months, and today he decided to take action.

He had no medical contact with the lady, but it was known that she loved sweets. His box of chocolates would come in handy again. How to get them to her? He could mail them. No, then he would have to go to the post office.

Why not send a small boy to take them to her? Pay him a dime and she'd have them the same afternoon. Dr. Brown looked at his wife.

"If any patients come in, I'll be busy about twenty minutes in the laboratory." She nodded, and he went in and closed the door. He reached for his vial of special poison and then his syringe and the box of chocolates. This was one the whole town would thank him for if they only knew. Grimly he put almost half a cc of the deadly fluid into each of two big hand-dipped chocolates, wrapped each in tissue paper, put them in a gold-foil-wrapped box and tied it with a ribbon. On the outside he pasted a slip of paper that said, "To

Madam Walker for all her fine services." He put the square box in a paper sack and went out to the street. He had put on a hat that came down well over his eyes and he wore dark glasses.

Down half a block he found a youngster playing marbles by himself. He didn't know the child. Dr. Brown took out a dime and called to the boy.

"Son, I have a package I need delivered. Can you take it for me for a dime?"

The boy's eyes lit up and he grinned.

"Sure, sure. Where to?"

"You know Madam Walker's house down two blocks and next to the bank only up the stairs?"

The boy grinned. "Yeah. I watch the ladies in the window there."

"Good. You take this down there, go up the steps and tell whoever you see that it's for Madame Walker. Can you do that?"

"For a dime, sure."

Dr. Brown tossed the dime in the air and the boy caught it, inspected it, then put it in his pocket. He took the package and hurried down the street. Dr. Brown followed him, saw him turn on H Street and go up the steps to the whorehouse.

Yes. That should do it for Madam Walker. One less house of prostitution on the main street.

When Dr. Brown got back to his clinic through the back door, he found three patients waiting to see him. Good. He would be busy.

When the boy ran up the steps to the brothel he was wide-eyed. He'd never had the nerve to come up here before. He was twelve and was getting all sorts of ideas about girls. Now he was in a real whorehouse! The very thought made him shiver. He charged up the steps and saw a door straight ahead. It was the only one. He pushed it open and looked inside.

Madam Walker herself sat at the desk this early in the afternoon for the "gentleman" trade, those gents who could afford to take off in the middle of the day. She was forty, frankly fat, ate well, enjoyed life as much as she could and loved it whenever she saw a man she wanted.

She frowned at the kid in front of her.

"A little young, ain't you, son?"

"Just . . . just got . . . just got a package for you. Got a dime to deliver it."

He held out the paper sack, and she looked in it carefully, saw the gold-foil-wrapped box and took it out. She grinned at the kid. "Thanks, big guy. You want a bonus?" She opened her robe and let one large breast swing out. The boy stood there frozen in place as he looked at his very first woman's breast. His eyes widened, then his mouth dropped open. She flipped out the other side of her robe to reveal the other breast, and the twelve-year-old-boy gaped in delight.

"Oh, wow, golly!" He stared until she covered up and waved her hand.

"Now, get out of here, kid. Go tell your little friends that you saw Madam Walker's tits. Scram."

The boy turned and fled down the steps, nearly falling, catching himself and bursting through the outside door with a silly grin still etched on his young face.

Madam Walker undid the wrapping carefully. She would save the gold foil paper. It was expensive, she knew. She took off the top and looked inside. Tissue paper.

When she found the first chocolate, she squealed in delight. She didn't hesitate. Madame Walker bit the chocolate in half and chewed it greedily. She didn't notice any bad taste. One of the girls came by, yelped in surprise and reached for the second chocolate, which Madam Walker had put on the table.

Madam Walker slapped her hand away. "Mine, you ninny. Get out of here." She held the second chocolate in her hand as she finished eating the first one. She had just eaten half of the second one when she made a strange face, then clutched her throat.

One of her girls came out of a room with a customer. They waved at Madam Walker, but her eyes glazed and she fell forward on the table. Both rushed to her side.

"My God, she's passed out," the woman screeched. "Run and get the doctor."

Nate Parmley looked at Madam Walker. He touched the artery in her throat but found no pulse.

Parmley looked at the girl and shook his head. "Sorry, a doctor won't do this lady any good. She's dead. Don't touch anything. Keep everyone back. I'm going to get the sheriff. Something doesn't look right here."

A few minutes after Parmley left for the sheriff, Dr. Edward Thatcher ran up the steps with a girl who had gone to fetch him. He checked for vital signs and shook his head.

"Sorry, Mrs. Walker is no longer among the living." He picked up her hand. The fingernails had turned blue. He looked at her face. There were definite blue streaks around her eyes.

"Has anyone removed anything from this table?" he asked, his voice stern with authority.

No one said anything for a moment. By then a dozen of the ladies of the evening had come out to stare at their former employer.

Dr. Thatcher looked over the table again, checked the box and the tissue, then stared at the faces around him. "Has anyone taken anything from this table since this poor woman died?"

One small hand went up and the girl who had been with Nate Parmley came forward. She held a half-eaten chocolate in her hand and slowly put it down on the table.

"It was here. It looked so good, I just grabbed it. I didn't think Madam would mind."

Dr. Thatcher nodded at her and she stepped back. He picked up the chocolate and sniffed it, then put it back on the table.

A noise came from below, and the sheriff and a deputy came through the door and stared at the body.

"She's dead, Sheriff. Some highly unusual circumstances that I'd like to talk to you about in private."

"Any witnesses?" Sheriff Raferty asked.

Parmley stepped forward. "Just me and Julie. We was here when she keeled over that way. Fell flat on the desk."

"I'll want you both to give me statements. You too, Doc. If you three will come with me down to the office, we'll get this taken care of quickly." He sent the deputy for the coroner to take care of the body.

One of the house girls came up, fists on her hips. "Sheriff, just what are us girls supposed to do now?"

"Don't know. Did Madam Walker own this building or rent it? Can you keep the business going by yourselves, or do you need a manager? I'd say you get together, find out the facts about the building and any other legal problems or situations, and figure out what you can do. That's up to you."

He turned and led the three down the steps and toward his office.

Dr. Thatcher kept up a steady stream of talk the block and a half. "Sheriff, something mighty strange about Mrs. Walker falling dead that way. I read an article about sudden deaths like this but I can't remember where it was. The blue fingernails are part of the clue, the rest of it I'll try to remember. I'll put it all in a statement for you.

"You have to know that I've been treating Mrs. Walker for some female problems. But her heart was as strong as an ox in heat. No problem there, so I'm positive she didn't have a heart attack. Be interesting to see if the coroner finds any problems with her body."

The sheriff nodded. He didn't need another unexplained death on his hands. Not now, he didn't. At least this one he couldn't blame on Spur McCoy. The sheriff liked the federal man, but strange things had been happening since he'd come to town.

Thatcher kept talking. "This is the second strange one I've seen in a week, Sheriff. First Keith Edison, the hardware owner, died. His clerk said he was grinning one minute, then fell down dead the next. I don't know what's going on. Edison had blue fingernails, too, just the way Mrs. Walker did. I read something about that somewhere. I've got to find out what it is. I'll get it all down in a report to you, a second report.

"I'm certain, Sheriff, that neither Keith Edison nor Madame Walker died of natural causes."

Chapter Eighteen

Lester Grundy found a boardinghouse where the owner didn't mind if he played his fiddle all day.

"Just so there's no playing after nine P.M. when all working men should be in bed," Mrs. Noritowski said. "I love music, and you can leave your door open when you practice during the day and the others are gone. Be nice. Kind of livens up the place."

He agreed to pay her a dollar a day or six dollars a week. If he wanted it on a monthly basis it would be twenty dollar a month. He paid her for three months in advance, and Mrs. Noritowski almost fell over.

"You sure, young man? Nobody ever paid me three months in advance. It ain't proper. Bodes ill somehow. I'll take a month in advance and then we'll see."

"I think you should take the three months."

The landlady shook her head. "Nope. Won't do it. Your playing might attract the wrong kind of girls to my place. I don't rent to women. They're too much trouble."

Lester chuckled. "I'm practicing to be a symphony orchestra violinist, not a fiddler for the barn dance. I can assure you I won't bring in any girls."

"Symphony? Oh, gracious, when I was a slip of a girl I heard the Chicago Symphony Orchestra play three times. It was simply grand." She frowned in thought. "Well, tell you what. I'll compromise and take your rent for two months. Still don't like it, but I will." The two twenty-dollar bills he gave her vanished into a pocket on her skirt and she went back to cutting up the beef for the stew for supper.

Lester grinned when he thought about that last talk with his father. It had been strained and a little angry, but when Lester had showed that he was moving to town with or without his father's approval, the senior Grundy had handed him ten hundred-dollar bills.

"Put this in the bank and take care of yourself," Archer Grundy had said. "Maybe we ain't all that alike, but for your mother's sake, I'll do this for you. If she'd lived, I'm sure she'd be pleased you were taking up music."

That had been two days ago, and Lester had come to town on a horse with his violin and little else. Now that he'd found room and board, he settled in to play. He practiced hard for three hours, then walked downtown and back. It was almost a half mile one way. The little town was starting to spread out, and he wondered how big it would be in twenty years.

He practiced again for another two hours, until he began to get bored. Whenever he stopped playing, he worried about Josefina. What was she doing? How was she getting along with his father? He'd sensed that she was pregnant the last time they'd made love but he hadn't asked her. He hoped his father would do the right thing by her, but he knew he wouldn't. He'd ship her back to Mexico with a hundred dollars the way he had three other pregnant Mexican cooks over the past two years.

Lester took his horse out of the stable and rode for his father's ranch. All the hands would probably be out on the range. His father would be set up in the bunkhouse, thundering his demands from there now that the house was gone.

Lester didn't care. He wanted to see Josefina. Somewhere in the back of his mind he had the urge to marry the girl . . . to bring her to town and make her his bride and live in Mexican Town if they had to. He wanted to do it, but he wasn't sure that he could. He had no money of his own, no job, and he was trying to be a musician.

That same morning, Spur McCoy slept late in the new hotel. He had a quick breakfast and went down the alleys to the back door of the post office. He arrived just before one and spent the first two hours watching the patrons who picked up mail at the H window. The girl did not come, and the clerk did not signal him that someone else had asked for the C. J. Herez mail. Maybe the clerk had scared her off yesterday when he followed her. Maybe the counterfeiter was on the northbound train right now with the plates, all of the real money and the counterfeit bills that he hadn't been able to sell yet.

Spur set his jaw and remained in position across the room from the H list clerk. If Consuelo came, he would find her.

Lester rode in from the west pasture and behind where the ranch house used to stand so no one in the ranch yard would see him. Two hands were there gentling a wild horse they had captured three months ago. Nobody could ride it.

Lester headed for the cook shack. He figured his pa would be in the bunkhouse. By now he'd probably walled off the near end to create a room of his own.

Josefina yelped in surprise when she saw Lester slip through the door of the cook shack. It was about ten feet square with two big wood ranges along one side and a pantry on the other. One table, two chairs and a working counter made up the rest of the room.

"You back to stay?" Josefina cried and ran to him. She carried a paring knife she had been using but was careful not to cut him. She threw her arms around him and pressed tightly against his body. He could feel the swelling at her waist.

He kissed her deliciously, and when it ended, he reached down and patted her expanding belly.

"How much longer he going to let you stay here?" Lester asked.

She turned away and shrugged. "Maybe he let me have his baby here."

He caught her and turned her around. When he could look into her eyes, he shook his head. "You know he's never going to let you do that. I told you about the three other girls he got pregnant and then sent back to Mexico."

"Maybe he won't do that with me."

"Maybe, but the odds are that he will. Where will you go? You have family close by?"

"Have family. Could work the streets for two, three more months, fucking the gringo bastards."

"No, don't talk that way. I truly wish you could stay with me in town, but I don't have a house." He frowned. "I could rent a house, then you could come and cook for me."

"Just cook?" she asked. She took his hands and put them on her breasts. "Josefina damn good at other things too."

He removed his hands and held her arms. "Yes, I know. Oh, how well I know. But I'm thinking you could stay with me until the baby comes. Then maybe you could go back to your family in Mexico."

"With a *niño?* No, no. That would be the worst way. Maybe I could live with you?"

"You mean live all the time?"

"Yes. Lots of gringos live with Mex girls down in Mex Town. Lots of them."

"No, not that way. I can't marry you, either. Pa would never hear of it. We'd have no money and I got no job."

"I come live with you anywhere, anytime." She kissed him, and he saw she had unbuttoned her blouse. Her breasts surged against his chest, and she pulled him to the floor.

"Right now, make me feel like a wife. Soft and tender. With me on my hands and knees. Right now!" She lifted her skirt and went to her hands and knees. She wore nothing under the skirt.

He couldn't stop himself. He ripped open his pants, went behind her and jolted forward into her as she smiled and yelped in delight. Then it was over and she stood and let down her skirt and buttoned her blouse while he fastened his pants.

She pulled him over where she had been peeling potatos. "See, it is always good with us. No screaming, no yelling, no hitting. Just lovemaking and tenderness and wonder. It will always be that way for us."

"So, you want to come live with me in town?"

She thought about it a long moment, then finally shook her head. "But you have no money. How would we live? You'll be practicing your fiddle all the time.

No time for lovemaking. What would I do with the baby when she comes? No, I think I better wait here until Grundy takes me back to Mexico."

Lester scowled and walked across the cookhouse and back again, his face still angry. "He won't make it right for you. He probably won't even give you a hundred dollars to live on. I'll take care of you, and the baby, too."

She shook her head at him. "Right now I must stay here, lover Lester. I must stay here. He will help me when we get to town. Help me get to the border, and with some *dinero*. I know he will. He will be fair with me."

She looked at the things to cook, then jumped back. "Oh, I must take him a cold drink from the well. He's in the bunkhouse and not happy. His leg still hurts."

"Then I guess I should be riding back to town. It was great being here with you, even just for a moment. Don't tell him I was here."

She shook her head, hurried to the door and ran out to the well.

A minute later, she went in the back door of the bunkhouse. A wall had been built eight feet into it to create a bedroom of sorts, and Archer Grundy sat in a big chair with his broken leg on a stool in front. He had been napping. He looked up at Josefina and nodded.

"About damn time you got here. Is it cold?"

"Yes." She handed him one of the crock jugs they kept in the well with various cold drinks in them. She had put down three jugs of lemonade the day before.

"Trying to think of some way to roust those damn brothers with their herd of cattle. My lawyer in town sent me a message that they're trying to sue me for assault and battery and attempted murder. Imagine that. He said it won't even get into court, but he's being careful. It's a criminal charge, but he says we shouldn't worry about it."

He pulled her over to him, put his arm around her and cupped one breast. "You got a fine pair of tits, I ever tell you that? Most of you Mex whores don't have much in the way of knockers, but yours are big and heavy. Yeah, I like that." He fondled one breast, then turned her around and put both hands on her breasts.

"Now, what the hell we gonna do about them damn homesteaders? Can't get careless. Got to force them off so they can't charge me with anything. Gonna be damn hard to do. I got two of my men to ride out and find their herd. It's up in the foothills out there at the far side of their land and then back north. To hell and gone.

"I can have two men go back and kill, say, four of them brood cows with rifle fire. No way to connect that to me. No proof. Just like I can't prove they burned down my ranch house."

He tipped the jug and drank some lemonade and grinned. "Yeah, four or five dead animals will get their attention. Then we got to find their wagon. Most of what they own must be on that wagon.

"Did I tell you they put their tent on the creek, but they haven't actually moved in yet? The wagon is the key. They either drove it halfway back to town or hid it in one of them patches of brush and trees up there. Must be fifteen or twenty of them out there. I'll put one man on it with some grub and two blankets and tell him not to come back until he finds their wagon and can lead me to it.

"Hell, yes, I can ride. Take a little doing, and I'll take some of old Doc Brown's pain powder, but I can do it. To see that wagon burn up I can take a little pain."

He swatted her on the bottom. "Now, get your fancy

little ass out of here and get supper ready. I'm gonna be hungry as an old she-bear who just got herself bred today. Roust yourself back to your cook shack."

She jumped away, then came back and rubbed his crotch, bringing a roar of delight from the big man. She dodged around his hands and hurried out the door.

Archer chuckled. What the hell, once a day was enough for him these days. He'd done her good just before breakfast. Yeah, he was slowing down a little, but the could still satisfy that little sex kitten. He moved his leg. The pain shot through it straight to his brain. He roared in fury and slammed his hand down on the arm of the chair so hard that dust flew.

Rico Montez now realized that he had to do the job on the federal lawman himself. He had followed him that morning and then seen him vanish into the post office. What could he be doing there? He watched the same door for two hours and the lawman had not come out.

Maybe he was sorting through the mail, looking for the package with the money in it. Damn, that wouldn't do. Montez figured he'd do it right here as soon as the big lawman came out of the post office. Couldn't do it any sooner. He told Consuelo not to check the mail today until late in the afternoon when he came back to ride herd on old Dennis.

He looked at his pocket watch. Damn, it was nearly four o'clock. He had to get back to the print shop. If the money came today, they'd be gone over the border by tomorrow. He grinned. At least, *he* would be gone by tomorrow. Little Consuelo would have to take care of herself.

He took the rifle and eased it off the box he'd set it

on in the alley across from the post office. He'd have to rush now to get back to the old tinware store. Damn, another chance gone to get a shot at the lawman.

Chapter Nineteen

Spur had varied his position a dozen times as he waited in the post office for Consuelo to come and ask for the C. J. Herez mail. It was almost five o'clock. The windows closed at five. Fifteen more minutes to go.

He had just stood up again when he saw a flash of black hair at the H window. The clerk said something and turned to his box of mail. He looked up at Spur and waved the red card with the Herez name on it. The clerk stalled a short time, as if searching through a stack of H mail, then turned back to the window and told the girl that there was nothing for Herez.

Spur watched the Mexican girl turn away from the window and walk out the front door. He followed her more closely than he usually would a suspect. He couldn't afford to lose her as the clerk had.

She didn't seem to be in a hurry. She went into two small stores where Spur couldn't follow her. He waited outside, and she soon came out. The third store she went in was a big general store, and he entered it as well and stayed away from her, hiding behind stacks of merchandise until she left.

Down a block, she went into a women's wear store, and Spur didn't feel comfortable following her in. But after he took two casual looks in the window and couldn't see her, he dashed inside and asked where she had gone. A woman clerk said the Mexican girl had asked if she could go out the back door. Spur charged the way the woman had pointed. He made it out the store's back door to the alley just in time to spot the Mexican girl going into the back door of another store whose front door was on the other side of the block.

He rushed through the leather goods store's back door. She was not there. He ran out to the street but could not see her. The street was only three blocks long. This section had few stores and a pair of older houses.

Twelve, no, thirteen buildings on this block. He would have to check every one. Spur moved to the first house and knocked on the door.

Consuelo slipped in the side door of the old tinware store and closed it silently. She wondered if that man had been following her. She wasn't sure. No one had seen her enter the tinware store. She went into the living area and found Montez with the tail end of a bottle of whiskey.

"Anybody follow you?" Montez demanded in Spanish.

"A tall man might have tried. I saw him in two stores, then one time behind me on the street. I went through a women's wear shop and lost him. Nobody saw me come in here. I'm smarter than that, Montez."

"I hope so. We getting anything to eat around here?"

"Not if you keep talking to me in that tone of voice. I don't like it. I'm not your slave, you know."

Montez looked at her sullenly. His eyes blazed for a moment, then cooled. "Where you get the smart tongue from all of a sudden? You used to be easy to get along with, a fun girl to be with."

"I learned a lot about you, Montez. Just don't try to cut me out of my half of the money. If Dennis has ten thousand in there, I get half."

Montez's eyes flared. He started to stand, then shook his head and sat down hard. "Sure, no problem, sweetheart. You brought me to this gold mine. Half of it should be yours. Don't worry, I'll take care of you."

"Have you found the real money yet?"

"No. Haven't looked too hard. Want the old man to get the printing done first, then I'll work him over and we'll get the money in a hurry."

"I'll have some supper in half an hour."

After they ate, she took a plate of food and a cup of coffee down to Dennis, who was shackled to the press. He sat beside it, evidently done working for the day.

He thanked her for the food. "The printing's all done," he said softly. "Wanted to tell you first. We could take out Montez tonight. Can you get him drunk?"

"He already drunk and be passed out in an hour," Consuelo said in her broken English. "I get him down here first so we no have to carry him down."

She started back up the stairs but stopped. "Oh, no package today at the post office. Maybe it come in tomorrow."

A half hour later she roused Montez where he napped on his folded arms on the kitchen table. She quickly got his attention by clanging a pair of pot lids together.

"Hey, Montez, wake up. Wake up, you lazy bones. I

think I've found the hidden money downstairs."

He blinked and rubbed his eyes, then shook his head. "You what?"

"I think I've found where Dennis hid the real money. I need help reaching it."

"Hell, I'll help."

He stood, weaved a little, but made it to the steps without falling down. He stumbled at the bottom of the stairs and crumpled to the basement floor. He was unhurt, and tried to sit up and giggled. He stood with an effort and followed Consuelo. They walked past Dennis, who stood beside the press, and then Consuelo stopped. Just after Montez staggered past, Dennis swung the heavy wrench, hitting Montez on top of the head and driving him to his knees. He sat there a moment, then toppled forward unconscious on the paper-strewn floor.

"Damn, that feels good!" Dennis shouted. "Been wanting to do that for a long time. Yeah, feels good. Now get me out of these shackles so we can get Montez tied up proper."

They found the key to the leg irons in Montez's pocket and took the shackles off Dennis. He swung them around in delight, then pulled Montez over far enough to shackle one ankle to the heavy press with the same chain that had held Dennis.

"I love this. At last I can get back at this monster who was going to kill me, or at least cut off my fingers. I know he would. I've seen his type before."

"We need to make plan," Consuelo said. "We better leave first thing in morning on train. You want go to San Francisco, right?"

Dennis nodded. "I've had a lot of time to think about it. We can live in San Francisco. There are a lot of mixed couples up there, and nobody would notice. We'll have money enough to live for ten or twelve

years. Then I'll buy a press and go back to work printing some more money. We can do this for the rest of
our lives and live in luxury."

"We can travel? I always want to see Mexico City."

"Why not? We'll have enough money."

"So what we pack? We take the counterfeit?"

Dennis grinned. "You bet. After a few months I'll set
up some more sales for it. Always a market for twenties. Should go in a traveling case."

"And real money. That be in the same case? We no
get it mixed up?"

Dennis laughed. "Don't worry, I can always tell the
difference. We'll get that the last thing before we go in
the morning. When is the first train, did you check?"

"Yes, leave at six-forty A.M. Really early. Or there
one at eight-fifteen."

"Let's plan on the later one. Now let's pack up the
bills. You know where that leather case of mine is?"

Ten minutes later they had the bills wrapped and
put in the traveling bag. Then they went upstairs. As
they passed Montez, he came back to consciousness
for a moment and groaned.

"Who the hell hit me in the head? Damn, that hurts."
He glared at Dennis a second, then passed out again
from the alcohol and the clout on the head.

Dennis kicked him as he went by. "No-good son of
a bitch," he said and laughed. "I want to find my bed
and sleep like a human being for a change." He
grinned. "Well, I'll sleep eventually, after I strip off
your clothes and do you about three times."

Consuelo nodded. "At least three times. Hurry up so
we get started. I missed you."

Dennis grinned and patted her on the shoulder.
"You're a fine woman, Consuelo, a fine woman. At last
the good guy is going to come out the winner in this
ugly situation."

Consuelo smiled and urged him up the steps as she unbuttoned her blouse.

Spur McCoy walked up to the small house between two buildings and knocked. The day was moving toward twilight. A small woman opened the door and looked at him.

"Yes?"

"Miss, I'm looking for a Mexican girl who just ran down the street. Did she come in your house or hide behind it?"

"No one is here but my husband and me. We didn't see nobody running or hiding."

Spur lifted his brows. "Thank you. Sorry I disturbed your evening." He went to the first big building. It was locked up and dark inside. There were no side doors. The second big building proved to be some kind of a warehouse. It was being used, but the big drive-in door was padlocked. There were marks on the ground where wagons had gone in or out of the place recently.

For almost an hour, Spur went up and down the long block trying to find someone who knew something about the girl. He had no luck. By then it was full dark. He waited to see which of the buildings blossomed with lamps.

About half of them were homes or businesses that were operating. He had been to each of them and found nothing. No one could remember seeing a pretty Mexican girl with bangs and long black hair to her waist.

He would have to continue his search in the daylight. Even if he did dig the girl out of where she was hiding now, she could easily get lost in the darkness. Daylight would be best.

* * *

Out on the Bar G ranch, two cowhands checked their rifles and loaded them as they prepared to take a ride. One was Burt Ambrose, ramrod of the Bar G and a man who knew what Grundy was going to do a second before he did it.

"As soon as it gets dark we ride out there and do it," Ambrose said. "You sure you can shoot when the time comes?"

The other cowboy, known only as Lefty, grinned. "Hell, yes. I've done a little shooting in my time. The boss said there was a five-dollar bonus?"

"Right, but don't spread the word, stupid. Get yourself a pocket full of rounds and let's ride. Be more than dark by the time we get off the Bar G range."

They rode for two hours, covered a little more than eight miles of open valley, then worked up a small valley toward the steeper hills to the north. The trickle of water that had been a creek at last gave out, and they came to the end of the narrow valley and there found what they had been hunting.

The fifty head of brood cows belonging to the Harding brothers were bedded down along the seep under a scattering of evergreen oak trees and an occasional sycamore.

They pulled up fifty yards away and watched the cattle. One old cow turned and stared at them. Probably she had heard the horses moving up. She ignored them and went back to chewing her cud. The moon had come out, and they could see the cattle easily. They sat their horses on the near side of the little valley where there were no trees.

"How many?" Lefty asked Ambrose.

"Three or four each. Boss didn't give me no figure. Don't want to slaughter them all. Might be able to buy the rest of them cheap one of these days."

"Let's do it," the taller cowboy said. Lefty stepped

down from his mount and pulled his rifle from his saddle boot. "I'll work on the right side, you take the left."

Lefty lifted the rifle to his shoulder, sighted in on the head of a brood cow lying down, and fired. He heard a bawling protest from the cattle, then fired again at the same animal.

From somewhere on the other ridge not one hundred yards away, a rifle barked, and the slug slammed through the air a few feet from the two Bar G riders.

Then another rifle opened up and more than a dozen shots jolted into the area. The two horsemen were in the open, and the moonlight made them good targets.

"I'm hit!" Lefty shouted. An instant later one of the horses took a head shot and went down pawing and screaming in her death struggles.

The firing from across the way stopped. A voice sang out.

"The two of you get on that last horse and ride before we kill it, and then you. Tell Grundy he's a fool and a bastard. He'll probably get himself killed before we can take over his ranch to pay off our lawsuit. Now ride, you cowardly, criminal no-accounts."

Ambrose had pulled his horse into the shadows of some trees as soon as he heard returning fire. His horse was safe. He called softly to the other man.

"Lefty, you bad hurt?"

"Got me in the leg. Hurts like hell. Don't think I can walk. My horse is dead. Let's get the hell out of here."

Lefty crawled into the moon shadows and snorted. "We killed one of their brood cows and lost a good cow pony, and I got a shot-up leg. Not a good trade. Old man Grundy gonna be mad as hell."

The two cowboys rode double on the way back to the ranch. They had no need for speed. The Harding brothers wouldn't follow them. If they had wanted to kill them, they would have closed in on them at the herd and picked them off.

"What the hell we gonna tell the old man?" Lefty asked, his voice showing more than caution.

"I'm thinking on it. We can say we killed ten of their cows and then got rousted by six guns. That sounds about right. Three to one ain't no odds even in the dark."

Lefty snorted. "You try that and you'll get us both fired. He's rawboned mean with that broken leg. Better to tell him just what happened and let the man's fury hit us. He needs us right now. No chance he'll fire us."

They arrived at the Bar G ranch buildings a little before eleven o'clock. The horse didn't make good time walking back carrying two riders. Both men went up to the end room built into the bunkhouse and knocked.

Grundy bellowed from inside, and Ambrose opened the door. Grundy lay on his bed propped up by pillows. Two coal-oil lamps burned, providing enough light for him to read the *Illustrated Police News*. It featured sex crimes and sex scandals with drawings and some photographs. He glared at them over the top of the magazine.

"So, you did it?"

"Almost, Mr. Grundy," Ambrose said.

"What the hell you mean, almost?"

"We shot the first brood cow, then all hell broke loose from across the way with two or three rifles firing at our muzzle blasts. They must have fired twenty times from some brush. We had no targets to use for return fire.

"We lost one horse, and Lefty took a slug in the leg. It ain't looking too good. Can that girl fix it up?"

"Idiots! Imbeciles! Fucking bastards! Didn't you clear the area for a guard before you started shooting? Lucky both of you ain't dead. Those boys know what they're doing. Must have had some good military training. You killed just one cow?"

"Near as we can tell, Mr. Grundy."

"Son of a bitch. Hell, I should've done it myself. Get the hell out of here. Have Josefina wrap up your leg. If it looks bad, you can ride into town in the morning and go see Doc Brown. Why in hell am I surrounded by brainless idiots?" He glared at them. "Go on, get out of here."

They left.

Outside the bunkhouse door, Ambrose slammed his fist into his palm. "Damn it! One of these days that old man is going to go just a step too far. I don't have to take his insults. I can ride for any cow outfit in the state."

"Yeah, you could," Lefty said. "But then they might find out about the flower garden, and then where would you be?"

"Shut up, Lefty. You just keep your yap shut and don't you ever say them words again. Hear me? I could put out your lights on any night I want to, remember that. You sleep so sound a five-year-old could slit your throat."

They stared hard at each other a moment, then Lefty nodded and they headed for the cook shack where Josefina had her small bed. Lefty developed a limp before they had moved ten feet.

They knocked on the door and opened it. Josefina sat up on a pallet at the side of the room. She rolled up the blankets during the day. She wore only a man's undershirt that was far too big for her. One breast showed below the sagging neckline.

Ambrose reached for it, but before he could touch

212

her, she pulled back and slapped him. "My titties belong to Mr. Grundy. Now what you want?"

She turned up the low-burning lamp and saw the blood on Lefty's thigh.

"*Madre de Dios,*" she said and told him to drop his pants. He did, and she saw where the bullet had entered in front of his mid thigh and gone out the back.

"Bad," she said. "*Muy malo.* You see doctor tomorrow." She put a square of cloth over each wound, then wrapped them tightly with a strip of cloth and tore the end in half down six inches so she could tie the ends around his leg.

"Now get some sleep and go into town in morning," she said. "This is bad one. Bullet hit bone, I think. You won't be riding for two, maybe three months."

"What the hell, Lefty," said Ambrose. "You'll miss all the fun. Looks like we're heading right into the middle of a range war. The good part is that our side has the most men and the most rifles. Should be interesting."

Chapter Twenty

Spur McCoy left the street where he had lost Consuelo's trail and had supper at Anderson's Cafe. Mrs. Anderson grinned when he came in and went to his usual table.

"Hope you're hungry, Lawman. I've got some roast beef that's so good I ate most of it myself. That with some horseradish sauce is enough to set up a man for life. How about a good roast beef dinner?"

"Sounds fine, Mrs. Anderson. That and a whole damn pot full of coffee. It's been a bad day."

The roast beef was some of the best he'd ever had. Mrs. Anderson smiled at him. "You want to see my display of pictures of naked women in the back room? I've got a few in case you're interested. Of course, I can show you something better than pictures. Want to take a break from your bad day and have a good time?"

Spur laughed. It was the second time she'd propositioned him, and he did enjoy it, but it would never happen. "Mrs. Anderson, I'm flattered and moved, but not moved quite far enough. I'm so tired I couldn't even get it up for you and we'd both be disappointed. I'm best in the morning. Maybe another day. I'm going to hit my bed and die for about ten hours."

She wiped the table again and scrunched up her face. "What the hell, at my age if I don't ask, I never get any." She winked at him and touched his shoulder. "You have a good rest, and come back often."

Spur meant what he said about bed. He got to his hotel, made sure no one followed him, then went up to the second floor and eased through the door to his room. He locked it behind him, then lit a match and looked for the lamp. It was right where he left it. He took off the chimney, turned up the wick and lit it, then put the clear glass chimney back in place and rolled the wick down a shade.

He heard something behind him and turned, drawing his iron as he spun. The Colt was up and aimed at the sound and the hammer back.

"No, no!" a woman's voice yelped. Then he saw her clearly. Ginny Lambeau sat up on the bed and rubbed her eyes.

"Hey, you came back. Wondered when you were going to get here. What time is it?"

"A little after eight, Ginny. How did you find me?"

"This is my little town, McCoy. I could find a matchstick in a forest. You get your case wrapped up yet?"

"No. Almost had my little Mexican girl today, but she ditched me by going through a women's clothing store."

"Sounds like a bright young woman. She getting poked by the counterfeiter?"

"Probably. Maybe she even cooks for him. I know

she picks up and probably mails things for him. Had a chance at her today and missed. Damn it."

"Hey, you're too tense. You need to relax. Come here." She held out her arms, and he sat down on the edge of the bed. She put her arms around him and nestled his head on her breasts.

"Now, isn't that a nice cushion for your head? Nice and soft and warm." She held him a few minutes. Then one of her hands went down to his crotch and she began to rub gently.

"Of course, if you have any other ideas about what might relax you, we could certainly try them."

"You're sneaky. I came in here ready for a ten-hour sleep."

"You're not so ready for that now?"

"Not a chance." He turned and breathed through her blouse.

"Oh, now that is nice. Do you do any other tricks?"

"A few." He sat up and opened the buttons on her blouse. She wore nothing under it. He fondled her big breasts.

"So beautiful, so damn sexy. Did you know that a woman's breasts are her most beautiful part? Photographers go crazy shooting pictures of women's tits. I guess I'm just a breast man."

He kissed them and licked her nipples, watching them firm and rise as hot blood poured into them.

"They like you too, nice man." She had the buttons on his fly open by then and pushed her hand inside. "Oh, my, what a big boy you have down here. Could I meet him?"

"Any time," Spur said. He lay on the bed on his back. She opened his belt and pushed his pants to one side, then pulled down his underwear. His penis sprang up ready and willing.

"Oh, my! This one doesn't look tired at all." She

216

caught him with her hand and stroked him a few times, then bent and kissed the purple head. She looked up at Spur. "Does he do any tricks?"

"Likes to go swimming."

Ginny giggled. "Like this?" She bent and lowered her mouth over him and stroked up and down a few times. Then she came away from him, straddled him above his erection and kissed him. The kiss lasted and lasted with tongue battles and defeats and new counterattacks. When the long contest ended, she sighed.

"I give up, you win. Just lie still, I'll do all the work." She pulled off her blouse, then her skirt and pink bloomers. She still straddled him and grinned.

"Now just relax. This won't hurt a bit. In fact you might enjoy it."

She moved backward on his body until she was over his crotch. She lifted his erection and aimed it carefully, then eased down with his lance penetrating her vagina, which was ruby red and oozing with her welcome juices.

"Oh, yes, yes, that feel so wonderful. It's a different angle, it just thrills me, it's so marvelous."

When he was fully inserted, she began to use her arms to thrust herself upward, then she jolted down, and he grunted in pleasure each time.

"You like that?" she asked, watching him.

"You're not the kind of girl I'd shut out in the cold on a winter's night, I'll tell you that, Ginny. More, damn it, more."

She grinned and complied. Four more times she did the lift and drop, and then she shivered and her whole body shook and she had to bend forward to keep from falling. He took advantage of the new position and began humping upward. He jolted hard and fast, and before her climax ended he had his own satisfaction.

It was like a steam engine roaring into the station,

like a bucking bronco heaving and spinning and bucking and coming down with all four feet at once. Then he drove upward harder four times and he felt as if he had half died. His breath came in huge gulps and gasps, and every muscle in his body tried to relax at once after being stressed to the maximum.

He sighed, and she wailed in delight and fell on top of him, then stretched out her legs until she covered him and they both rested.

It was twenty minutes before she moved. She rolled to the side and then snuggled back against him.

"Glad you came home. I figured the only way I'd see you again was to find you and break into your room."

"How did you get in?"

She laughed. "You know how. These hotel locks are about as cheap as they come. Skeleton keys. There are three basic types. If you have all three you can get past ninety-nine percent of the locks all over town. I don't know why people even lock their doors. Of course, most of us don't. I never do. If you want to break into my house sometime, just turn the knob and open the door."

They sat up, and she scooted off the bed and brought a picnic basket and set it between them.

"What's your pleasure, sir? I have snacks of all sorts. Wine and cheese, apples and cheese, four bottles of beer, a small flask of whiskey and a jar of branch water. So what is your pleasure, kind sir?"

The nibbled on the cheese and crackers, sampled the wine. He dribbled some wine on her bare breasts and licked it off.

"Nice, that was nice," she said. "Now lay down on your back." He did, and she took the wine bottle and poured a little puddle in the depression in his chest and lapped it up like a puppy.

She looked up and laughed. "I've always wanted to

do that. Fantastic, amazing. Salty wine. Might be a new trend. Maybe we can bottle some just for dribbling on your sex partner."

She undressed him and they made love again, this time fast and furious with him on top and her legs locked together behind his back. It was a shouting, braying and screeching kind of climax that left them both breathless and panting.

Later they attacked the fried chicken she had brought. She offered Spur some buttered slices of bread and produced a salt shaker from the basket.

"It's like a chicken sandwich without the trouble. First you have a bite of the salted cold chicken, then take a bit of bread and chew them up together. Your stomach won't know the difference between that and a real chicken sandwich. The big deal is that I save about an hour by not making the sandwiches."

After the chicken was gone, she nibbled on his ear, then kissed his eyes and down his face and throat to his nipples. She licked them and bit them gently until he reacted. Then she turned over in his lap with her bottom up and looked over her shoulder at him.

"Spur, greatest lover man of all time, spank me."

"I don't do that."

"No, I don't mean hurt me, just spank me until my little ass gets red. It really gets me hotter than a fireball. I mean I can show you some real wild fucking after I've been spanked good. Go ahead. Not too hard, but hard enough."

He whacked her with his hand and she nodded. He spanked her until she turned red, and she turned over and pulled his face down toward her crotch.

"Oh, damn, but that feels so wonderful. You want to chew a little on my favorite spot?"

He kissed around her nether lips, then brushed them with his lips, and even as he did she climaxed, jolting into one spasm after another, her whole body writhing and shivering. Her voice came out as a high keening that he wouldn't have recognized as human if he didn't know she was doing it. He'd seldom heard anything like it.

After she tapered off, she lifted up and kissed him, then flopped back on the bed, recovering.

He stretched out beside her, caressing her flattened breasts. She caught his hands and held them.

"Let me cool out a minute. You really got my old pussy motor running that time. Damn, but that was marvelous. Now let me enjoy it a minute more."

Later they dug again into the picnic basket and found fresh strawberries and whipped cream. They ate them and talked and laughed, and Ginny cried when she realized that Spur's assignment in town was winding down.

"Then one day you'll be gone and I won't have a lover and I'll be so sad. What will I do?"

"A beautiful girl like you won't have any trouble finding a new man. You'll fall in love, get married and have six kids before you know it. The way you love to make love, you'll be barefoot and pregnant for the first six or seven years of your marriage. You'll love it."

"All them little kids?"

"Motherhood will magically transform you into a woman devoted to her children and loving it. You'll see. Amazing what even the first child will do for a woman."

"Not yet," she said.

"Good." He kissed her eyes. "Now, it's time for us to get some sleep because tomorrow I'm going to catch a counterfeiter." He pulled a sheet over them, then blew out the lamp.

She snuggled against him.

"Sometimes I think I like this part just as much as

the other. So soft and warm and comfortable and feeling so . . . so safe and loved and protected."

"Yes, I think you've got it. Now, go to sleep."

Out at the Harding homestead on the land Archer Grundy claimed as his own, the three Harding brothers sat around a small campfire in a deep patch of brush and live oak trees. Their wagon sat nearby and six horses had been tethered a short way back.

"What you think they'll try next?" Ira asked. He and Brody watched their older brother, Oliver, who had led them this close to their own spread.

"Been thinking on that. The shot at our brood stock didn't work for them. We lost one cow, and she's made some good steaks and fry meat for us, but they must have figured to kill off half our herd. No sense moving them now. I don't think they'll be back up there."

"Told you I saw a lone rider checking out some patches of brush and trees," Ira said. "They looking for our wagon?"

"Bet your britches they are. If they could burn our wagon it would come nigh close to whipping us. So we guard it all the time. We'll move it every two days from now on, working it back toward San Diego. Can't hurt.

"I'll ride out and stand guard on the herd tonight, but I don't think they'll be back. Old man Grundy must be mad as hell by now. We lost one brood cow last night, but he lost one or two horses."

Ira pushed a small stick into the fire and watched it blaze up. "I'll go back to the building site. We've got that platform started for the tent. Don't want them to tear that up."

"Couldn't hurt," Oliver said. "That leaves you, Brody, to take care of the wagon. You'll have the shotgun and double-aught buck. Anybody comes around and doesn't call in first the way we do, you give them a load of that double-aught. That'll discourage them in a damn rush."

Brody grinned. He'd learned to shoot three years ago and could do well with a rifle or six-gun. A shotgun was a scare weapon, he knew, and an effective one.

The two older brothers finished their supper, gave the dishes to Brody to wash in the creek, and mounted and headed for their guard posts. It would be a long night.

Oliver got his horse and rifle ready, then went over to where Brody sat beside a tree.

"You scared, little brother?"

"Yeah, a little."

"Good. A scared soldier is a soldier who stays alive. We're all a little scared. That helps us to do a better job. We're fighting for our land here, Brody. If we let Grundy push us off this land, we might as well quit and ride back to Ohio. I ain't about to do that."

"Me, neither, Oliver. We gonna keep our land. We can do it. Nobody gonna get to our wagon. I'll make sure of that."

Oliver whacked his thirteen-year-old brother on the back and went to his horse. If anyone bothered their brood cows tonight, they would get a surprise. He'd planted dynamite at several points on the eastern slope of the hill with markers on them. If he hit one of them with a rifle round he would set off a four-stick dynamite blast.

Oliver grinned. He almost hoped that Grundy and his rawhiders would try something tonight.

Chapter Twenty-one

Archer Grundy knew he'd have to do it himself if anything was going to get done. He called Burt Ambrose into his temporary room at the end of the bunkhouse and scowled as the cowboy stood there with his right hand near the butt of his six-gun.

"Ambrose, you and I have been through some hard times. Now we've got a good ranch and some respect and we're selling five hundred head of steers a year. Next year we'll go to maybe six hundred. What we have to do now is maintain our position, keep up the hard work and not let some sons of bitches walk all over us."

Grundy cleared his throat. "By that I mean those bastard homesteaders who moved in on us. Got to get them out of there before some other assholes decide they can do it, too.

"Tonight we're going to pay another visit to the bastards. It'll be a visit they won't forget. I want you to find five good men. Men who aren't afraid to shoot where they're told to. I don't want any of those men who failed to charge the other day when we took that first rifle fire.

"I need men who want to earn an extra twenty-five dollars and know they might get shot in the process. Get the men's names and come and tell me about them. Don't take more than a half hour.

"Has that man we sent out to find the bastards' wagon come back yet?"

"No, he was to report to me when he got here," Ambrose said.

"Too bad. We'll have to go anyway. We'll leave here two hours before sunset, so we can get to their place just before dark."

"Begging your pardon, Mr. Grundy, but can you ride with that leg?"

"Got a damned hard cast on it. Doc Brown made it out of plaster of Paris and it's hard as a rock. Damn right I can ride. So it hurts a little bit. Got me some pain powder I can take. I'll put a cushion between the cast and the horse. Should work fine. Now get out of here and find me those five good men."

Burt Ambrose nodded and hurried out of the room to the front end of the bunkhouse where he knew of two men who would shoot their own mothers for twenty-five dollars.

Grundy bellowed for Josefina. She couldn't hear him, but someone in the bunkhouse did and went and called her. She came, wiping her hands on a towel.

"Mr. Grundy?"

"I want a small pillow maybe a foot square. Find one and bring it here. Then bring me something to drink. We've got that bottle of whiskey in the cupboard."

"You want some branch water, too, Mr. Grundy?"

San Diego Slattern

"Hell no. A real man drinks his whiskey straight. Now get your little buns out of here. Scat."

She hurried away.

Two hours later the seven men saddled up and left the corral at the Bar G ranch. It had taken them ten minutes to get Grundy mounted on his horse. They set up a series of wooden boxes he could hop up on and then they boosted him the last two feet into the saddle. He bellowed in pain, shook his head and wiped sweat off his forehead.

"Let's get the hell out of here. We've got a two-hour ride before the fun starts."

They rode. Grundy asked Ambrose to stay beside him as they led the pack.

"First we head to where we found the brood cows that first day. I figure that's where they want to build their ranch house if it gets that far. They might have started, and we can bust something up for them. From there we hit the brood cows again. Hell, this time we play it smart and not ride out in the open or into any traps. I want to kill off half of their brood cows tonight. The damn bastard homesteaders won't be able to prove who did it."

"Yeah, Mr. Grundy. This time we'll be more careful. No rush, we have all night to get this done."

At the end of two hours, Grundy pulled the men to a stop and gathered them around him like a cavalry officer.

"Men, we have only a little way to go. I think the place is just over this next small rise to the west. The one with a few trees and brush on it. I'll send Ambrose up to scout it out when we get close. No noise, no talking, no cigarettes. Let's move out."

When they were on the reverse slope of the hill, fifty feet from the ridgeline, Grundy again stopped the men and waved at Ambrose.

"Dismount and walk up there and see what you can find out. Enough moon still out, you should be able to tell if they started to build or if the wagon or cows are there."

Ambrose dropped off his mount, ground-tied her and jogged up to the top of the ridge. From down on his belly he scanned the area below. Brush and some trees to his left, clear and to his right. He could see a tiny stream. No brood stock here. They must be still at that other spot. He scanned the area again, then saw a splash of light that looked like fresh lumber. He ran through the brush to get a better look.

Yes, it was the start of a cabin or maybe a tent frame. He'd seen both start out that way. He hurried back and reported to Grundy.

The old rancher nodded. "Ambrose, I want you to find some cover in the edge of the brush, get behind a thick tree or something, and send three shots into that construction down there. Want to see if there's anybody on guard. The rest of us will be in the brush and trees to your right. If there's any return fire, it should be at you.

"If somebody shoots at you, all six of us will unlimber our long guns at the bastard and drive him away from the building. Then we ride down there and tear the damn thing apart and drag the lumber to hell and gone with our ropes. Got it?"

Ambrose nodded, took his rifle and led his horse into the brush. Grundy took his five men uphill, then cut into the brush and had them dismount and work up through the growth until they could get a clear field of fire on the whiteness of the construction below.

Grundy made a call that was supposed to be a mourning dove. It wouldn't fool another dove, but Ambrose heard it. That was the signal that Grundy was in position. Ambrose fired three shots at the new construction. A moment later seven shots from the construction slashed through the air, aimed at the muzzle flash of Ambrose's weapon. None of the rounds came close.

"Shoot!" Grundy yelled, and the six men fired all the rounds in their repeating rifles.

When the echoes of the rifle fire faded in the valley and the outback country took on its usual quiet again, Grundy stared at the scene below. He saw one figure leap from what looked like a pit of some kind, run for a horse and ride away.

"Yeah, flushed him out," Grundy said. "Let's go down and take that thing apart."

When they got there, they saw it was a floor and uprights for a tent frame. They used their ropes and horses to pull down the frame, but the floor was made of two-by-sixes and too heavy and well nailed to make a dent in. They started a fire in the middle of it and heaped on wood.

"That fire should burn up the whole damn floor by dawn," Ambrose said. He looked at his boss, who stayed on his horse. "What's our next target, Mr. Grundy?"

An hour later, Ambrose found the fifty head of brood cows in the same area as they'd been when they'd hit them before. This time the men came up quietly and kept in the woods. Grundy waved Ambrose over.

"Same routine. I want you down farther away from us this time. If anyone fires back, we'll try to blast him out of there with more rounds than he's got. Worked before. We get rid of him and concentrate on the cattle. When you draw the fire, stay down behind a rock or something. Then when we finish firing, come back with the rest of us."

Ambrose grinned and ran along the reverse slope

and followed the ridgeline for fifty yards, then went up to the top and looked over. Yes, an easy shot. He picked out a spot halfway between the cows and the brush on the far side, then changed his mind and put two rifle rounds into the brush just above the pregnant cows.

He fired and edged down below the lip of the protecting ridge. Three shots came blasting back at him, and a few seconds later the six rifles in the woods blasted at the homesteader. Ambrose didn't know where the homestead shooter was, but he didn't want to rise up and look. The rifle fire tapered off into silence. He could hear the men mounting and moving out of the brush to a spot where they could get good shots at the brood cows.

He mounted and rode in that direction in the safety of the reverse slope. Then he heard a pair of rifle shots. Almost in the same instant the cracking roar of an explosion ripped through the hills.

Ambrose had to hold his horse in close check to keep her from running away. He heard one horse crashing through the woods, then another.

Before he heard anything else, another rifle shot cracked, followed at once by a second explosion.

Dynamite bombs. The bastard must have rigged up bombs he could explode with a rifle shot. Ambrose spurred his mount forward into the heavier brush and found two riders coming toward him.

"It's a damn war up there!" one of the riders yelled. "I didn't sign on to get blown up by no damn dynamite bomb."

By the time Ambrose got to where Grundy sat his horse, only two of the other riders remained. They had pulled back in the woods for protection, away from the forward slope where the dynamite must have been hidden.

"How in hell did he do that in the dark?" Ambrose asked.

Grundy shook his head. "Damned if I know. It's suicide to try to get out there where we can get shots at that herd. Let's ride out of here before we lose any men."

They rode for half an hour before Grundy called a halt. He opened a paper from his pocket and poured some powder from it into a small cup he carried. Then he filled the cup with water from a saddle canteen, mixed it with his finger and drank it.

"Yaaaaaagh," he brayed. "What a foul-tasting brew. Maybe it'll help a little. Damn it, let's ride. I'm getting too old to be out this late playing at being a damn cavalry soldier."

Oliver Harding listened to the men riding away over the ridge. He could hear them leaving just as he had heard them coming. He pushed up from the breastwork he had made of four-foot-long two-by-sixes nailed to two small trees. He had created two firing ports in the three-foot-high barricade.

He smiled grimly. It had worked once more. He didn't know how long he could work all day and defend his herd at night. Maybe they'd have to take turns, him and his brother Ira.

At least the explosions hadn't upset his lady bovines. He'd set off three smaller charges during the day in the same area, and the cows had not minded. They seemed to adjust to the sudden explosions.

He looked out at the hillside just past the cows. He could see five more pieces of white cloth he had staked to the ground. Each cloth was about six inches square and covered a three-stick charge of dynamite. All he had to do was shoot into the center of the cloth to set off the powder. It had worked. He wasn't sure what to try the next time.

He knew there would be a next time. Maybe he should make another strike at the Bar G to keep them off stride. He'd think about it. He settled down with his blanket sure that there would be no more trouble here the rest of the night.

He wondered how Ira had made out. It was conceivable that the riders from the Bar G had hit the cabin site before they came up here. He'd find out in the morning.

This was their land. They had homesteaded it all legal and proper. No high-handed son of a bitch with twenty riders and more money than he could ever spend was going to force them off their land. They were Hardings, damn it, and a Harding never, never gave up his land to anybody. They had learned that from their pa back in Iowa.

What happened back there ten years ago wasn't Pa's fault. Four years of bad crops and a year of no cash crop at all, together with the depression, had taken the last dollar out of their pockets. When their ma died, the fight went out of Pa and he just sat in the house and waited to die.

At the age of fifty-two he'd told them that his life was over. When the bank man came to take over the land, Pa had shot at him with a rifle, missed and fell over with a stroke. He never lifted his hands again. He died a day later from another stroke, and the boys moved out and headed west, each with a horse and dreams of a cattle ranch.

That had been more years ago than Oliver wanted to remember. He looked up at the cowboy's clock. The Big Dipper took a nightly ride around the North Star. A cowboy could tell what time it was to within fifteen minutes by the position of the pointer stars in relation to the North Star. Right then it was a little after midnight. He could still get a good six hours of sleep and be back at the wagon for breakfast at six-thirty.

Downhill, at the site where they had started to build a platform for their tent, Ira had ridden off a quarter mile and stopped after the rifle fire slammed into his barricade. He turned back and saw a gang of men tearing down the platform. Bar G men, he was sure.

He listened to them shouting, heard nails coming loose as boards were torn apart. Then he saw a fire start, and he cursed. That would ruin most of their work.

He stayed out of sight and waited until the riders rode away, shouting, to the north. He knew the herd was up there, but Oliver was guarding it, so all would be fine.

As soon as he was sure the men had left, Ira rode up and stared at the destruction. The uprights had all been torn down and scattered. He could find the two-by-sixes in the morning.

The fire was the problem. He rushed to it and shovcled dirt on the flames eating slowly at the center of the platform. They had piled brush and limbs and some of the two-by-sixes on top of the platform to feed the fire. He pitched all of that off with the shovel, then smashed the rest of the fire out with the shovel and more dirt.

When he finished, he had sweated through his shirt, and the chill of the evening breeze made him shiver. At least he'd saved most of the platform. A hole was burned all the way through in the center, but it was less than a foot wide. They could put a patch on it without much trouble. If he hadn't stayed, the whole platform could have burned up.

He went back to his blanket and rolled up in it, keeping his rifle close at hand. Bess, his mount, was a talker. That's how he knew the other horses were coming before. She had whinnied at them half a dozen times before they rode up. Now he settled down. With Bess as his watchdog, he would know if any other rider came within a quarter mile of the site. He slept soundly.

Brody Oliver was too far away to hear anything that happened at the other two sites. He sat in the dark twenty feet to one side of the wagon against a giant sycamore tree. He loved the big trees with their light-colored bark and huge leaves. They were spreaders, with lots of limbs and branches, and would be great for climbing or even building a tree house in if he had the time and the lumber.

The only lumber they could afford had gone for the planks to make a floor for their tent. It was a step up from a dirt floor, and he looked forward to it.

Brody tensed. He heard something in the brush. He looked at the horses. None of them had been bothered. One or two of them would have whinnied if other mounts came anywhere near. He listened again.

Brody relaxed. It was probably a rabbit or maybe a possum. He'd seen a lot of possum around and knew that they did their roaming and feeding at night. Almost never did he see a possum during the daylight unless it was a dead one.

He moved to a more comfortable position with his blanket around him and shifted so he could see the North Star through the branches overhead. The pointer stars showed that it was a little after twelve. He wondered if anyone would come now.

Maybe and maybe not. He'd learned to sleep lightly. He'd put in his time riding herd as their cattle slept at night. Sometimes he'd fall asleep riding and wake up

232

only if a coyote barked or a wolf howled.

Now he edged lower against the tree and put his head on his saddle. A little nap wouldn't hurt a thing. He figured it was past the time when anyone from the Bar G ranch would come. If they did, the horses would awaken him.

Yes, the horses would talk, and he'd hear the hoofbeats if they came at anything other than a slow walk. A little nap would be good. Brody closed his eyes, testing. He grinned, then closed his eyes and slept.

Chapter Twenty-two

Consuelo walked up and down in front of Rico Montez, who was chained to the leg of the heavy press. He had slumped down and stretched out on the plank floor with one leg bent. Consuelo stopped and shook his shoulder, ready to jump back out of reach. He didn't wake up.

She went upstairs and poured a glass of water from a pitcher, carried it down the steps and threw it in Montez's face. He sputtered in anger, his eyes popping open. A frown creased his face.

"What the hell? Where am I?" He sat up and tried to move his left leg.

"Hey, who chained me to the press? What in bloody hell is going on here?"

He looked around and saw Consuelo standing six feet away from him, smiling.

"Well, good morning to you, Senor Montez," she said in Spanish. "What does the master wish this

234

morning? How may I be of service to you? May I lick
your boots and scrape my head on the floor, bowing
to such a noble person?"

Montez grabbed the chains and shook them. They
were solid, forged with half-inch links. His surprise
turned into anger and he roared at her.

"I don't know what game you're playing, little
whore, but it's over. Unlock me from this leg iron right
now or you're in more trouble than you can ever have
nightmares about. Do it now!"

Consuelo laughed at him. "You are a bastard, Montez. You intended to get all the money and leave me
behind, didn't you? Admit it. You have probably sold
your tiny little saloon by now and are all ready to
charge across the border and set yourself up as a rich
man.

"Don't bother looking for that little hideout gun you
carry. It's gone, and so are the two knives. I've never
liked knives, Montez. The gun may come in handy
later, we'll see. I haven't quite made up my mind yet.
You have all day to think about it. We can't leave until
tomorrow morning."

Montez stared at her, and slowly the gravity of his
position came to him. He calmed down.

"Consuelo, no, on my mother's grave, I was going to
take you with me. I *will* take you with me. We'll go
together and you can pick where we stay. Mexico City,
Ensenada, Cancun. Wherever you want to go. You get
half the money. I told you that the other night. At least
I intended to. You're the reason that I'm here, I owe it
all to you."

"Right, you sure do. The only trouble with that is
that I owe it all to me, too. Oh, just wanted to tell you
that Dennis and I are having a big platter of eggs, bacon, and toast and oranges. Doesn't that sound good?
Sorry, you don't get any breakfast." She turned and

walked toward the stairs but stopped when he called.

"Come back," Montez bellowed. "You can't just leave me down here chained up this way. We can work this out, Consuelo, I know we can!"

She went to the top of the stairs, turned and waved at him. "Montez, you are a real bastard, you know that? Were you going to kill both of us before you left with all the money, or just Dennis?" She frowned. "Yeah, probably both of us so nobody could come hunting for you and get even. You're as bad as the worst of the gringos."

She slammed the door and went in to see Bernard Dennis. He really had treated her well while she had been with him. She realized that now. He even let her buy new clothes. He sat at the small table working on his bacon and eggs. She went to the wood range and fried three more eggs and put them on his plate along with two pieces of toast she finished on the top of the iron stove.

"Is enough, or you want more?" she asked in her broken English. "I make all you want."

He grinned. "No, this is plenty. It's just so damn good to be free again. How long was I down there, a day and a half, two days? Seems like a year. I have some more packing to do downstairs. We're still set to leave tomorrow morning on the train, right?"

"That the plan. You want I go to post office? Another thousand dollars be good."

"No, no. Too big a risk. We'll go with what we have. I have enough counterfeit to bring in another three or four thousand. We'll have that and my reserve." He smiled. "Don't worry, I won't forget it. I'll get it out just before we leave. I don't want there to be any chance that Montez could get it. He might chew off his leg just to get free."

They both laughed, and she sat down to two eggs,

bacon and toast. They both had coffee. He finished his.

"I'm going downstairs to pack up my ink, a few sheets left of the good paper, and the plates. I don't want to forget those. They're more valuable than all the money we have. Remember, *don't* go to the post office. They must have figured out the C. J. Herez name and are watching for anyone who uses it."

She smiled and waved.

Dennis went down the steps and grinned when he saw Montez working at the chain, trying to pry loose a link.

"You'll never get out of that chain, Montez. I tried for two days, remember? Strange how things change around, isn't it? First you had no idea there was lots of money in San Diego. Then you changed things and thought you had captured me and all of the gringo money.

"Now you're chained to the press, hungry and thirsty and knowing that we aren't going to feed you a thing. Somebody will hear you in a few days before you starve to death. Probably, if you yell real loud."

Dennis chuckled and packed up the rest of his ink. It wasn't a lot but he wanted to keep it. He could see how close he could come to duplicating it in San Francisco.

When he finished putting the ink, the paper and the engravings in a small carpetbag, he went near Montez.

Suddenly Montez swung a wrench at him. He had to step back to avoid the savage swing.

"Keep trying, Montez. That way you'll use up all of your energy and you'll die quicker." Dennis frowned. "I still owe you a pistol whipping. Don't worry, I won't forget. I'll get to it before we leave."

He turned and walked up the steps with the carpet-bag and the priceless twenty-dollar-bill engravings.

* * *

Spur McCoy had returned to the street at eight A.M. as he told himself he should and worked the remaining business firms and empty buildings on the block. When he last saw Consuelo, she came out of the store about in the middle of this long block. She had to be here somewhere. He didn't like this part of his job, but it had to be done. It was routine drudgery, but it could find him a counterfeiter.

The second business he went to was a saddle repair shop. He talked to an old man with white hair and hands scarred and twisted from long years of holding reins and a cowboy's rope.

"Yeah, I seen that one once or twice. Made me wish I was fifty years younger. Slender little Mex girl with long black hair and bangs across her face. Young, tight little body with good breasts. Pretty as a newborn colt standing up for the first time."

"You see what building she went into?"

"Nope, can't say as I did. Seems she was walking west in front of here, but I couldn't tell you where she stopped. Saw her twice, as I recall."

Spur moved to the west and checked three other business-type buildings. One was vacant. It seemed that this had once been a busy business area, but the stores had mostly moved to H Street. One man said he'd seen the girl, but that was about all. The second man had no idea who Spur talked about.

He eyed the houses, four of them. None in good repair. Not much pride in ownership down here.

By eleven-thirty he had checked out every building on the long block. He'd even gone to the next block and worked those houses, but no one could remember seeing the girl.

He decided he was in a rut and walked to the *Union* newspaper office and found Natasha. She looked up from a desk and came forward quickly.

"Is it all over yet? Can I write the story?"

Spur grinned. She was so bright and quick and eager. He shook his head. "No story yet. But it's lunch time. You do eat lunch, don't you? I'm here to take you out for a nice quiet little bite to eat."

"Oh, darn! I hoped it was settled. I am working on another story, though. I'll tell you all about it. It needs a detective on it, too. But the sheriff can't get excited about it. Lunch? Sure. Let me get my hat and I'll be right with you."

They ate at a sandwich shop she suggested and had ham and cheese on a bun with everything on it, a plate of corn chips and a bowl of fresh chopped tomatoes with chopped hot peppers, chilis, onions and garlic to dip them in. It was so hot Spur went through his glass of water in a hurry.

"What's your new story?"

"Oh, it's about five people who have died here in town in the last year. Three of them in the last week. One was running for the school board and another was a city councilman. Then of course there was the notorious madam who wouldn't move her business off H Street. I've talked to Dr. Edward Thatcher, who says he's sure that one of the men died by poisoning. He says he has the word of the coroner, but the sheriff won't help him dig into the matter.

"He said he examined the madam and he's positive that she was poisoned. Her fingernails turned blue right after her death. He says that's one of the results of a kind of rare poison that comes from the jungles of South America. The natives down there use it on their arrows to kill birds and things."

"The sheriff won't open an investigation?"

"No. He says maybe San Diego is better off without these certain people who had been getting in the way of progress. He said he for sure wasn't going to investigate an old whore like Madam Walker no matter how she died.

"So that's about where I am. I don't have any facts linking all of these deaths, but Dr. Thatcher says he saw a medical article on this poison and that when he finds it, it will go a long way to convincing the sheriff that there's a murderer in our town."

They finished lunch and walked out into the seventy-degree weather. "Is it always this nice in San Diego?" Spur asked.

Natasha smiled. "Almost. It rains now and then, but not often enough. We have a water shortage even now. When it gets down to fifty-five degrees we start talking about how cold it is. Most of the time it's pleasant like this. Not too hot and not too cold."

"I'll have to invent some reason to come back. Right now I better get down to the post office. Kind of a last shot at hoping to catch my girl and the counterfeiter. But don't print that." Spur took her arm and walked her back to the newspaper.

Spur found his usual chair in the post office back room and watched the H window clerk like an eagle looking for food for its young.

Across town, Dr. Edward Thatcher rubbed his forehead. He'd had a tough morning with patients. Now he had an hour all to himself, and he ate the sandwich his wife had fixed for him and had coffee that they boiled on the small heating stove in the back storage room.

He took out his journal again and looked at the loose sheet in the front of it. The heading read: SUSPICIOUS DEATHS IN SAN DIEGO.

Under that were five entries going back a little over a year. The first was a county supervisor who had opposed a small dam going in up toward Ramona to hold back some of the winter rains that could be used for San Diego's water district. He was found one morning slumped over in his buggy. He hadn't been home the night before.

His wife said he had a meeting of county supervisors to attend, and she didn't miss him until she awoke about six A.M. There was no sign of violence. He hadn't had any health problems. He hadn't been Dr. Thatcher's patient, but the decision by the county corner to list the death as from a heart attack seemed strange to Dr. Thatcher. The supervisor had been in a violent argument the week before about the dam, and now he was dead.

Dr. Thatcher held his thoughts to himself.

Six months later a man running well ahead for city council suddenly took sick and died in three hours. He had been Dr. Thatcher's patient, and the death puzzled the medic. The dead man had no history of heart problems, no apparent illness or sickness. He didn't complain and hadn't been to the doctor's office for six months, and then for a urinary infection. Dr. Thatcher remembered that the man's fingernails had turned blue shortly after his death.

The fact triggered a memory of some research he had done at one time, but he couldn't connect it with any definite area.

Then about two weeks ago one of Dr. Brown's patients died after a two-day illness. Lothair Clinton had been running for the school board. Now Dr. Thatcher wished that he had insisted on checking the man's fingernails. He'd asked the coroner, who said he didn't remember anything about Clinton's fingernails.

The last entry on the page was about the town's most famous whore, Madam Walker. Dr. Thatcher had been in the area when she died and he had got there before the sheriff arrived. After determining that she was dead, he checked her fingernails. Under some garish polish he saw the blue creep into the nails. He looked at her face and saw blue streaks around her eyes. It was another poisoning, he was sure.

Still the sheriff would not budge. He said he needed concrete evidence, something he could take into court. What better evidence could the court want? Of the three most recent sudden deaths, all three of them had blue fingernails.

Where was that damned article he had read? He had been so impressed with it that he had torn it out of the medical journal and saved it, but where? He had almost an hour to hunt.

Systematically Dr. Thatcher began searching his office. It had to be here somewhere. As he searched, he kept thinking of the phrase that had been spinning through his mind ever since he'd begun digging into these sudden deaths. It was "For the good of San Diego." From one way of looking at it, there was a case for that.

It would be better for the town if Madam Walker's whorehouse was not in the center of San Diego's business district with her bare ladies sitting on their open second-story windowsills calling out to prospective customers and offering a look at the merchandise.

It would be better for the city if it could keep the marching band. Keith Edison had led a drive to cut off funding and use the money for the water system. Somebody liked the marching band, and Keith Edison's death had derailed the drive to eliminate it.

As Dr. Thatcher thought back, each of the suspicious deaths had some element of civic pride or civic good attached to it. The dead were obstructionists or trying to hurt San Diego in some way.

Who in hell would be bold enough, no, crazy

enough, to do something like that? It would have to be someone who knew a lot about chemistry or medicine. How would anyone get hold of such a poison? Dr. Thatcher had no idea how he could get any.

He kept searching his office. He even looked at files he had on pain, but it wasn't there. How had he filed it? Or had he? He kept looking.

A knock sounded on his door and it opened. His nurse, Betty, looked in. "We've got a young man who tried to cut off his finger. Think you'll have a minute to sew it back on?"

Dr. Thatcher nodded. That would be the end of his search for today, but he would get back to it. There were just too many similar circumstances here for the deaths to have happened by chance. Someone was killing off the people he or she thought were hurting San Diego or holding back progress. He wanted to find out who it was even if the sheriff wasn't interested.

He would find out. But first he had to find that damned article.

Chapter Twenty-three

Spur McCoy shifted his position on the post office chair, then stood and walked around it. It was almost three o'clock and no one had come to check at the post office for mail in the C. J. Herez name. Maybe he'd scared her off yesterday. But would they leave a thousand or two thousand dollars just sitting in the post office?

He didn't think so. She'd be here. He just had to wait. That didn't mean he had to be happy as he waited. He walked around the back room of the post office, keeping an eye on the H window.

Then he went back and sat in his chair. The clerk at the H window held up his hands in a helpless gesture. They both had to wait.

Lester Grundy sat in his room at his boardinghouse practicing. He still had a tremendously long way to go in developing his skills on the violin. He knew that.

However, he was willing to take the time and do the work to develop into a classical violinist.

He played another difficult series of scales his teacher had assigned as a warm-up. Then he moved on to an actual piece of music.

After two hours he was tired. He had started practicing at seven. Now at nine o'clock he felt so lonely that he could scream. He didn't have Josefina to confide in.

He'd go see her. Why not? His father was laid up in his room in the bunkhouse. He'd never know. He could slip into the ranch from the back side the way he had before. Yes!

He put his fiddle away, pulled on a pair of heavier pants and hurried out the door.

Two hours later, he rode up to the brush line of the small creek 200 yards behind the ashes of the Bar G ranch house and looked out. There were few horses in the corral. That meant most of the cowboys were out doing the ranch work.

Keeping the cook shack between himself and the bunkhouse, he walked up to the back door of the cook shack and edged it open. Josefina was alone, working at the long counter, preparing some kind of food.

He slipped in and called, "Josefina, visitors."

She looked up and her face burst into a big smile and she rushed to him, hugging him tightly, her face against his chest.

"Oh, Lester, I'm so glad you came. I've been feeling sad lately. I have a *niño* but nobody to share the good news with. I've been hoping all morning that you would come. Look what I made."

At the side of the room she had hung a blanket, and behind it someone had built a bunk against the wall with rope strung between rails to form a kind of mattress holder. On top of that were four blankets.

She pushed the blanket aside and pulled Lester behind it. "Here I can have a little privacy." She kissed him, and he felt his blood boiling. He felt her stomach and could tell the baby was growing quickly now.

She smiled. "I call him Joseph in honor of the Holy Mother's husband. Do you think that's all right, even though he'll be a bastard?"

"I think that's fine, Josefina. He'll be beautiful and strong and a comfort to you."

He pulled her down to sit on the bunk beside him, then kissed her again and fondled her breasts.

"I've missed your tender lovemaking so much," she said. "Do we have time now?" She frowned. "No, not now. Right after the noon meal. Only three men are here, but they will be starved."

She kissed him again. "You stay here until I get the men fed, then we will be together and love each other and it will be wonderful."

She slipped past the blanket, and he heard her singing as she fixed the rest of the noon meal. A cowboy came to the door and looked in.

"Boss wants to see you pronto," the man said. "He wonders where his dinner is. He's mad as hell."

"He's always mad these days. Tell him I'll bring it right out."

When the cowboy left, she peeked past the blanket. "I have Archer's dinner ready. I'll take it to him, then come back and fix the rest of the meal for the cowboys. Then we'll make love. You just stay quiet and I'll be back soon."

Lester heard her go out. He leaned back on the bed and found it quite comfortable. Not as good as a real mattress, but better than sleeping on a plank floor or out on the range.

He drifted off to sleep and woke up when Josefina kissed him. She tried to smile, but sadness wreathed her face. She kissed him again and lay on top of him.

"What's the matter? Did he hit you again?"

She shook her head. She tried to talk, but the words wouldn't get past the crying. She sobbed and turned her face away, trying to control herself.

"I must leave. He told me just now that he's taking me into town and to the border this afternoon. We leave in two hours. I have to get everything I own and put it in a carpetbag so I can take it to Mexico with me. He said we'll take the buggy and leave at three o'clock."

"Less than two hours. Do you have your things?"

"Not much. Most of it was lost in fire. Everything I own is here." She indicated a cardboard box at the end of the bunk and two skirts and two dresses that were on the clothesline when the house burned.

She sat up and so did Lester.

"So, we're going to have to do something. I won't argue with Pa. When his mind's made up, it's no use. We'll outsmart him. When you get to town, you tell him you want to stay with your sister in Mex Town until you can contact your parents in Mexico. That way he won't have to take you the last twenty miles to the border."

"But I don't have a sister—"

He put a finger over her lips. "He doesn't know that. Get off the buggy in Mex Town and tell him you can walk the rest of the way. I'll meet you there and we'll rent a house and live in town. Or maybe, if I can get ten thousand dollars from my father, we'll move to San Francisco. Yes, we talked about that before."

She kissed him tenderly. "Wonderful, Lester. How can I ever thank you? I'll do whatever I can. You'll see. I'll cook and sew for you and be a wife to you and keep you happy."

She stood and took an old carpetbag from under the

bunk and folded her clothes and put them in the bag. Next came one small crucifix and a small book in Spanish.

"That's all. I don't own much."

He touched her swelling belly. "You own a son, the most glorious gift of all. You must protect him and take care of him. We'll be sure you eat right and go see a doctor to be sure all is well with the child."

She sobbed again, unable to contain her feelings. He held her until the crying stopped. Then they heard someone coming. Lester slipped behind the blanket just in time.

The door opened and Burt Ambrose marched into the cook shack.

"You ready to go? Boss changed his mind. Says he wants to leave as soon as he can so he'll be back before dark. Got your bag?"

"Yes," Josefina said. She looked at the blanket, then back at the ranch foreman. "I don't have much." She picked up the bag, looked at the blanket again and left with the cowboy.

Lester hurried to the door after they left and looked out through a crack between the door and the jamb. The buggy had been hitched up and his father was already sitting in it. Josefina put her bag behind the seat and stepped into the rig. She looked back at the cook shack.

"Mr. Grundy, I don't want to leave. Don't I do good work for you? Aren't the men happy with their meals?"

"Yes, Josefina. Your cooking is fine, that's not the trouble. You got yourself pregnant. That's the problem. You and I both know that you'll be better off with your in-laws back in Mexico. No argument. It's settled. You're going." He looked up at his foreman.

"Burt, you take care of things as usual. I should be back before dark."

With that, Archer Grundy slapped the reins and they moved off down the trail west toward San Diego.

Lester watched through the partly opened door of the cook shack. He figured his time there was limited, since one of the men from the bunkhouse must already have been named as the new cook until the boss brought back a real cook, another Mexican woman from San Diego.

Lester stood there, so furious he couldn't think rationally. He had to get his horse and follow the buggy well back and out of sight, then find them in town and watch where Josefina got out. They could live for some time on the thousand dollars he had. After that they would take things as they came.

He was about ready to slip out the back door of the cook shack when he saw Burt Ambrose get his horse from the corral, slide a rifle in the saddle boot and mount up. Lester watched him a moment, curious about where he was going. Then Ambrose looked down the trail that the buggy had taken and rode ahead slowly, following the buggy from a good half mile back.

Why would Ambrose follow the buggy? Lester had a sinking feeling as he rushed to the back door, ran full speed until his lungs screamed at him, and then stopped, panting heavily. He was still fifty yards from his horse. Why would Ambrose follow the buggy, and why so far back? There seemed to be only one explanation but Lester didn't even want to think about it.

He screamed into the sky as he got to his horse, then mounted and rode. All he had to do now was shadow Ambrose and see where he went. If he turned off for some range work, Lester would be relieved. If he didn't, then it was a good thing that Lester had brought along the six-gun in his saddlebag. He often carried it when he rode the trails in case he stumbled

on a rattlesnake. Now he might have found two of the
evil creatures. He certainly hoped not, but the more
he thought of it, the more it seemed logical. He choked
down a sob and rode faster until he saw Ambrose on
the gray plodding ahead at a walk with the buggy a
quarter mile ahead of him.

Oliver Harding didn't like leaving his new ranch, but
Ira and Brody would be there. He had to ride to town
to sign some papers. The lawyer told him to be there
today at two o'clock. He rode south and then west to
pick up the Bar G trail into town. Over the years, riders, buggies and wagons had created something of a
roadway through the rolling hills and valleys on the
way to and from the Bar G ranch. The path was the
easiest and quickest way to San Diego.

He had ridden for half an hour when he saw a
strange procession moving along the trail. A black
buggy with one horse pulling it and two people inside
led the way. A quarter mile or so back a lone horseman
followed, and behind him about twice that far, and
using brush and gullies for cover, a second horseman
followed the first.

Oliver was certain that the last horseman didn't
want the one in front of him to know he was there.
The rider behind the buggy would have been in plain
sight often if the buggy riders had looked behind, but
evidently this didn't bother the horseman. Curious.

Oliver followed the group like an outrider from a
changing distance to the side. Often he was closer,
sometimes farther, but he usually had them in sight.
The important thing was that they not see him.

Two miles farther on, the buggy stopped in a grove
of live oak. The trees grew along a small stream and
were in leaf the year round, dropping dead leaves almost continually. Around the live oaks there was al-

most no brush. The rig stopped, and a woman in the buggy jumped down and moved toward the stream. She carried a small pail.

Before she got to the stream a rifle shot cracked in the afternoon silence. Oliver saw the girl jerk to the side and tumble to the ground. She got to her hands and knees and tried to stand, but another rifle round slammed into her and drove her to the ground. This time she didn't move.

Nobody left the buggy. Oliver saw movement from the left, and the horseman who had followed the buggy galloped up with a rifle in his hands. He rode to the girl on the ground, studied her a moment, then put his rifle back in the boot and dismounted. He ground-tied his gray and went over to the buggy. After a short conversation there, the rider came back with a shovel.

"Murder and now a burial," Oliver said softly. He had to get close enough to identify the killer and the man in the wagon. There could be little doubt who that would be. Who else would be coming from the Bar G in a buggy but the owner? Oliver left his horse and worked down a brush line until he was thirty yards from the man with the shovel. He was digging a shallow grave, working quickly in the soft ground along the small stream.

He was only partly done when the second rider, who had been following the first, galloped into the area. He shouted and screamed. Oliver couldn't hear all of it, but he heard the words "Pa" and "How could you do this?" Then the man on the horse fumbled with his saddlebags, pulled out a six-gun and fired twice at the man in the buggy, who was twenty feet away.

By then the grave digger had pulled out his own .44 and shot twice at the rider. The man on the horse pivoted, lifted his hand to fire again when he took a third round in the chest and slammed off the horse, hitting the ground in a death sprawl.

The man in the buggy screamed.

"What the hell you doing, Ambrose? You've shot my son. Why the hell'd you do that? See if he's alive. You better pray that he's alive and that Doc Brown can save him. Go look at him, you bastard."

Ambrose holstered his gun and knelt beside the body. He looked up and shook his head.

"I'm sorry, Mr. Grundy. He's gone. He was shooting at you. I was trying to save your life. Are you hit?"

"Dead? My son is dead? You killed the one bright spot in my life. You killed the only reason that I've been working so damn hard the last thirty years to build up a ranch I could leave to my son. I should kill you right here, only I can't. With this damn broken leg, I need you. Damn you, Ambrose!"

Grundy leaned out of the buggy and looked at his son. He wiped his eyes, then glared at the foreman. "Well, pick him up and put him in the seat beside me. At least I can give him a decent burial. Come on, move. Then you bury that girl deep and make sure you make the place look like it's never been disturbed. I'm counting on you for this. Remember what I can tell the sheriff if I have to."

Ambrose drew his .44 but didn't aim it. "Old man, you'll go a step too far one of these days. You just remember what I can tell the sheriff as well, if I have to. This has been a good arrangement up to now. Let's keep it that way."

Ambrose holstered his iron, then picked up Lester Grundy's body and with a lot of effort carried it to the buggy and put it in the seat beside his father.

Grundy scowled at his foreman.

"Dig that grave at least four foot deep. We don't want the coyotes digging her up. Now, make it happen quickly before some saddle bum rides by and sees you."

Grundy sat there in the buggy for a few minutes watching his foreman digging. He called to the man, "Make it four feet deep, Ambrose, not a hair less." He slapped the reins on the mare's back and the buggy with its sad cargo rolled forward.

When they got to town, Archer Grundy drove to the sheriff's office and gave a boy fifty cents to get the sheriff for him. It was three minutes before Sheriff Raferty came out. He nodded at Grundy, then looked at the body in the seat beside him.

"Dead?"

"Yes, Sheriff. We were on our way to town and three damn rawhiders hit us. Rode up and didn't say a word, just drew iron and started shooting. Got Lester three times. I got by with just one round in the leg. I think we killed one of them before we drove them off."

"Where did this happen?"

"About five, six miles out of town toward my ranch. Just hope they don't hit the ranch while I'm gone."

"Can you describe the rawhiders, Grundy?"

"A little. All bearded and dirty as sin. Wore old clothes looked like they never been washed. Old stained hats. One smoked a pipe. Rode horses that were mostly bones and skin. Two bays and a roan. Never saw a wagon, but they usually work from a covered wagon. Two of them was in their twenties, I'd say, and an old man about fifty. Might have been sons of his."

"I'll write up a report. You best get over to the doc and let him treat that wound. Still got a cast on your leg?"

"Right, Sheriff. That's why I had to have that boy come get you. I'm not moving around much yet."

Oliver Harding sat on his horse a short distance

from the sheriff's office and listened to the exchange between the lawman and the rancher. Oliver would be telling the sheriff a different story about two murders, just as soon as he talked to his lawyer. He was already ten minutes late, but what he knew had made it well worth it. The lawyer had said it might take two or three hours of work on the lawsuit, but even then there would be time afterward to see the sheriff.

Oliver Harding nodded grimly and rode on down the street to his lawyer's office. At least from now on there would be no problem with Archer Grundy and the Bar G causing problems at their new ranch. That was over. Grundy would be hanged or spend the rest of his life in state prison. It didn't matter if he had pulled the trigger on the rifle or not. He must have ordered the foreman to do it. That was the same as killing the girl himself.

Oliver wondered who the dead girl was and why she died. He lifted his brows. It would all come out at the trial. He'd plan on being there.

Chapter Twenty-four

That same afternoon Spur kept his vigil at the post office. It wasn't until another train came in that the registered mail clerk came and talked to the H clerk, then went over to Spur.

"A registered package came in for C. J. Herez. She'll have to prove who she is and sign for it at my window."

"Thanks a lot. Now the game becomes more interesting."

It was nearly four o'clock when the H window clerk looked over at Spur as he served a young Mexican woman.

"Yes, Miss Herez. That's right. There is something for you. Take this slip to the registered mail window and pick up the item there. Just as usual. Thanks."

Spur slipped through the door into the main part of the post office and saw Consuelo move to the registered mail window. She was dressed in a different skirt and blouse today, more colorful. She handed the registration clerk something that looked like an envelope. The clerk nodded and wrote on a slip, then had her sign something and handed over a package.

Spur had been careful to wear different clothes today so she wouldn't spot him that way if she had seen him before. She left the post office and began her shopping tour down the block.

Spur chuckled. She was good, but he knew her routine. He walked quickly to the last place where he had seen her, behind the store on that block he had worked so hard on that morning.

He walked to a spot where he could see the girl when she came out of the same store or one nearby. He could stand at one corner and see the whole street without being spotted.

He settled down to what he figured would be a ten-minute wait, but had barely taken a second breath when the girl in the colorful blouse and skirt and long dark hair came out of a store and sprinted down the street. She didn't look behind, and Spur walked in the same direction.

She went past the end of the block and halfway down the block Spur had not checked that morning. No wonder he hadn't found any sign of her; she had run a block and a half.

He paused against a store front. She had slowed to a walk, looked over her shoulder and turned in casually at the fourth store.

"Gotcha!" Spur said to himself softly. He ran the same way and saw that the fourth building was a closed-up and run-down tinsmith's store. It looked as if it had been shut for years.

He walked past the front and came to an open space between buildings. The girl evidently had gone in here and used a side door. As Spur entered the space, he could see that the grass and weeds had been beaten down where people had walked in and out of the building.

He had found them.

He listened against the side door but heard nothing. He took out his Colt and cocked the hammer, then turned the knob. The door was not locked. He turned the knob until it stopped, then pulled the door open. It moved on oiled hinges. He opened it farther and looked inside.

The darkness fooled his eyes for a moment, but when they became accustomed to the light, he saw that part of the area had been cleaned up and turned into living quarters.

He paused. Where had the girl gone? For a moment he thought he heard someone call, but as he concentrated the sound disappeared. He stepped inside the building to check the rest of the area.

No one was there. The sound came again, a bleating, hoarse call. Spur frowned. Then he remembered the lay of the land outside. The building was set on land that sloped away behind it. Could there be a basement or half basement?

He saw two doors. Quietly he moved to the first. It opened into a small office, which had the dust of a year's abandonment on it.

The second door was across the room. He moved as cautiously and silently as possible. The second door was not locked either. He opened it and heard the call again. A human voice, but hoarse and weak.

The open door revealed a set of steps that led down, and he could see lamplight from below.

He went down the steps slowly, watching closely. No one moved.

Then he saw a man chained to a support beam. A leg iron had been padlocked around his leg. When the man turned, Spur saw his face and the large purple mark that disfigured it.

"Help me! God's sakes, help me!"

Spur hurried to the man after quickly scanning the rest of the area. No one else seemed to be there.

He knelt by the man who sat on the floor with his back against the beam.

"Get me out of here. My name is Bernard Dennis. Please get me out of these chains."

Spur saw the printing press.

He sat back on his heels and grinned. "I'd say you're the man I've been hunting, the counterfeiter, right?"

"Yes, yes. That don't matter now. She's getting away. Told her not to go back to the post office. That's where you followed her from, right? Damn crazy woman. She's smart and she's getting away right now."

Spur frowned. "What do you mean?"

"Consuelo, the girl you followed in here. You see her anywhere around here? She took all the money and the plates and left out the back. She's disguised as an old Mexican woman. Look for her in a brown coat with two traveling bags. Hurry before she gets away."

Spur saw a door at the back of the building. He started for it but stopped quickly. He saw a second man also chained, this time to the heavy printing press. He lay sprawled in death on the floor. His throat had been slashed, and so had his genitals. Blood had poured from both places. He also had a small blue hole in the side of his forehead.

"That's Rico Montez!" Dennis shouted. "He's not going anywhere and neither am I. Go get the girl! She's got all the counterfeit money."

Spur passed Montez and raced for the back door. Now he was looking for an old woman in a brown coat with two bags.

He ran outside, down the small hill to the street below and saw footprints in the dust coming out of the dirt into the street. They were small and headed to the left. That was the way to Mexico. Now he knew he had to hurry.

A block later he saw an old man sitting in front of a small house. He asked him if he'd seen an old woman carrying two satchels or carpetbags.

" 'Deed I did, young man. She looked like an old Mex woman in a hurry. I yelled at her but she kept going. She headed on down the street. You're maybe five minutes behind her."

Spur jogged along asking questions, getting answers. Every block or so another person had seen the old woman with two bags.

Soon the route was plain. Consuelo was headed for the border with her money and the counterfeits, maybe the plates, too. He wasn't worried about the dead man. They could sort that out later. If the girl got away, the whole case would be a disaster.

The bay was about fifteen miles away, then it was another nine miles to the U.S.-Mexican border. She was going to get tired carrying those two carpetbags.

"Sí, I see her. Pretty girl. She want my cart. I tell her I need cart. Not even sell for the twenty dollars she offered me."

Spur thanked the man and looked ahead. There were few people and almost no buildings along this part of the long San Diego Bay. Then why couldn't he see her ahead?

Two buildings stood alone on the edge of a salt marsh that ended in the bay. He would have to be wary. Consuelo must have a pistol if she killed Montez.

He slowed as he jogged along, until he noticed that the near side of the closest building had no windows.

He ran faster and stopped at the side of the building, breathing hard. He listened.

He heard nothing.

Spur worked around the side of the structure, found a blank wall and kept going. He was at the corner of the second wall when he heard a scream. Then a shot. He rounded the corner and saw Consuelo with a revolver held to the head of a Mexican woman. Consuelo led a horse, and she stared at Spur.

"Don't take another step or this woman dies," Consuelo said. "Drop your gun in dirt. Now, or she die, then you die."

Slowly Spur bent and put his Colt on the ground beside his feet. He stood.

"There are three San Diego sheriff's deputies waiting for you at the border. I alerted them before I followed you from the post office."

"You lie, you no have time."

Consuelo looked at the Mexican woman and jabbered at her in rapid-fire Spanish. The woman nodded and took off her blouse, ripped it into long lengths and tied the two carpetbags together so they would hang on each side of the horse right behind the saddle.

All the time Consuelo kept her gun trained on the woman. At last she was satisfied that the cloth would hold the bags. She stepped into a stirrup and swung up on the horse. She spoke again in Spanish, and the woman nodded.

"Senora Romero here help me get to Mexico. She know a good route. She come with me. If I see you again, Treasury man, this woman die. *Comprende?*"

"I understand, yes. You'll never make it. Did you play the two men in the tinshop back there against each other and then double-cross the winner? Was that how you outsmarted both of them?"

"Montez was a pig. Always a pig. A pimp, a killer. I

owed him. Dennis was kind but I could never live with his face. Now, stay here, or more people die."

She rode ahead at a walk, the carpetbags swinging and bouncing with each step the horse took. It was plain to Spur that the horse would not tolerate the banging if she was asked to run. As soon as the pair moved out beyond pistol range, he bent and grabbed his Colt and looked in the building. There was nothing and nobody there.

He took off after the horse, jogging until he was within twenty yards, then walking. A mile ahead he saw a settlement, houses along the water. Probably a small town that had grown up down here. He would find a horse there to rent, or steal if he had to.

The older woman was crying. Consuelo talked with her, then gave her a number of bills, probably counterfeit ones.

The old woman squealed in delight, jerked away from the horse and ran as fast as she could to the rear. Consuelo must have been surprised. She tried to turn on the horse and shoot. She fired one round, but it missed, and then the woman was out of range.

Consuelo looked at Spur. He was out of range, too. She scowled and kicked the horse into a faster walk. The carpetbags full of money bounced harder on the horse's flanks.

They were in the village soon. It had one main street a long city block back from the high-water mark of the bay. A few stores and a dozen streets. Spur saw a rider coming up behind him, and when the young man was near him, he waved two twenty-dollar bills at him.

"I want to rent your horse for today," Spur called. "I'm a federal lawman after a counterfeiter."

The young man shook his head. "Can't do it. Late to see my girl. She'll skin me alive if I don't get there fast."

He dodged around Spur's grab at the halter and rode down the street.

Spur jogged to keep within forty feet of Consuelo.

The next man he offered the forty dollars to grinned and took the money. But by the time Spur had mounted and turned forward, he had lost sight of the girl.

Where was she? He rode ahead, saw a side street and galloped down it, but he couldn't see her. He went back to the main street and saw the horse he had been following. Consuelo and the two bags were gone.

He asked three people before one remembered seeing the girl.

"Oh, yeah, the one with the two heavy bags. I offered to carry one and she swore at me. Surprised the dickens out of me. She went into that store right there."

Spur looked at the small general store. He drew his six-gun, ground-tied his mount and ran to the screen door. He flung the door to one side while staying hard against the outside wall. A shot blasted through the door. He ran two steps, dove through the door and rolled on his shoulder to his feet. He heard a second shot as he rolled, but it missed him.

Quiet settled over the store. A woman sniffled. A sound like a slap came. The sniffling stopped.

"Consuelo, you're getting yourself into more and more trouble," Spur called. "Is that what you want? You turn the bags over to me and the engraving plates, and I'll let you continue on into Mexico. If I have to shoot you, I might kill you. If I capture you alive, you'll spend the rest of your life in a federal prison. Is that what you want?"

Another shot blasted, and a copper pot above Spur's head took a direct hit and clattered to the floor. He heard her move. Two people were moving, one a shield and not cooperating. He'd seen it all before.

He judged his timing, then leaped out in the main aisle. The two women were almost at the rear door. Consuelo held both of the carpetbags for added protection. She shot again. Her aim was bad. That was round number five if she hadn't reloaded. He doubted that she had.

Spur darted part way down the aisle and jumped behind a counter with horse collars. The rear door banged shut and Spur ran and pushed it open. He looked out from the side of the door but couldn't see either woman.

Then he did. Consuelo and the woman were in a buggy that surged away from the building and went rolling down the alley with Consuelo driving. Spur swore.

He reversed his field, ran through the store, found the horse he had rented, and mounted. At the first cross street he turned to the left and rode hard to the alley, then examined the rig's tracks. It turned to the left, away from the bay, deeper into more streets and houses. He looked up and saw the rig turning to the south a full block to the west. He kicked his horse in the flanks and raced after them.

Spur knew that his horse was faster than a horse pulling a buggy and two women. He knew it, but that didn't help much. He spotted the buggy again a block down, then it was gone. He followed the tracks.

Consuelo turned at almost every corner, sometimes going to the north to confuse him. At last they came out on an open road that ran along the bay again.

He kicked his mount into a gallop and gained on the buggy. From forty feet away he waved his six-gun at her.

"Give it up, Consuelo. That gun won't do you any good. You already fired five shots. You don't have any rounds left. You're through."

263

Consuelo laughed and sent a shot toward him. It fell short.

"I reloaded. You think I stupid or something? You come close and I kill this woman. Same as before. Back off."

"Good. Shoot her dead, then I can kill you and take the money and your body back to town. This has gone on long enough."

"You bluff, McCoy, no? You bluff. You a lawman, you no let me shoot this woman. So stay back."

Spur's bluff hadn't worked. He hadn't thought it would but he had little else. How could he stop her? At this rate, she'd ride out of the U.S. past the partial barbed-wire fence that marked the border between the two countries, and she'd be free with all the money and the engravings as well.

He was sure that she had cleaned out Mr. Dennis, he said his name was, of all the real money he'd been getting in those registered packages.

Spur figured he could ride up directly behind the buggy, then burst around the side and shoot the girl. He shook his head. Too great a chance of hitting the innocent woman.

He did the only other thing he could think of. He rode to the left thirty yards and thirty yards ahead of the buggy, then turned his mount and rode straight for the women at a hard gallop. When he was twenty feet away he swung to the left, putting the woman between him and Consuelo. He heard her fire but waited a fraction of a second longer, then shot the horse twice in the head as he stormed past it.

He pulled up when he was away from the rig and turned to see the horse going down in its traces. The buggy bumped to a stop and Consuelo shrieked in rage. She jumped down from the buggy screaming at him and waving her weapon. He was out of range. He taunted her.

"Well, well, the queen of Mexico is without her royal coach. What will she do now?" As he talked he saw the woman in the buggy step down and run away from Consuelo. By the time the pretty girl turned back to her, the hostage was out of range of the little six-gun. From the sound of it, Spur guessed it was a .32 or .38 caliber.

Consuelo ran back to the buggy and stepped into it. She looked at Spur and shouted at him, swearing in Spanish and English.

Spur saw someone coming toward them. When the rider got closer, Spur saw he was a well-dressed Mexican man on a fine-looking horse. He stopped when he saw the dead horse and asked Consuelo something in Spanish. Spur fired a shot over the stranger's head.

"Senor," Spur called. "I'm a federal lawman. This woman is a criminal who has just robbed a bank of ten thousand U.S. dollars. If she asked you to help her, I would advise you not to do it. I may have to kill you, and if you help her and live, you will spend twenty to thirty years in a federal penitentiary."

The man spurred his horse and bolted away from the buggy. When he came near Spur, the lawman nodded. "Good choice. Now would you like to help me?"

The man shook his head. *"No hablo Ingles."* He touched the brim of his fancy big hat, smiled and rode away to the north.

"Well, Consuelo, it's just you and me and all that money. I'm surprised that a smart girl like you didn't do a little more planning. I even bet that Dennis told you not to go back to the post office today, didn't he? He figured I had you spotted by now, and you had to give yourself away by using that fake C. J. Herez name. Are you ready to take me up on my offer to take a hike for the border and leave the two carpetbags there for me?

"Oh, you can fight it out with me. But from what I've seen, you're not that good a shot. Also, remember that my forty-five Colt has twice the range your little gun does. Let's say I'll give you five minutes to think it over. Then I'm going to ride up there and shoot you dead. No rush. You have five minutes to live."

Chapter Twenty-five

Spur hadn't seen the men coming. There were six of them, walking along the ill-defined road by the shore of the bay. They all looked young, all were Mexican and poorly dressed. He figured they were working-men.

He rode toward them, but by then Consuelo was screaming at them in Spanish. He wasn't sure what she said, but the men glared at Spur and shook their fists at him.

Suddenly the six men broke and ran for the buggy. Spur rode toward one man and angled him away from the rig, but when he looked back, the other five had surrounded the buggy and were talking with Consuelo.

He rode the sixth man well away from the buggy, then came back and surveyed the scene. Consuelo stood there beside the men. Her old brown coat had been abandoned. Now her pretty new blouse had been torn and one breast showed.

She waved at Spur.

"Now what you going to do, shoot all of us? I told these men you assaulted me and shoot my horse. You try to rape me and tear my blouse, but I beat you off and shoot you once. They protect me. I pay them each twenty dollars, counterfeit. They walk me all the way to Mexico, where each get another twenty. That is more cash money than they see in six months."

"Won't work, Consuelo. They'll see all the money and rob you and abandon you. Then I get you, tie you up and go after them."

"You wish it happen that way. They poor men, not criminals. They believe what I tell them. You the gringo bastard enemy."

She turned and the men formed a shield around her, carrying the carpetbags. The group began moving away. Consuelo pulled her blouse together to cover herself. She looked back at Spur and laughed.

He rode to the front of the group, then walked his horse straight at them. When he was thirty feet way, Consuelo fired at him. The round came close but missed. He spurred his mount forward, and the horse's chest slammed into the outside man in the marching formation, tumbling him backward into the dirt.

He jumped up, evidently not hurt badly. Spur rode at him again and soon had him herded fifty yards away from the group. Spur pointed north and yelled, "*Vamoose.*" The man stared at him, took out the twenty-dollar bill and shrugged. He kept on walking to the north.

Spur rode back to the group of five and positioned himself in front of them again. He tried English. Maybe some of them understood enough.

"Bad woman," he shouted. "Stole money, robber.

Bad woman. *Mujer muy malo.* Go now and no harm to you. Leave her. I am a lawman, a *federales.*"

One of the men looked at Spur hard, then nodded. He chattered to his friends in Spanish, and one of the men surged away from the pack and ran to the north. Consuelo threatened the others with her gun. One of the three men slapped her hand, and she dropped the gun.

That was the key. The other three Mexican laborers dropped the two bags of money, turned north and ran well out of range of her gun.

Spur rode closer. Consuelo bent to pick up the weapon and aimed it at Spur, but he was still out of range.

"Bastard!" she shouted. "I beat you yet." She picked up one of the bags, opened it and took out a handful of bills. She threw them into the air, and the gentle wind whipped them along the roadway.

"You want counterfeit, go get it," Consuelo shouted. She threw another handful of money up and then another. Spur watched it blow past him. He couldn't let the money lie on the road. It would break the economy of San Diego and could bankrupt some business firms. He'd have to gather it after he corralled Consuelo.

He had a horse, the big advantage now. He spurred his mount forward, leaning in against the animal's neck away from the woman, angling close to her, hoping to knock her weapon away. At the last moment she jumped to the side, but had no chance to shoot at him. He charged her again, and this time she moved the same way but got off a shot that missed both rider and horse.

Now he pushed her away from the two carpetbags of money. Each time she tried to get back, but he used the mount like a cutting pony, driving her farther and farther from the bags.

She fired twice more, but the third time she pulled the trigger there was only a click.

Spur reined up and stared at her. "Are you ready to come back to town now and go to jail?"

She screamed at him, pulled a knife from her skirt and charged the horse. He kicked at the knife hand, took a small cut on his leg, but drove her off.

She charged him again, then shifted her target and stabbed the four-inch blade deep into the horse's side. The animal bellowed and charged forward. Spur barely held his saddle but got the horse controlled quickly, turning back to push the woman farther from the bags.

Just ahead was the salt marsh along the bay. It was home to a thousand small creatures, but right now it looked like a smelly, rotting swamp.

Consuelo turned and ran into the marsh. She splashed through the mud and slime and salt brine. Soon she was fifty feet into the muck and she kept going. Spur walked his mount into the mire. The animal didn't mind. It was cooling to her hot feet.

Spur looked across the bay. This was the widest part. It must be two miles across here. She might be able to swim it, or swim out a ways and then south toward Mexico before she came to shore.

He moved the horse faster and rode in front of her. She stopped, glaring at him.

"Shoot me, get it over with," she screamed. "I had worse days in my life. Go ahead, shoot me."

"Are you ready to come back to town and go to jail?"

"Hell, no." She waded around him, then ducked under the horse's belly and ran forward. Soon she stepped into water over her head and began swimming. Spur swore and rode after her. The horse took to the water gratefully and soon was swimming in the bay after the girl. She was good in the water. Spur knew the horse wouldn't catch her overhand crawl stroke. He tied his hat to the horn and slid off into the water.

They were fifty yards from shore when he caught her. He trapped one of her kicking feet and pulled her underwater. She came up coughing and blowing, and he caught her by the hair and pulled her in with a choke hold.

He treaded water hard to keep them both afloat.

"Now are you coming back to San Diego with me?"

She nodded, coughed and spit out some salt water. "Yes. I swim back."

He let go of her and she sank underwater and avoided his grasp. When he spotted her, she came up for air twenty feet away and farther into the bay. He had to catch her again.

This time it was harder. Twice more she dived when he came near and swam underwater. He waited. The third time she tried to dive, he caught her long black hair and jerked her up to the surface, then with the hair as a handhold he began a strong kick and side stroke and towed her back to where he could stand up.

This time he grabbed her with his arm across her stomach, hoisted her on his hip and carried her out of the water to dry land, close to the carpetbags. He tied her ankles together, then her wrists and sat her in the warm sand. He had seen two men ride by on horses, but neither had stopped at the buggy or the bags. A man had followed them and picked up a number of the bills. He yelped in delight and turned and ran back toward Mexico.

Spur spent the next twenty minutes picking up the bills. He grinned when he found that they had different serial numbers. She had thrown out some of the real money, not the counterfeit.

When he got back to Consuelo, she had freed her hands and was working on the leather bootlaces he had tied her feet with.

Her fingernails clawed red marks down his cheek as he tried to grab her hands. He finally got them and tied them again, this time making sure she couldn't get away.

He sat beside her and the carpetbags. Then he went and brought the horse out of the marsh.

"Now, young lady, anything to say? You're going back to town and to the county jail."

"I not in jail yet."

"Damn close."

He untied her ankles and sat her on the saddle, then tied her hands to the saddle horn. She glared at him. He stacked the two carpetbags behind the saddle and tied them on with straps from the saddle. Then he took the reins and began the walk back to San Diego's "Newtown."

He took a shorter route than they had come by and went through a section called Mcx Town where most of the Mexicans in the area lived. They came to a street where there were four saloons in a row. Idle workers lounged outside.

Consuelo began shouting at them in Spanish. They laughed. She kept talking, and they stopped laughing and stood and followed her. Spur drew his six-gun and waved them back.

"I'm a United States lawman. This woman is a prisoner for counterfeiting. Anyone who helps her is breaking a federal law and will go to prison."

The men listened, then looked at Consuelo. She shouted at them in Spanish, and six of them ran out and got in front of the horse, stopping it. Two lunged at Spur, and he swung his pistol, knocking one down, but missed the second. He hit Spur with a shoulder

272

and slammed him backward.

Spur saw eager hands reaching for the girl. Knives flashed as her bonds were cut, and they pulled her off the horse. Spur gained his feet and stepped into the saddle. The carpetbags remained tied on.

By that time, Consuelo was in the middle of ten or twelve young men. They stood around her cheering.

Spur rode as close as he thought prudent.

"Told you I not in your jail yet, gringo," Consuelo called. "These my people. Besides, I tell them I give each two free pokings if they get me free."

As she said it she pulled off her blouse and turned so the men could see her bare breasts. A shout went up, and the twelve men ushered her into a saloon. She looked back at Spur and grinned.

Spur watched the last of the men vanish into the cantina, then rode forward. He had most of it. He had Dennis, he had the plates and the counterfeit and the real cash. He'd settle for that. Let Sheriff Raferty worry about the murder charge for whoever killed Rico Montez.

He encountered no more trouble as he rode down to the courthouse and carried the carpetbags into the sheriff's office.

"Need to use your safe for a few days. Then we need to get a witness in here and take an inventory of what's in these bags."

They spent an hour counting the real money and the counterfeit. When they were done, Spur realized that the engraved plates for the twenty-dollar bill were not in the bag.

"Where are the plates?" Spur shouted.

"Supposed to be in here?" the sheriff asked.

Spur grabbed his hat. "Come on, Sheriff. We've got to make a house call on Mr. Dennis, the counterfeiter. I hope to hell he has the plates or knows where they are."

273

Chapter Twenty-six

Dr. Edward Thatcher had just bandaged up his last patient and given out his last pills of the day. He sat in his office and stared at his shelves. He was not a neat man. Papers, magazines, studies and literature about new medicines littered his desk top and his two bookshelves. He hardly knew where to start to clean up the mess.

He would have to straighten it up if he was to find the medical journal article about that strange symptom of poisoning, as well as how the poison could be used in some experimental projects in a highly diluted tincture form. It had been about a year ago that he saw that article. He'd torn it out of the journal, but what had he done with it?

He began the painful job of searching the rest of his office. Then he stopped, grinned and sat down in his big chair. It had been right after that Julian boy died of poisoning when he drank that fluid he thought was cod liver oil his mother had set out for him.

The fluid had been diluted coal oil his mother was going to throw out because it wouldn't burn in the lamps. The boy's throat had burned and his stomach was damaged beyond repair. They had induced vomiting, but it was too late.

That was when Dr. Thatcher set aside a file in his Symptoms and Cures file drawer for poisons. He stood, went to the file drawer and pulled it out. The third file back was marked "Poisons." He pulled out the article he wanted and with a sigh sat down and reread it.

He found the passage he remembered but hadn't marked.

It has come to the attention of this researcher that when this particular poison is ingested, it will result in death within two or three minutes. One strange effect on the body is that the fingernails and toenails turn a soft blue color. The color can't be washed off and is spread through the nail tissue, not just on the surface.

Dr. Thatcher smiled, stood and grabbed his hat, took off his white work coat and hung it up, then stopped. He had planned to dash over to the sheriff's office and show him the evidence that he said he needed. Dr. Thatcher frowned.

Actually, this wasn't evidence. It was simply information about how one rare poison worked and the effects it had on the human body. Evidence would be if Dr. Brown had any of this poison in his laboratory. More convincing evidence would be if Dr. Brown had any chocolates like the half piece they'd found at Madam Walker's. He needed to figure out some way to find out if Dr. Brown had any of the poison.

What had the writer in the magazine named it? He looked at the article again and found it in the first paragraph. They called it *bicarri*, and some primitive tribes in the jungles of South America tipped their arrows with it to kill animals, birds and fish.

He read the next paragraph with interest.

Some researchers have said that a diluted tincture of bicarri has been used in the treatment of epilepsy and other brain-induced physical breakdowns and central nervous system electrical imbalance problems. No double-blind testing has been done that is recognized, but one researcher is optimistic about how the poison can be used to benefit mankind.

He put the article on his desk and rubbed his jaw. So his problem was Dr. Brown. He had no idea how the doctor way out here in California might have obtained bicarri poison. It wasn't in any of the medical supply house catalogs that Dr. Thatcher used.

How could he approach Dr. Brown? He remembered the boy from Ramona who had been in to see him about epileptic seizures. The seizures were caused by imbalances in the central nervous system. Perhaps he could discuss the case with Dr. Brown, and maybe even get him to offer some of his new drug to try on his epilepsy patient.

He put on his coat and went to Dr. Brown's office. There were no patients in the waiting room. Hilda Brown smiled at him.

"Dr. Thatcher. How nice. I hope it's a social visit. Philip has been a little out of sorts lately. He enjoys it when you two get together and talk about medicine."

"Is he through for the day?"

Dr. Brown came out of his office and held out his hand.

"Edward, I certainly am through for the day. Do you have time for a talk, or are you here about that heart of yours?"

"No, the heart is as good as it will ever be. I'm sure of that. Just wanted to talk a minute. I get tired of lancing boils and treating difficult cases like poison oak and dislocated fingers."

Dr. Brown chuckled. "I'm on a run of colds, bunions and chicken pox. Why don't you come into my office?"

They rambled on for ten minutes, mostly making humorous complaints about patients. Then Dr. Thatcher led the talk into more serious matters.

"I do have one case that has me stumped. A boy about ten in Ramona has epilepsy. Has seizures quite often, and I don't know what to do about it. I can't find anything in the medical journals about it.

"Oh, they say it's an imbalance of electric impulses in the brain or the central nervous system, but that doesn't tell me much. I heard about somebody back East making some experiments with some new medication, but I don't remember what it was."

"Epilepsy," Dr. Brown said. "That's one thing I haven't had any contact with. Never had a patient with it, thank God. About all I'd think to do would be to give them a helmet of some kind to protect their head when they fell down during a seizure."

"There must be something. I thought maybe you've read about it lately. I'm frustrated, really at a dead end with Johnny."

"I might have seen something on epilepsy, but you know how it is," Dr. Brown said. "If you don't have a patient with that problem, you skim the article or skip it entirely." He frowned. "I'm doing a little experimental work, but nothing that relates to your case. At least I don't think it does.

"I have this one patient who has some kind of a nervous disorder. It comes and goes. When it hits, he can't stand up, he can't walk, can't even sit in a chair. His whole body just rebels and shakes and his arms and legs sprawl out and he can't control them."

"Sounds a little bit the same," Dr. Thatcher said. "Central nervous system. What are you doing for him?"

"I'm trying a tincture. You remember some nature nuts use a highly diluted tincture of arsenic for certain disorders. I tried the one hundred-to-one tincture on this patient. Didn't do a bit of good. Now I'm onto something else. I'm not sure over the long haul, but it might be helping."

"Central nervous system. Do you suppose . . . I mean, do you think it might help my patient with epilepsy?"

"Frankly, Edward, I don't know. I've talked to some chemists and they say that at greatly diluted mixtures, this drug can't do any harm. You might give it a try."

"What's the drug and how can I get some?"

"That's a problem," Dr. Brown said. "Fact is it's illegal in this country just yet. I got some through a friend who had a missionary friend in South America. It's like gold to me. If this works, I'll be doing a paper on it for any medical journal I can find."

"If it works for your patient, maybe it would also help my young patient."

"It could." Dr. Brown hesitated. "Tell you what. I'll give you ten cc's of it in a one-hundred-to-one tincture. I won't even tell you the name of it. If it works, I'll figure out how we can get some more. We might just have a medical discovery here, Edward."

"You'll get the credit if we do, Philip. All I want to

do is help my patient. Would now be too soon to ask for that tincture?"

Dr. Brown smiled. "You're an impulsive guy, aren't you? Just sit here for five minutes and I'll go in my lab and mix you some. The measurement is critical."

After Dr. Brown left, Dr. Thatcher sat drumming his fingers on the arm of his chair. He was almost there. Now if he could somehow get the name of the poison out of Philip. He'd use the old medical records dodge. He should have it for the patient's medical history. Of course, he'd never tell the patient what it was unless it was fantastically successful. Yeah, it should work.

He picked up a copy of the new medical magazine just out last year, the *Journal of the American Medical Association*. He had heard about it but hadn't subscribed. He was deep into an article about the heart when Dr. Brown returned.

"I made it a twenty-cc tincture because it's more precise to mix it and get precisely the right amount of the drug. I want you to keep exact records on how you use it and what amounts."

Dr. Thatcher took it and hesitated. "Maybe I went overboard here, Philip. I want to help this patient, but I feel strange about giving him some tincture when I don't know what it is. I mean, I need to put it down in his medical records in my office and all that kind of thing."

Dr. Brown laughed. "Yes, Edward, I know how you feel. Some of us like to keep records. Hell, why not? Oh, I see you found the AMA journal. Lots of good things in there, if I get time to read them. I guess you won't turn me in to the medical board for having an illegal substance. Most people in South America call this bicarri. The primitives use the poison full strength to tip their arrows and blow darts to kill small animals. They use it straight, of course, just the way they

279

get it from some poisonous snake down there."

Dr. Thatcher nodded. "Good, Philip. Good. Now I best be getting home or Ethel will think I've run off with your nurse."

Dr. Brown nodded. "Been thinking of doing that myself." They both laughed, and Dr. Thatcher waved goodbye and left.

He'd done it. He had the evidence he needed to put a stop to this medical murder rampage by Dr. Brown for the good of San Diego. He wondered if he should go to the sheriff right away but decided it could wait until morning. He just hoped Dr. Brown didn't decide to slaughter somebody else that night.

After supper, Dr. Thatcher sat down with his wife and told her what he had discovered so far.

"Not a word about this to anyone," he warned. "Not even Beth. I'll talk to the sheriff first thing in the morning. What I want your help on is the people who have died. You keep the records for our church on the births and deaths. I hope you have your book here."

"I do. You know I always keep it here." Ethel took it from a small stand and opened it. "How far should we go back?"

They decided on two years and went over the names of the deaths. Twenty-two had died in their parish. They made a list of the names and put beside each one the reported cause of death.

Dr. Thatcher studied the list. Then he nodded. "Look at this. Paul Curlow had been a city councilman before he died. It lists the cause of death as a heart attack. He wasn't my patient. But here's Adolph Streib. He was running for county supervisor. His cause of death is shown as a sudden seizure. Streib was my patient and hadn't been to see me for a year. He was strong as a range bull. His heart was stout, he had good lungs, and he just seemed never to get sick.

"Then one morning he died in two minutes. Damn, I wish I had looked at his fingernails. I bet you a dollar they were blue."

By bedtime they had found six people who had died suddenly. Five of them were in local government and one a state representative.

Dr. Thatcher shook his head. "I'd bet the homestead that all six of these people, plus the four in the last few weeks, were all murdered by Dr. Brown. He must think he has to cleanse our town of bad politicians."

"How terrible," Ethel said. "He seems like such a nice man, and such a good doctor."

"He's both of those, except when it comes to this one hare-brained crazy streak he has about protecting San Diego. Maybe I should go see the sheriff tonight."

He shook his head. Tomorrow would have to do. He was too tired and emotionally drained to do more than get up the stairs to his bedroom. One thing he did was take good care of that tincture of bicarri. That was going to catch a killer.

Chapter Twenty-seven

Spur McCoy, the sheriff and three deputies ran for the tinsmith store. McCoy beat them all there and tore in the side door and down the steps.

Bernard Dennis was gone.

The empty leg shackle lay with the heavy chains by the pillar that held up the first floor. Spur took a quick look around. The plates might be anywhere here, but they were not to be seen. Dennis had them and at that moment was trying to get out of town.

Spur ran back up the steps and met the four men coming into the side door.

"He's gone. We've got to check the railroad station. He's short, maybe five-two with the left half of his face covered by a purple stain. Let's get to the railroad. It's a little after six-thirty. When does the next train go north?"

"Seven-oh-seven," one of the deputies said.

"Cover the ticket counter and the cars. Don't let anyone get on that train unless you can tell for damn sure it isn't this short man with the purple stain on his face."

The sheriff pointed to two of his men and they left at a run.

"Now, the other way. Is there any kind of gate or crossing guard or anything at the border with Mexico?"

"Not much. A shack and one inspector, but he usually has nothing to do."

"Send a man down there and have him stay there the rest of the night. Dennis is from the East. To escape he'd think railroad. Mexico is a foreign country. He doesn't know the language. He probably won't try to run that way." Spur frowned as they hurried toward the train station.

"Is the train that goes out a passengers only or a mixed train?"

"Mixed? Oh, yeah, it has some boxcars and freight as well," the sheriff said.

"So we check every empty freight car and every undercarriage before the train leaves. Let's move fast. The dead body back there in the basement won't go anywhere. He'll be there tomorrow. We've got to find that sneaky Dennis tonight."

Spur and the sheriff jogged toward the railroad station at the foot of D Street, which some people were calling Broadway.

When they got there, the deputy at the ticket counter said the ticket salesman hadn't seen anyone with that kind of stain on his face. He'd watch for him.

The deputy on the tracks had been checking boxcars. He came up to report.

"Nothing yet, Sheriff. Some of the trainmen say that the place for the bums to run and jump in the boxcars is about a block up north after the train gets a slow start. They're out of the station area that way, hide in the bushes and weeds, then jump on, and nobody can get to them until the next stop."

"We'll cover that area, too. Can you get any more deputies, Sheriff?"

The lawman nodded and sent a deputy back to the courthouse to bring up five more deputy sheriffs.

Spur checked the train. It had two passenger cars with twelve freight cars in front. He searched four of the empty boxcars. There was no one in any of them.

He looked under each freight car. Some bums preferred to ride down there, lying on the rods as a kind of platform. It was also a good way to roll off and get killed.

Spur walked through the passenger cars. He nosed into each of the small bathrooms. Both were empty. No one had been allowed on the train yet.

A wagon from the post office arrived and workers pitched mail sacks into the mail car. Spur went up to the car and found the doors on each end locked. He jumped up where the mail sacks were going, and a man pushed the muzzle of a sawed-off shotgun in his stomach.

"I'm a federal lawman," Spur barked. "Take that scatter gun away or I'll ram it down your throat." The railway express man gulped, saw the sheriff nod and pulled back.

"We got to be careful in here, mister. Nobody allowed. What do you want?"

"You see a short man, five-two or so with a purple stain on the whole left side of his face?"

"Never have seen one."

"Anywhere in here he could hide?"

"A couple. Let's have a look."

They kicked aside mail sacks, pushed into the corners and came up with the verdict that no one was hiding in the car.

"Make sure it stays that way," Spur said. "When these mail sacks are all on, do you lock this side door?"

"Absolutely."

"I'll stay until you're locked up tight."

When the mail was all on, Spur dropped down to the tracks and the express man slammed the door shut. Spur heard the locks click into place.

Spur looked at the sheriff. "Now we wait."

The extra deputies came. Spur stretched them out for a hundred yards along each side of the tracks to the north of the station. He told them what to expect.

Dusk settled in over San Diego. By that time it was nearly seven. The conductors began to let people board the train. Spur stood at one car while the people filed on. No one he saw could have been the counterfeiter, even with the help of an expert makeup artist.

When all the passengers were on board, Spur went through a gate and up the tracks 150 yards past the engine. He warned the deputies not to let anyone get on the train. He ran off two bums who were waiting for the train. At first they hesitated, but when Spur put a .45 round into the dirt at their feet, they scampered away with blankets and scrubby carpetbags.

The train pulled out on time at 7:07.

No last-minute passengers ran for the last car.

No one tried to jump into the moving train's empty boxcars.

Darkness closed down solid, and Spur and the deputies walked back to the lights of the station.

Spur talked with Sheriff Raferty.

"The man has to eat. Let's check every eating place in town that's still open. Split up the deputies. Dennis may have some money, but if I know Consuelo, she took every dollar he had. Let's get the deputies moving. Show me the place closest to the tinsmith store. I want to check eateries on that street."

Spur spent the next hour jogging from one small cafe and restaurant to the next. There were four on that street, but no one in them had seen a man with a massive purple stain on the left side of his face.

Spur went to the next street and saw a deputy rushing toward him.

"Found out where he ate. Had a full meal and darted out of the cafe without paying."

Spur nodded. "Okay, so he has no money. That means he won't be staying in a hotel. Most of them would ask for payment in advance. Have the men make these same food checks when the cafes open in the morning, probably about six A.M. Now send them home. I'll be roaming the streets all night watching for him."

Spur walked around the area near the cafe where Dennis had eaten. Lots of vacant lots and unoccupied buildings where a man could sleep through the night. He might even try to get back to the tinsmith shop. That was covered. The back door was locked, and a deputy was watching the side door. He couldn't get in there.

So where? Spur began walking the streets, watching for someplace he would hole up if he was hiding and wanted somewhere safe to sleep. He walked into three abandoned buildings, listened, made a torch of some paper and determined that no one was hiding there.

Spur went back to the tinsmith shop. The sheriff was there checking on the murder of Rico Montez. Lamps and lanterns blazed upstairs and down.

The coroner had just determined that the cause of death was either the slit throat or the bullet to the head.

"Had to be the girl," Spur said. "Her name is Consuelo. The people who work at the El Razza saloon should know her last name if she had one. She slashed his crotch before he died. See all the blood? She hated the man for former times, I'd say. He was a pimp as well as a saloon owner. Not a great loss to the community."

Spur watched as the body was dumped in a wheelbarrow, rolled out the door and down to the street to the undertaker's wagon.

"When does the first train go out tomorrow morning?" Spur asked.

The sheriff looked at one of his deputies, who fished out a schedule.

"First train for passengers at six-thirty," the deputy said.

Spur frowned. "Is there ever a work train that goes out of here at night? A rig with maybe one or two cars to work on the tracks or bridges, maybe repair some washout?"

The sheriff nodded. "Happens now and then. You'd have to check with the stationmaster at the depot."

Spur hurried that way.

Five minutes later he talked with the night manager at the station.

"Yep, we got one work train heading out tonight just after eight o'clock. Not many places on it where a man could hide. This one has an engine and one flatbed car. It's got a few new rails that we need up the line, a handcar and about a hundred wooden ties."

"Where is it now?" Spur asked.

"Should be sitting on the main line, getting warmed up," the night man said. "Let's go take a look."

Outside they found no work train either at the station or just to the north in the train yards. The night manager talked with a man in a booth lit by three lanterns that made it brighter than day. He came back quickly.

"Well, that takes care of that. New orders came down by wire. The work train is rescheduled. It'll leave here at nine-thirty tomorrow morning, get the work done at two points, and go on to the Oceanside siding before the regular scheduled main liner comes through there at eleven o'clock."

Spur swore softly. He thanked the trainman and headed for the small station house where there were benches for passengers to wait for trains. He saw two men stretched out sleeping. A train detective rousted them before Spur got to them. Neither one was Bernard Dennis.

The next best chance for Dennis to get out of town would be that work train. The passenger train would be covered in the morning like a thick, wet fog.

Spur gave up and hurried back to his hotel. He could get six hours of sleep and be at the train station at five A.M. watching for the counterfeiter.

Six hours later, Spur awoke, shaved, dressed, had a quick shower and walked to the four other cafes and eateries closest to the rail station. Still he found no one who had seen the small man with the purple-marked face.

He walked to the rail yard and watched it come alive. Few worked there at night. Starting at six, things began to move. He told the trainmen who he was hunting, and they said they would watch for him.

"We don't like them bums getting free rides north," one brakeman said. "That don't help pay our wages. We watch for them guys good."

Spur waved and moved on. He found the work train idle on a siding pointed north. It would go at 9:30 and the passenger/mixed train at 8:00. He had some time. He roamed the area, peering into baggage racks, behind closed doors, behind a small building—anywhere he figured that Dennis might be hiding or had spent the night. He found nothing.

He kept moving and looking. The deputy sheriffs came at 7:30 and worked the passenger train, repeating the procedures of last night. All empty and unsealed boxcars were searched, all passengers boarding were carefully scrutinized by Spur. When the train pulled out at 8:07, there were six deputy sheriffs down the line watching for anyone trying to jump into the boxcars before the train picked up speed. They found no one.

Spur slumped in the depot. Now he had an hour and a half to wait for the work train. Somehow he felt that that one would be more productive. He told the deputies to leave. He'd take care of the work train himself.

Then he went into the depot and looked out a window, trying to find a spot where he could watch the work unit and not be seen. Maybe they had scared off Dennis with too many deputies. Maybe Dennis had to think it was safe to make his way north. Yes, it might work.

Dr. Edward Thatcher walked into the San Diego County sheriff's office three minutes past eight o'clock. Sheriff Raferty had just sat down at his desk with a steaming cup of boiled coffee and hadn't even had a chance to sample the breakfast roll that the bakery had sent over as usual.

"Dr. Thatcher, not often I see you. Sit down. Can I get you a cup of coffee?"

The medical man shook his head. He was too nervous to even think about coffee.

"I have something serious to talk to you about. May I close the door?"

The sheriff nodded, and Dr. Thatcher closed the

door and set the bottle of the tincture of bicarri on the desk. "I'm going to tell you a story you might find hard to believe, but let me finish it and show you the proof.

"There's a man in San Diego who has murdered at least ten men and women during the past two years. He's a respected man in the community and does all of his killings in what he figures will help the progress and development of San Diego to grow into a fine city.

"He seems totally dedicated to his 'calling' to make this a better place to live. He does it by murdering those he thinks are getting in the way of progress or good government or causing harm to our town."

Dr. Thatcher began detailing those persons who died of sudden attacks, or in suspicious ways, and finished with the death of Madam Walker with the half of a chocolate on a table nearby.

"Sheriff, it's my medical opinion that all of these people were killed by a fast-acting poison called bicarri. This is an illegal substance in the United States. It's used by some primitive South American tribes as poison for their darts and arrows.

"One of the effects this poison has on the body is to turn the victim's fingernails blue. Did you notice the nails on Madam Walker? They were blue. That's what got me thinking. I'd seen the blue nails before on dead people.

"Then I remembered an article about bicarri and how one man in the country was testing it as treatment for epilepsy in highly diluted form."

He brought out the article. "This story in a medical journal mentions that if used at full strength bicarri is deadly and will turn the victim's fingernails and toenails blue."

"All right, Dr. Thatcher. You've made a good case. Now who is the killer?"

"Dr. Philip Brown. I got this tincture of bicarri from

him last night. He has a supply of the drug. He could use it with some of his own patients who were 'troublesome.' He could inject the poison into chocolates like the one Madam Walker had eaten half of before she died."

The sheriff reacted in surprise at Dr. Brown's name. He stood and walked around his office, rubbing his neck and face, staring at Dr. Thatcher.

"You're making a serious charge, Dr. Thatcher."

"I know that, and I'm ready to back it up with proof. This is a tincture of bicarri Dr. Brown gave me last night. I bet we can find in Dr. Brown's office some of those fancy chocolates to match the half of one that killed Madam Walker. All you need is a search warrant to check out Dr. Brown's office and laboratory. You'll find the bicarri and I'd wager some of the chocolates as well."

Sheriff Raferty sat down. "We might have enough evidence to convince the judge to give us a search warrant. Anything else?"

"Two of the dead men had been my patients. One of them was strong as a bull elephant. In fine physical condition. His heart was stout enough for two men. He died suddenly from unexplained causes. It couldn't have been a heart attack. But there was nothing suspicious, so the coroner had no reason to do an autopsy."

"That helps. Would the coroner remember any of these blue fingernails and toenails?"

"I haven't talked to him, but I would think that he would. He sees dead bodies all the time, and not many of them would have that blue tinge."

The sheriff nodded. "All right. I want you to put all of this down for me in a statement. Write it out for me with all the details you can remember. Then I'll talk to the coroner and see what he can recall. You have that list of names you think Dr. Brown killed? Good. We'll keep this confidential until I talk with the coroner. We don't want Brown to find out about your suspicions and leave town."

"Can I write it out here? That way you'll have it faster."

The sheriff gave him a pad of lined paper and two pencils and left the office to talk to the county coroner, who was also the undertaker.

Sheriff Raferty stopped in the doorway and looked back at Dr. Thatcher.

"If this is true, this is the biggest scandal to hit this town in many years. Nobody will know who to trust around San Diego anymore. A lot of people are going to be suspicious every time you suggest they take some medicine."

Dr. Thatcher looked up from his writing. "Thought about that. But I'll put up with that if Dr. Brown isn't killing off the politicians he doesn't like anymore. It's a good trade."

The sheriff nodded and went out the door.

Chapter Twenty-eight

Oliver Harding had spent longer than he expected with his lawyer the afternoon before, and when he got out the sheriff had already gone home. He rode back to the wagon at their new homestead and helped guard the brood cows. Nothing happened and he had a good night's sleep.

Now he was up with the sun, had breakfast at the wagon hidden in another stand of trees and brush, and rode for the place where he had seen the woman murdered the day before. This time he carried a pointed shovel and wore a grim expression. He knew what he would find. The whole scene had seemed so routine for the killers, he wondered if the rancher had done it before. He had no idea who the woman was, but he'd heard that Grundy was a widower.

When Oliver arrived at the site, he dug a few spadefuls of dirt from the woman's grave. The soil was still soft, and the man who'd filled in the grave had not even tramped it down or tried hard to conceal it with brush or leaves.

Would there be any more graves here? Oliver looked around with a practiced eye and soon found a suspicious spot not too far from the first one. The ground had sunk slightly in a roughly rectangular shape.

Oliver pushed his spade into the soil and found it harder than that in the previous grave. He marked the spot with one shovel of dirt on the side and looked for more graves.

Before he was through, he had found what he was certain were three more graves, making a total of four. Some were older, with vines and some small plants growing on them. But all had the unmistakable sign of a sinking area.

Oliver leaned the spade against a live oak and rode for town. He wanted the sheriff there before any serious digging took place.

When he got to town it was a little after ten. He went directly to the sheriff's office and was shown inside.

"Sheriff, I saw a woman killed yesterday out toward my ranch in the east county. Then just a few minutes later I saw a young man gunned down. The man was evidently some relation of the man in a buggy who was there along with a man on horseback. I believe the driver of the rig was Archer Grundy."

The sheriff looked up in surprise. "You say you saw the Grundy boy get killed?"

"Yes, sir. Looked to me like a cowboy who did it. I wasn't too close, but the man knew Grundy, evidently took orders from him. He was the one with a rifle who had just shot dead this young woman who had been in the buggy and headed for town."

Sheriff Raferty frowned. "Wait a minute. You're telling me you saw two murders yesterday?"

"Right, Sheriff. I saw this buggy with a rider following it a ways back. Then another rider was following him. Looked suspicious, so I stayed in some cover and watched. The buggy stopped under some trees, and the girl got out with a bucket to get some water.

"That's when the guy with a rifle shot her, killed her. Then the other rider came up and yelled and screeched and pulled his six-gun and shot at the man in the buggy. That's when the other gent killed the boy."

The sheriff had been taking notes. "Then they buried the woman and Grundy brought his son to town. He told me some rawhiders attacked them. Three men."

"That's a lie. I went back to the spot where they killed the woman. I found three more spots that I think are graves as well. Looks like a regular cemetery out there. Figure you'd want to come take a look. Might help to bring four deputies to do some digging."

The sheriff shook his head. "Lord almighty. I don't know what this town is coming to. Yep. I guess we better ride. I'll get some help and have them bring long-handled shovels. That will be five murders if we find bodies in all those graves."

He looked at Dr. Thatcher's statement. It would have to wait. A pair of fresh murders yesterday had to take first call. He told his deputy where he was going and headed out of town east with his shovel-toting posse of four deputies and Oliver Harding.

The sheriff hoped this was the way he would finally nail old man Grundy for murder. He knew that Grundy had killed the other homesteader and his wife. He just couldn't prove it. This time he had an eyewitness. It didn't matter if Grundy hadn't pulled the trigger. He was just as guilty of murder.

They arrived at the grove of live oaks and the trickle of a stream just before noon. The buggy tracks were

Dirk Fletcher

still showing in the dirt road. A pile of horse droppings marked the place where the rig had been stopped for some time. Two deputies went to work on the freshest grave site.

Oliver pointed out the other three spots to the sheriff, who shook his head.

"Damn, Grundy's getting sloppy. Usually you put a pile of dirt over a grave so when it settles it'll be level. He didn't even bother to do that or to try to hide the graves with brush."

A cry came from one of the deputies. He'd found a shallow grave. Less than two feet under the ground they found a skirt. A few shovelfuls later they came to the body. They uncovered it and lifted the girl out of the ground.

"Mexican girl," Sheriff Raferty said. "Could have been a whore for his men, or maybe his cook." He looked at the body again. "Be damned, this girl is pregnant. She can't be over sixteen or seventeen and three or four months with child."

Oliver scowled. "The son of a bitch. I'd like to gun him down myself. Need any extra men on your posse when you go and bring him in?"

Sheriff Raferty rubbed his jaw. "My guess is he'll never stand trial. Man like him wouldn't take well to jail or a trial or prison. He's not going to be easy to arrest. Yes, I think he'll fight us, and get all of his men to join him who will. Could be a battle.

"One more thing. Can you identify the man with the rifle who killed the girl?"

"Don't think so, Sheriff. I was back too far. Didn't want to give myself away. Seems to me he rode a gray and wore a tan hat. About all I can say."

Another cry went up and they moved to another hole. They found what was left of a body. Most of the flesh was gone from the bones. They found a small

leather bag. Inside was a book that had been inscribed: "To Conchita Juarrez on her 17th birthday."

"Good of Grundy to leave identification with the body," the sheriff said.

Before they were done, they had uncovered four bodies. Three of them, including the latest, were young Mexican girls.

Sheriff Raferty set his mouth and half closed his eyes. Oliver watched him.

"How far is it to the Grundy ranch?" he asked Oliver.

"A little over two miles, I'd say."

"Men, put down your shovels. We're going to make an arrest. You've all got your rifles and six-guns. We may have to use them. Let's ride."

They came up on the Grundy ranch a half hour later. The six men rode side by side as they approached the ranch. A rider came out to meet them.

"Is Mr. Grundy at home?" Sheriff Raferty asked.

The cowhand nodded. "He is. You the sheriff?"

"I am. Ride along with us. Yesterday Mr. Grundy took the buggy to town. You see him leave?"

"Yep. I was working a horse in the corral."

"Just after he left, a cowboy rode out on his horse. You know who that was?"

"Sure, our ramrod, Burt Ambrose."

"Is he around?"

"Not sure. I can find out."

"No, son, you just stay with us."

They rode into the ranch yard, saw where the ranch house had been and angled for the bunkhouse. Just before they stepped down from their mounts they heard a gunshot. The men drew and dismounted but saw no one firing.

"Where's Mr. Grundy?" the sheriff asked the cowhand.

"Far end of the bunkhouse. Made a room down

there. Outside door in back."

Sheriff Raferty took two men, walked to the back of the bunkhouse and knocked on the door with the butt of his six-gun.

"Grundy, this is Sheriff Raferty. Need to talk to you."

There was no answer. The sheriff unlatched the door, stood against the wall and swung the door open. Nothing happened. He looked around the door and let down his revolver.

"Mr. Grundy won't be standing trial," the sheriff said. The rancher sat slumped forward at a small table. The side of his head had been blasted off and the six-gun had frozen in his hand.

The sheriff stood there a moment, then turned to the cowboy, who gawked at his boss.

"Now, young man. Where is Burt Ambrose?"

They came around the bunkhouse just in time to see a rider spurring his mount away from the corral.

"That's him," the cowboy said.

"Ambrose! Stop!" the sheriff called. One deputy pulled his rifle from the boot.

"Stop him," the sheriff ordered.

The deputy sighted in and fired twice. The rider, less than forty yards away, jolted forward off his horse, fell under the hooves and tumbled over three times before he came to a stop.

"Looks like Burt Ambrose won't stand trial either," Oliver Harding said.

Back in town, Spur McCoy had watched the work train from a second-story window in the railroad depot. He had a good view of the engine and flatcar. He figured anyone jumping the flatcar would do so down the tracks a block or two. He had no idea how agile Bernard Dennis was, but desperation would give him a big shot of frantic energy. Spur had seen it happen before.

Ten minutes before, the engineer had checked over the engine. It had been fired up and had steam ready. A fireman kept stoking the furnace with coal. Four rail workers would ride in the cab or on the coal tender. They considered it beneath them to ride on the flatcar.

At 9:25 Spur left his perch, walked down a block and then parallel to the tracks for a block before he headed toward the tracks. He found a spot where he could observe the tracks and not be seen. A small bush covered him.

The work train pulled out precisely on time at 9:30. Spur watched it critically. It was a block from the station when he saw a man move. He came out of some tall weeds near the track, ran along, caught hold of the edge of the flatcar and vaulted on board.

Spur ran down toward the tracks. He was still thirty yards ahead of the train. He let the engine roar by, then looked at the flatcar. Not much to hang on to. He found a tie-down loop and caught it as he ran alongside. The train moved at less than a brisk walk. He jumped, pulled himself up and landed on board.

Before he could move, something swung at him. He ducked as a two-by-four whispered over his head. It had been swung by Dennis. Spur jumped to his feet and looked into the muzzles of a double-barreled derringer hideout.

Dennis snorted. "Never thought I'd see you again, lawman. I won't for long. Get off. Jump off right now or I'll kill you where you stand."

"I caught Consuclo. I thought you'd want to know. I got back all of the money, the good and the counterfeit. Figured you'd be interested."

"Why would I want to know? The little bitch double-crossed me. I was going to take her to San Francisco. Get a new start."

"She didn't have the engravings. You still have them, Dennis. I want them."

"You don't need them. I do and I have the gun. Now jump off before I shoot you."

"Ever shot a human being before, Dennis? It isn't easy. Goes against all of your bringing-up. Hard to do, to kill a man. I never like it. How in hell did you get those plates?"

Dennis laughed. "Fools at the bureau. They were set to be melted down when we got a new signature for the twenty. I simply substituted some blank plates the same size and carried the good ones away in my pocket. Same with the paper and the ink."

"The only thing you couldn't control was the serial numbers," Spur said. "Why did you spend those counterfeit bills?"

"I didn't. That bitch Consuelo did. I gave her all the money she wanted. She must have found some counterfeits or stole them out of the bin when I was asleep."

"She did you in. Next time never trust a woman."

"Don't worry, I won't. Now jump off."

Spur shook his head, and the counterfeiter lowered the weapon and fired one round near Spur's leg.

Spur jumped but dove the other way behind a stack of wooden railroad ties. The pile was head high and six feet wide.

The noise of the engine prevented anyone in the cab or the tender from hearing anything that happened on top of the flatcar.

Spur drew his six-gun. "Now, Dennis, we both have guns, only you have just one more shot. I have six more and then twenty more rounds in my gun belt. You want to have a shooting contest?"

Spur looked around but didn't see the small man.

He scoured the front of the flatcar. Dennis wasn't there. He looked on both sides of the ties. No Dennis. He looked back along the track and saw the small man dusting himself off. He had jumped.

Spur moved to the side of the car, picked a soft spot on the right of way and jumped.

He hit the ground and rolled, almost lost his six-gun but grabbed it. When he stopped, his head spun for a moment, then cleared. The train was down the tracks. He looked back for the counterfeiter.

He was gone.

Spur jogged down the right of way until he found the spot where Dennis had jumped, then followed his tracks into some brush. On the other side of the thin veil of growth he saw a dozen buildings. The train had not yet left the city of San Diego when he and Dennis got off.

Where was the little man? Spur heard a scream from a building that could be a house or a small workshop. He raced to the building, found it was a hardware store and hurried inside.

Ten feet ahead, he saw Dennis holding a weapon. There was no time to draw or dodge.

"You die!" Dennis shouted and pulled the trigger on the double-barreled pistol. The hammer hit an empty chamber.

Spur heard the click, whipped his Colt .45 out of leather, cocking the hammer, and the second the muzzle cleared leather he shot from the hip.

The Colt went off in an ear-crunching roar in the small store. Spur wasn't trying to be fancy. In any situation like this he aimed at the largest part of the body, the chest. The round hit squarely in the left side of Dennis's chest and he flew backward as if someone on a rope had jerked him. He slammed against a display of kettles that tumbled down on him as he

301

bounced off and sprawled on the floor.

Spur advanced on the small man slowly, his Colt cocked again and ready. The counterfeiter must be dead.

Dennis groaned. He turned over and sat up, rubbing his chest. He glared up at Spur. "You bastard, you've ruined everything. It's all over now."

Spur knelt beside him, pushed the six-gun under Dennis's chin and stared at him.

"Why are you still live?"

Dennis slowly moved one hand up to his chest and opened his jacket. The shirt had two large pockets, and in each Spur saw an engraved plate protruding. The pocket on the left showed a long tear in the cloth.

Gingerly Dennis lifted out the plate. The .45 slug had hit it on the face, scored a long streak through the fine lines of engraving and bent it at a thirty-degree angle.

"You ruined it, you imbecile. Now it's worthless. Now I can't do any more printing with it."

Spur took both plates, bent the crooked one almost straight and put them in his own pocket.

"You won't be doing any more printing anyway, Dennis, except maybe in the prison print shop. That plate saved your worthless life. Now the taxpayers have to cough up hard-earned dollars to keep you in prison for the next thirty years."

Spur lifted Dennis up and headed him toward the door. He turned to the store owner. "Sorry about the pots and pans. Hope we didn't ruin anything."

The young store owner shook his head. "These aren't the breakable kind." He waved and began picking up his display.

It was a mile and a half back to the sheriff's office. When they walked in about ten-thirty, the sheriff wasn't there.

"Put this guy in an escape-proof cell," Spur told the deputy on duty. "He's a federal prisoner and I don't want to track him down again."

When the deputy came back and gave Spur a paper saying that he had accepted custody of a federal prisoner, Spur asked about the sheriff.

"Oh, he and a guy named Oliver Harding headed out toward the Grundy ranch. Something about two murders and maybe as many as five."

"That should keep you boys busy for a while. My little problem is all wrapped up. I have the rest of the counterfeit and the real cash and the engraving plates. Tell the sheriff when he gets back."

"I'll do that, Mr. McCoy."

Spur walked out of the courthouse, stretched and smiled at the sun. It was a beautiful day. Then he remembered Natasha at the newspaper. He had promised her.

He went back to his hotel, had a long hot bath and a shave, then put on clean clothes and his best boots and headed to the newspaper office. It was just after noon when he got there. He hoped that he hadn't missed the lady reporter.

At the *Union* office, Natasha came forward quickly when she saw him.

"Now I hope it's all over. You've caught him and you can give me the story?"

"Over lunch I'd be glad to tell you the whole thing. You pick the place to eat."

She chose a cafe with large tables so she'd have a place to write. She had a cup of coffee and took down the whole story as Spur told it to her. When he was done, she frowned.

"What about the girl, Consuelo. Did she kill Rico Montez?"

Spur grinned. "You'll have to ask her that yourself.

I think the sheriff will be wanting to ask her the same question. Then again, Dennis himself might know who did it. If Consuelo did, you can be sure he'll be glad to testify against her."

Natasha nodded and made another note. She turned her pad to a fresh page.

"Now, remember, I told you before that I was working on a story about several community leaders who had died under what could be called suspicious circumstances?"

"I remember."

"Something's happening on that story. You've been with the sheriff. Has he said anything about it?"

"I haven't heard him mention it."

"Darn. I know something is going on. Dr. Thatcher is mixed up in it somehow. I saw him go into the sheriff's office bright and early this morning and not come out for two hours. I just don't know what's happening."

"Why don't you ask Dr. Thatcher?"

"Yes, good idea. First I have to get this story written. I heard there was a search warrant issued early this morning, but I don't know who got searched." She smiled. "Oh, well, I'll get that story tomorrow. First, there's something I want to do." She pushed closer to him in the small booth and her hand moved under the table and lay on his thigh. She moved it upward, and he looked down at her.

"There's something I want to show you," she said. "If you have an hour or so. Could that be arranged?"

"It might. I'm in room twenty-four at the Pacific Hotel."

"You go up first and I'll be there before you know it."

He paid the tab and they walked to the hotel. He went in first and she came in behind him a doz steps. He went to the second floor and she walked up a minute later.

Spur held the door open and she stepped inside. She put her arms around him and kissed him hard on the mouth, then eased off and opened her mouth, letting his tongue slide in.

He picked her up and carried her to the bed. She broke off the kiss, went back to the door, locked it and grinned.

"I want to write the news, not be the news myself on the front page. I do need to thank you for helping me land this job. With this story, I'm a sure winner."

He helped her undress. She was young and firm and had slender legs tapered to perfection. Her shoulders were broader than he had guessed and her breasts were firm and pointed up slightly with their youth.

She toyed with the hair on his chest, then brought his hands up to her breasts.

"They enjoy being played with. Just a little."

He caressed them, listening to her breathing speed up and watching her nipples rise and harden. She kissed him again, then pulled him down on the bed. Natasha fumbled at his fly and he helped her open the buttons.

When she worked her hands inside his underwear, she squealed in delight.

"Oh my, so strong and firm, so huge. It always amazes me that you men can do this. From a little soft thing he springs up like a giant sword."

She stroked him twice, then turned over on her back. "Please, right now, quickly. I still have that story to write about you and your counterfeiter."

He laughed softly and caressed her breasts again, then slid his hand up her inner thigh until she yelped in wonder. When he touched her softly wet nether lips, she jolted into a climax that was quick and potent.

She finished and opened her eyes in wonder.

"Damn, nobody's ever made me do that before. Do me right now. Right now."

She pulled at him until he rolled over between her thighs. She had lifted and spread her knees, and he saw her soft brown swatch of hair and the pinkness of her heartland.

"Now, damn it, Spur McCoy. Right now."

He eased forward and worked into her gently. She was ready for him and he plunged in until their pelvic bones met.

"Oh, yes, yes! I knew it would be this good. Why don't you stay here and we can get married and fuck ourselves silly three or four times a day until we're old and so frail we can't get it up anymore?"

He kissed her and she laughed.

He began to move slowly and she matched him. Gradually they increased the pace until she was panting and he knew he had broken over the top of the hill.

He moved faster and faster until she wailed. The climax was soft and gentle with her spasms racing fast but not as violent as before.

His climax matched hers and he thrust gently six times, then twice more and eased down on top of her. She grinned and circled his shoulders with her arms, pinning them together.

"Just see if I ever let you go," she whispered. Then they rested.

Ten minutes later she moved and he lifted away from her.

"That story. I've got to get it done before five-thirty. I've got to run." She pulled on her clothes quickly. He helped her with buttons and she grinned at him as he sat beside her still naked.

"I like you this way," she said. She patted his limp penis, laughed softly and grabbed her notepad and scurried for the door. She unlocked it and looked back. "You going to be here tonight? If you are, I'll see you about eight. I don't have anything else to do the rest of the night."

Then she was gone.

Spur got dressed, put on a clean shirt and his best boots and went to see if the sheriff was back. It was after four o'clock when the sheriff walked in. He looked tired but pleased.

"That son of a bitch Grundy is dead by his own hand. We don't have to worry about him any more. You get your man?"

"In your lockup, safe and sound."

A man rose from a chair in the lobby and walked over. "Sheriff, did you use the search warrant? I never knew what you found out."

"Oh, Dr. Thatcher. Yes, we found the poison and a partly filled box of chocolates that match the half a chocolate we found on Madam Walker's table. He said he wanted a lawyer. He hasn't been charged yet, but I had a long talk with him about the victims. He admitted nothing. Said the idea was outlandish and I had no proof of any kind."

"You think he'll run out of town, Sheriff?"

"Don't see why he should. Our evidence isn't strong. I was hoping I could talk him into confessing. He won't do it. He intends to fight it."

Spur frowned. "You two talking about the people around town who have been killed because they were against some civic improvement or some progressive ideas?"

"The same, McCoy. I didn't want to bother you about it."

"Good. The newspaperwoman is interested."

"Tomorrow I'll give her two stories."

Spur waved at the lawman. "Looks like you have plenty to do. I'll leave that cash and the man who made it with you until tomorrow. Then I'll probably get directions from Washington what to do. See you then."

Spur walked out of the office and down the street. The weather was beautiful. Not too hot, not too cold. All he had to do now was wire his boss in Washington that the case was wrapped up. He sighed. Maybe he'd do that tomorrow. Maybe tomorrow Natasha could show him something about wave surfing that he'd heard about.

His arm twinged and he decided to let Dr. Brown take one last look at it. It hadn't bothered him much. He walked up to the office half a block away and told the nurse why he was there. She said there would be a little wait.

Five minutes later, she showed him into a room and Dr. Brown came in and checked his wound.

"Broke the wound open again. Now it'll take another three or four days to heal. Take it easy, no lifting or throwing, anything like that. Lie in the sun for a couple of days." Dr. Brown put some salve on the wound and tied it up tightly with a bandage. Then he nodded. "Good as new, almost. Remember, take it easy."

Spur heard loud voices from the other room. The doctor looked up and lifted his brows. A moment later the door to the examining room flew open and a woman stood there with a big six-gun in both hands. The hammer was back.

"Dr. Brown, you murderer! You might think you got away with it, but you killed my husband. Poisoned him. He tried to tell me just before he died, but all I heard was 'chocolates.' I didn't understand until I heard the talk around town."

She lowered her aim and fired a round into the doctor's groin. Dr. Brown staggered back against the wall and slid down to a sitting position, screaming in pain. Spur's weapon was too low to reach from where he sat on the treatment table.

The woman screamed and fired three more times, hitting Dr. Brown in the chest with each thundering shot.

Spur shook his head. He couldn't hear a thing. Smoke hung thick in the room, and he lunged forward and knocked the gun from the woman's hand. She fell to her knees sobbing.

Mrs. Brown rushed past them and looked at her husband. Spur knew from the placing of the rounds that the medic had to be dead. She held his head in her lap and swayed back and forth.

The woman who killed Dr. Brown knelt there on her knees sobbing. "You killed my husband. You murdered my husband, Keith Edison. You'll never kill again, you bastard!"

Spur sat there watching the scene. He held Mrs. Edison's six-gun. They were still that way five minutes later when the sheriff came running into the room.

"My God, another one," he said. Spur got up and nodded. "I'll tell you all about it tomorrow, Sheriff. Right now I've got to take a walk and clear my head."

That night he had things sorted out enough to be on time at his hotel room at eight o'clock. He had brought a basket filled with wine and cheese, a whole cherry pie, three kinds of crackers and cookies and a dozen bottles of beer.

Natasha squealed when she saw all of the food. "We're going to need all of this to keep our strength up," Spur said.

They ate most of it.

The next morning Spur sent a wire to his boss, General Halleck in Washington, D.C. He said he had caught the counterfeiter, recovered the plates and the rest of the money and some $11,000 in real money. He said he would await instructions as to what to do with the prisoner.

That afternoon he sat on the beach by a place called La Jolla and watched the waves breaking on the shore. Three men rode the waves on twelve-foot-long boards. Now and then one of them would paddle furiously sitting astride the board, then when he got to the top of a breaking wave, he would stand up on the board and go shooting down the face of the rolling wave into the beach.

Spur figured it would be no harder to do than riding a bucking horse. He watched them for an hour and was about ready to swim out and ask if he could try it when one of the board riders fell off, was smashed down into the sand by the wave and limped along the sand trying to recover his surfing board.

Maybe not, Spur decided.

He rolled over so he would get sun on both sides and looked up in time to see Natasha pedal up on her bicycle. She carried a basket and two towels.

"I just turned in that second story, the one on Mr. Grundy. The sheriff says it looks like Grundy hired these young Mexican girls off the street here in San Diego as cooks, then used them for more than cooking. When one of them got pregnant, he would pretend to take her into town to go back to Mexico, but one of his hands would follow their buggy and kill her and they would bury her in that grove of live oaks. Then Grundy would go on to town and bring out another cook. Isn't that terrible?"

"Yes, terrible. What's to eat? I've been swimming and I'm starved."

"First we swim again. Race you to the first wave."

Spur struggled to stand up, let her beat him through the warm sand and was surprised when she threw off a robe and continued on to the water in a skimpy bathing suit that barely came to her knees. She dove in and swam out, then waited for him while she treaded water.

"Now, Spur McCoy, what could be more wonderful than this? Perfect weather, no hard work to do, and a girl who just loves to keep you company in that bed of yours, or in hers."

"Sounds perfect for today and tomorrow at least."

She pouted. "Just two days?"

He smiled and kissed her lips, and they both sank under the blue Pacific. They held the kiss as long as they could, then came up as a huge wave broke over them and washed them toward the beach.

They ran laughing to their towels and dried each other off, then lay in the sun sampling the still cold beer.

"You're right, Natasha, nothing could be better than this. Someday I'll come back to stay. Until then, I'll have to take my prisoner to Los Angeles or maybe on to San Francisco. Then another case."

She caressed his chest. "You could take me with you."

"The general would have a seizure. You would get bored and hate me. Besides, you have a new job as full time reporter on the San Diego *Union*."

"Yeah, you're probably right." She leaned over and kissed him hard on the mouth, then moved back and lay on her back in the sun.

Spur smiled. He wondered again where he would be sent next. What would his next job be for the Secret Service? He relaxed. He'd find out in a day or two. Until then his main worry was not to get too sunburned.

DIRK FLETCHER

TWICE THE LEAD, TWICE THE LOVIN'— IN ONE GIANT EDITION!

Wilderness Wanton. Everything comes bigger in Montana's Big Sky country—the rustler's rustle more; the killer's kill more; and the lovelies love more. So the Secret Service has to send its top gun to clean up the territory. Spur McCoy has hardly set foot in the region before robbers set upon him, dollies fall upon him, and a rich S.O.B. puts a price upon him. With renegades after the bounty on his head, and honeys after the reward in his bed, McCoy will have to shoot straight to wipe out the hard cases, then wear out the hussies.
_3624-X $4.99

Klondike Cutie. A boomtown full of the most ornery vermin ever to pan a river, Dawson is the perfect place for a killer to hide—until Spur McCoy arrives. McCoy knows the chances of mining gold are very good in the Klondike. And to his delight, the prospects for golden gals are even better. With the help of the local Mounties, Spur is sure to get his man sooner or later. But when it comes to getting the ladies, he will strike the mother lode quicker than a dogsled driver can yell mush!
_3420-4 $4.99 US/$5.99 CAN

TWICE THE FIGHTIN' AND TWICE THE FILLIES IN ONE GIANT SPECIAL EDITION!

GIANT
SPECIAL EDITION

SPUR

COLORADO CHIPPY
Dirk Fletcher

It seems everyone in Colorado wants Spur McCoy. Uncle Sam wants Spur to shoot some bank robbers to hell. The desperadoes want McCoy cold in the earth. And a hot-blooded little angel wants to take him to heaven. But Spur isn't complaining. It is his job to uphold the Secret Service's record. It is his duty to aim straight for the renegades' heads. And it is his pleasure to bed down every fiery vixen in the Wild West.

__3911-7 $5.99 US/$7.99 CAN